The
Unremarkable
Uneventful
Life of
Harvey Henderson

J.R. BAUDE

Dedication

To my guide and inspiration,

My love

Lisa

Acknowledgements

My deepest thanks to Mary Ellen Baude for her learned assistance and staunch dedication in seeing this work was as true to itself as possible.

I unlocked the lock and pushed up the door to reveal boxes, more cardboard boxes. There were numbers on the side of each box. They were all taped shut. I used one of my keys to slice through the tape on one of the boxes. I opened it to find something rather ordinary, but, if what was in this one box was also in the others, it was almost unimaginable, incredible, monumental, really. The tumblers fell into place. I looked at all the boxes again. The numbers made sense now. I said out loud to myself.

"He wrote it all down. The son of a bitch wrote it all down."

One

◆◆

It was the last way I wanted to spend my Sunday afternoon, but after my father passed, I promised my mother I would empty her rented storage unit and find a good home for everything - all the remnants of a more vibrant time in their life that didn't make the cut when they decided to downsize from our family home to an empty-nester, golden-years, condo-munity. I made that promise three and a half years ago. Six months ago, I had even worked a deal with my sister where all I had to do was simply empty the unit and unload the contents into her garage, leaving her to manage the details. Still, I procrastinated.

I hate moving things. Maybe because I have moved a half dozen times in eight years or because my chosen profession requires a good deal of random travel, but there was more to it than that. My resistance was more than just the physical grind of transporting junk from point A to point B. I just couldn't put a finger on it. But, winter was only weeks away, and knowing I was looking at possibly performing this thankless task in single-digit temperatures was enough motivation for me to finally pull myself together and be done with it.

I set the DVR to record a couple of football games, knowing they would later be a welcome companion to a few celebration beers and some juicy homemade brats from Fellman's Deli. I was confident there was no danger of learning scores or outcomes, since I would be completely occupied and completely alone until my return to a night on my comfy couch.

The couch had become my best friend since April, when I put the wraps on my latest free-lance assignment. I had gone a few months here and there between gigs, but this stretch was unusually long. I've never been one to panic about such things, because something always comes along sooner or later. I felt I was becoming a bit too comfortable with boredom though, and I knew I needed to get something going.

Sure, I picked up an odd check here and there for some corporate speech writing. I penned some copy for a line of vacuum cleaners which didn't suck (the pay, not the vacuum cleaners), and I even ghost-wrote a blog for a local talk-radio personality for a brief time - all good work, but whether he admits it or not, a writer wants most to tell a story, one of his choosing. And maybe, if he's lucky enough, he gets to touch a soul or two along the way. I needed something meaningful, and the more I looked for it, the more elusive it became. One thing I was certain of was that this Sunday was not going to be any different from any other day in the last six months.

Behind the wheel of the Ford F-150 I borrowed from my friend Vince, I slowly trolled through the labyrinth of cinder block and corrugated metal searching for Unit 538. I wondered what trash and treasure lay behind all the other doors, no doubt items that at one time seemed a must-have now resting dormant, forgotten, banished to the purgatory of consumer goods, not even worthy of a second chance on a thrift store shelf - keepsakes and heirlooms too precious to let go, but too out-of-place for the modern world. I mused there had to be at least one stuffed moose head among the accumulation imprisoned here, several pinball machines, wood burning stoves, classic cars, perhaps even a dank steamer trunk containing the hidden bones of some unfortunate soul. With these flights of fancy I was trying very hard to take my mind off the mundane task that lay ahead. Besides that, there was an unsettling anxiety welling up in me that I couldn't assign to anything in particular.

I nearly drove past it. I didn't even notice the unit number, but for some reason, among the indistinguishable monotony of homogenous storage units one of them stood out. It just looked like "Dad". Chalk it up to a reporter's keen sense of intuition I suppose, but sure enough, up above, the number "538". My last chance at reprieve, the key I was given not matching the padlock, thus sparing me the anguish now at hand, was not to be. I raised the door. "That's *so* Dad," I said to myself. If there were eight square inches of unfilled space in that entire ten-by-ten-by-twelve foot unit, I couldn't see it. My heart sank, my shoulders slumped, and I felt the involuntary movement of my hand, still on the door handle, trying to pull back down. I thought, I could just close it, back up and pretend I never saw it, say, 'I lost the key' or something. No, I thought. Do this. Finally do this.

3

The cause of the anxiety was apparent now, and it had nothing to do with the physical toil that lay ahead. It was the stuff. I knew that the next few hours would involve me coming into close contact with pieces of my past - the bittersweet experience of wading in the remnants of days gone by. Yes, some of the memories would be good ones, like being home again, but much of it would only be a brutal reminder of the ruthlessness of time, the nagging, inescapable physical tokens that lay before me as cold, hard evidence of my fragile and swiftly approaching mortality. Ahead of me was an afternoon of humility on slow drip, of realizing the time for "someday I will…." was boomeranging right back to me as "I guess I'll never get to…" My anxiety turned to something just short of anger, which was just the energy I needed to get me through transporting over one thousand cubic feet of yesteryear.

It took almost exactly one hour to load up the truck, trek the thirteen point six miles to my sister's house, unload and then head back to the storage unit again. This repeated seven times. The autumn sun was quickly fading, and I still had one load left. I was tired. I had moved rocking chairs, a king-size solid cherry bed frame with headboard, TV trays, gardening implements, snow tires, Tupperware containers full of odd nuts and bolts, and books, and books, and more books. "Who writes all these books?" I blurted out loud, only to immediately realize the irony as the last word leapt from my lips.

I was down to the last six boxes, then four, when the realization hit me that the boxes I was moving now were quite familiar. I was moments from closing up the unit for the last time, but my unsatisfied curiosity got the best of me, and I quickly peeled the tape from one of the boxes, pulled open the flaps and was greeted by my distant past. Not the past of my father and mother, but *my* past, *my* childhood.

Dumbfounded, I rummaged through the cardboard time capsules examining and analyzing each item as if I were handling antiquities from the tomb of a long lost pharaoh. Random as they were, each artifact told a story, a story I had lived, but with enough time between now and then to have a modicum of objectivity. One-by-one, memory after memory came rushing forth as I examined the relics deemed too vital to a young boy's existence to discard into oblivion. There was a compass from my Scouting days, a rabbit's foot keychain, Matchbox cars, even small rocks, one of which had a small fossil of a seashell.

Lastly, and I almost dismissed it as packing material, I found a memento wrapped in several layers of opaque plastic, but wrapped with a certain care, as if I had actually discovered a mummy's tomb. Strangely enough, when revealed, it turned out to be something once living, at least in the mind of a very young boy. It was my childhood companion, a doll, a football man. I instantly recalled his name. The name I gave him the day I got him. A name that was so inventive as to tip all others that, even as a child, I had an unusual gift of imagination and creativity, I named him "Football Man".

His jersey still a brilliant red with white pants – the shirt made of a velvety fabric, the pants of simple cotton. The shirt survived in relatively good shape, the pants as well, except for a few spots lovingly worn down to the delicacy of the Shroud of Turin. His number is that of a running back - "44". His head and hands are made of molded plastic, not a hard plastic though, more rubbery than rigid. His helmet is part of the head molding, and it has no facemask. I brushed that off as an aesthetic manufacturing decision, and not a representation of the common characteristics of the football uniform from the era. After all, the latter option would be yet another reminder of the time spanned by the doll's owner, one that was surely not so long ago as to be from a time before the evolution of the facemask.

In his right hand, he holds a football, indeed it is part of the hand molding itself. A football fixed in his iron grip since before the term "Super Bowl" even existed. OK, I guess that is a few years. But, this reminder of my past was not one to mock my years. He was a welcome surprise to an otherwise exhausting enterprise. He rode home next to me buckled in the passenger seat, my boxes right behind us in the bed of the pickup.

Finally, my tortured bones found their way to the comfy couch. The self-promised beers and brats were soon history - well, at least the brats. The beers were still part of the present. Sharing the couch with me was Football Man. I even opened a beer for him. After all, it had been forty–plus years since he had a beer!! While we watched the recorded games, after explaining the technical marvel of the digital video recorder, I filled him in on the changes in football since he was "active". I hadn't realized how much the sport had evolved in the last four decades, until I started going into the details.

He had many questions, but I patiently answered each one with precision. We reminisced about other great number "44's". Especially the triumvirate of Syracuse greats Floyd Little, Ernie Davis and of course Jim Brown (Brown changed to thirty-two when he entered the pros). The last great forty-four I could recall was John Riggins. He had a vague recollection of that name.

As the evening progressed, the flood of memories and emotions were settling into place. I recounted back as far as I could. And as far as I could was to the actual day I received Football Man. He was given to me by a neighbor who lived in the other half of the duplex my parents rented at the time. By my calculations, I was just two years old. Perhaps the day itself was even my second birthday. I barely recall the man's face. I remember my parents in the room, our living room to be exact. I was on the couch (I guess some things never change). It dawned on me just then that I have no other conscious memory before then.

Perhaps it was the excitement of the moment, the awareness of someone for the first time, a stranger at least, giving me a gift, or just a coincidental critical breakthrough in my brain development where memories had begun to process for later use. Regardless, I had now traced my memories back to my original conscious memory, a moment all others would be compared to - a moment of utter joy.

I awoke after apparently drifting off. It was hours later. I was still on the couch. Without even a thought, a name rolled off my tongue - Harvey Henderson. That was his name, the man at the genesis of my first recollection. I soon drifted off again, but not before I had made a promise to myself, to the universe, I guess. I was going to tell this man's story. No particular reason, and perhaps it was my beer-soaked psyche skewing rational perspective. I resolved to reassess my commitment in the morning with a clearer head. My internal critic chimed in with a chuckle at my alcohol-fueled altruism and advised it would be apparent, in the sober light of day, that I would surely be back to my routine work of doing nothing in no-time.

When I did finally wake for good, it was approaching 10 A.M. Sleeping that late was a bit unusual, even for me, but I chalked it up to recovering from my physical ordeal the day before and a little bit to the beer, and possibly the fact that I was up until 3 A.M. I brewed a half-pot of Sumatran Sunrise and contemplated the logistics of taking on the Harvey Henderson project. The fateful words of my internal critic were echoing in my head, to my disappointment. I considered the time needed, the probable slim possibility that there was anything of even remote literary interest here and of course the resources, namely money, I would need to complete the project. I was confident that my skills as a writer were up to the task. I was sure I could bring a story to life, even if there wasn't much to tell, but if there were doubts, this was the time to bring them to the table.

I poured another cup of coffee and decided a Google search was in order. I resolved if the gods wanted the story written, then something would present itself, give me a starting point. The search yielded a few thousand short of four million references to Harvey Henderson. I surfed the results for an hour or so, and I learned a good deal about all manner of Harvey Hendersons. I encountered four Real Estate Agents, three Dentists, a Butcher and a Baker (no candlestick maker), even a sandwich with all, or parts of their names being Harvey Henderson. There was a doctoral candidate whose thesis examines the comparative history of hybrid techniques for corn growth developed by the Aztec, Toltec and Mayan cultures, a graphic artist whose specialty is designing fictitious insects from worlds unknown, and my favorite, a performance artist whose shtick is acting Shakespeare's most famous scenes while in character of another famous person.

As much as I was intrigued at the thought of viewing Hamlet's "To be, or not to be" soliloquy as performed by Richard Nixon, I resolved my life would not be considered incomplete having missed that theatrical tour de force. Based on dates, locations and other basic details, there was no way any of the hundred-plus HH's I looked into could have been my HH.

The phone rang. It was a job. Not even a writing job. A friend of a friend's lawyer needed some research done. Writing was involved but, you know, not *writing*. The natural by-product of being a free-lance journalist is marketable skills as a researcher. It was decent pay plus expenses for ten weeks of work. I took that as my sign. There was nothing to the Harvey Henderson tale. At least I had my Football Man and a marvelous memory.

Two

◆ ◆

It wasn't the first time I had done research for pay. If the subject matter was right, it could even be very rewarding. The assignment was to find the descendants of a small town in South Dakota named Fortune. The town's name turned out to be ironic. It sprang up almost overnight in 1877 due to the discovery of gold in the Black Hills of South Dakota.

The town was situated roughly three miles downstream from the single largest gold mining operation in the Black Hills. The geological make up of the gold from that area necessitated a method of extraction where one step of the process was to bind the gold to mercury. The legal angle here was a potential class action against the mining companies, the ones still in existence, for multi-generational health hazards caused by high levels of mercury concentrations in the stream feeding the water source for the town and residual in the soil. The additional irony was not lost on me, that the law firm that hired me was itself mining for gold. My two cents, which I kept to myself, at best, this was a frivolous legal case. But that wasn't my concern. For my part, the work was historical, genealogical sleuthing. I even considered that I might stumble upon a nugget of my own here in the form of material for a historical novel.

Thanks to the Internet, and the Mormons, the task of locating a significant portion of the town's original ancestors was more productive than I anticipated. Some of the data were easily obtained online, but some required travelling to county records offices and even conducting face-to-face interviews with learned locals. This aspect was (pardon the pun) a "gold mine" of information and backdrop for my secondary purpose. My potential novel was even finding some legs.

Initially, I thought locating Fortune's descendents might be a challenge. Fortune's life was brief. When the gold dried up, the town did too, but surprisingly, about one third of the direct ancestors of the original inhabitants of Fortune lived within a 125-mile radius. Fully another third were found via information provided by the first third.

Early on in the project, if you had asked me my impression of South Dakota, I would have suggested that the words "South Dakota" were Apache for "Get the hell outta here". At least, that was my initial reaction to sojourning the backwater towns of this humble state. Once I shed my snobbish bias, I was quite drawn to the area. It is remote, quiet and beautiful in its own way, like the shy girl at the dance, sitting in the corner of the gym, all alone, awkward and unsure. Yet, when you really take a good long look, you become enamored by her unassuming, undiscovered beauty.

South Dakota is a sportsman's paradise and a geologists dream. I hear the weather can be a bit brutal now and then... like all winter! But, it was early fall and the angled light of day gave stark majestic contrast, depth and character to the inherent natural beauty.

The people couldn't have been any nicer. Guarded and suspicious at first, sooner or later they warmed up to me, once they decided I wasn't there to put one over on them, or possibly because there might be some eventual financial gain in it for them. Regardless, I was charmed by their hospitality, and even though a decent number of these folks were living rather modestly, they pulled out all the stops on my account, and I was the beneficiary of some fantastic home-cooked comfort food.

When not partaking of the generosity of others, I found myself frequenting an establishment located roughly 16 miles southwest of where Fortune once stood. Just about where Custer County Highway 284 meets Interstate 385, there is a diner called the Crazy Horse Café. If you look in Webster's under the word "quaint", you should see a picture of this landmark. The outside of the diner is weathered and in need of a facelift, but the inside is genuine Americana at its best, not the pseudo-kitschy version of Americana you find hanging on the walls and in the rafters of countless corporate restaurant chains, but the real thing.

The décor is catch-as-catch-can regional paraphernalia scattered about the log cabin style interior. Huge pine trunks make up the walls and ceiling all stacked and finished with a glossy varnish. There are a couple of Bison heads, some impressive eagle feather headdresses in glass cases, spittoons which may not be entirely for décor purposes and photos that could qualify the building as a museum. Period black and white stills from the heyday of the gold rush, chiefs and warriors, from the indigenous tribes of the area, share the walls with U.S. Cavalry soldiers with whom they may have even clashed at one time or another. All are presented proudly in their own respective glory.

A medium-sized dining room capable of seating 80 or so patrons includes rustic chairs, tables and a dozen or so booths. I will say they serve up a mean Buffalo Strip Steak presented with homemade skillet potatoes and garnished with half a Bermuda onion which they grill, butter and then dust with freshly ground black pepper. The coffee is really quite good too and it arrives black.

Don't even think about ordering a grande, no foam, double shot, extra hot, free-trade, soy latte, or you may get summarily shown the door. In fact, I would wager dollars to a dozen Rushmore glazed doughnuts (another fine establishment I frequented) that you couldn't find a latte within 75 miles of the Crazy Horse Café.

One particular unseasonably cold afternoon, I stopped by the CHC (my own crass urbanizing acronym for the diner) and ordered a late lunch-early dinner. Seated in a six-person booth by myself, I took the opportunity to spread out my research notes and papers so I could enter the details into my master spreadsheet. Outside of a few records requests which could only be snail-mailed and would arrive at my home address in four to six weeks, the research was essentially completed, with the exception of some data entry and a final once-over. I would finish that task before night's end, which would bring the whole project in four weeks ahead of schedule.

I dined in quiet solitude, making entries in between bites and sips of whatever beer was on tap. I finished my work about the time my warm slice of apple pie a la mode arrived with a piping hot cup of the house joe. My eyes wandered the photos gracing the wall above my booth eventually stopping at an eight-by-ten photo of a high school football team. It was as out of place as the aforementioned latte. The header on the faded black and white picture read "1940 Kansas Area Division II Champions" and, beneath that the name of the school, "Hays High School". There were only twenty-six players and three coaches, their names listed across the bottom of the photo partly obscured by the picture frame.

The players wore what appeared to be wool jerseys and leather helmets (with no facemask, I might add) and black high-top cleats. I

13

looked around the diner, and seeing that no one was paying attention, I took the photo down to get a closer look. I nearly dropped it when the cardboard backing in the frame dislodged. I pulled the picture from the frame. All the names were visible now, "Top row from left to right: Timothy Benson, Frank Jamison, Karl Schuster" and twelve others. Below them, the front row, all on one knee, "Bottom row left to right: Spencer Wilson, Bartholomew Warrick, Harvey Henderson, James Patterson, William Kennedy, John…. Whoa!! Harvey Henderson!! "IMPOSSIBLE," I thought.

I sat and read the names over and over each time looking at the player listed as Harvey Henderson, trying to look in his eyes for a "yes" or "no" to the question at hand. I tried to scrape my first memory for a better recollection of the man's face who handed me my Football Man, but to no avail.

A voice interrupted.

"Is something wrong with the pie?" It was my waitress, Molly.

"Uh….no…," looking at the vanilla ice cream that was now a creamy lake surrounding my slice of pie.

"…uh…I was um…" unable to bring myself back from my amazement to actually put a sentence together.

"Did that fall off the wall?" Molly said apologetically. "That happens sometimes. Some of these pictures have been hanging here since before I was born."

She said it meaning to foster incredulity on my part, but looking at her young, bright face I could probably have trumped her with any number of things in my personal possession at that very moment, like the jacket I had hung on the hook at the side of my booth. Then, matter-of-factly, as if only to impress me with her deductive, observational abilities, she said,

"I bet some of them have been hanging here since before even YOU were born."

My ego assumed a consistency similar to that of my vanilla ice cream. I chuckled to myself a bit at the circumstance and the absurd undoing of my vanity that was earlier bold enough to entertain the thought of asking Molly if she would like to join me for a drink at the bar when her shift was over, strictly for research purposes, of course. I pulled myself together and embraced the beat-down saying,

"Oh, I'm sure there couldn't be any hanging here for THAT long."

I expected a laugh, or better a flirty, girlish giggle, but instead she paused blankly for a moment, then said,

"Is there anything else I can get for you tonight? Would you like a new slice of pie?"

"No thanks, dear. You've done quite enough," I said with a smile.

As Molly walked away, I remembered where my mind was before she showed up. I turned in her direction.

"Molly?" She stopped.

"Yes, sir?"

15

"Do you know anything....?" I caught myself and started again.

"Is there anyone around here who knows about this picture?"

"Sure, I'll get him."

Three bites of pie later, a strapping fellow in his late forties emerged from the kitchen. He carefully wiped his beefy hands on the cleanest part of his apron that he could find. He had striking black hair which topped his leathery face and expressionless demeanor.

"Molly said you wanted to talk to me?"

"Yes, my name is Denny Preston. I was looking at this picture from your wall, and I think I might know...well, know *of* one of these fellows in the front row here."

I pointed to Harvey Henderson.

"Hmmm." He bent over to get a closer look then pulled some reading glasses from his shirt pocket, again, "Hmmm."

"I don't really know much about this picture, but I know someone who will."

He pointed to the top row third from the left.

"Karl Schuster," I confirmed. He nodded.

"Can you be here tomorrow morning around eight o'clock?"

"Sure," I said.

16

"He will be here then. He comes in every Thursday for breakfast and then plays gin rummy with some friends."

"Thanks," I replied. "You don't think he'd mind if I joined him?"

His expression softened a bit. He looked me in the eye and said with a subtle pride,

"No, quite the opposite. If you want to talk about this picture, be warned, he'll talk you under the table." He smiled a bit. "He's my father. He built this place."

"Thanks...uh..."

"Wolf, Wolf Schuster."

He offered his hand, and I met his with mine. I wondered if that might be the last time I would have good use of that hand when he tightened his grip and shook. I think I hid my grimace well though. He disappeared into the kitchen.

I settled my tab and found my way back to the motel, where I thought I would surely be deep in sleep moments after hitting the pillow. Instead, there was one more thing my psyche had to reconcile, or at least consider, before it would shut down and allow me the rest I so badly needed.

Bogart's "of all the gin joints" line from Casablanca popped into my head. But, for me, my angst wasn't a matter of Ingrid Bergman. It was how it came to be that I found myself sitting in the booth of a diner in Custer County, South Dakota, the ONLY booth in that diner that had a single, out of place, seventy year-old photograph hanging on a wall - a photograph containing the image of a man I was unable to locate using state of the art search algorithms designed to query trillions of bytes of data in mere seconds, data that represents the vastest network of information ever known to man. Any thoughts of a historical novel were a distant memory, and the project I had summarily dismissed weeks ago was now front and center.

◆ ◆

So, if this were a movie, one of those "If you build it, he will come" Hollywood real-world fairy tales, this is the place in the story where the main character would wake the next morning a changed man because of the profound revelations unfurled in his dreams the night before. His mission now clear, his purpose well defined, and with unshakable resolve, he realizes his destiny is at hand.

But this was not a movie. I awoke to the strains of "The Pina Colada Song" playing from my clock radio, without any recollection of dreams at all. I had slept like a rock, straight through for seven hours. I did have a growing feeling of dread washing over me though, the dread that I would be prisoner to the incessant torment of "The Pina Colada Song" looping in my head for two or three days. I quickly killed the radio and headed for the shower with one detour, the four cup coffee maker on the vanity.

I hate to disappoint, but I'm not a real subscriber to "the gods", as in "the gods" of this or that making things happen "for a reason". I am a realist, a healthy skeptic. I'm not a cynic either. I do have an open mind about most everything, but if "the gods" are so powerful as to orchestrate elaborate happenstance events to "send a message", then why don't they just tell us what to do straight up. What's with all the cryptic hocus pocus? I know I drew a conclusion

18

earlier about the merit of the Harvey Henderson story based on the timing of a phone call, but that was really just an easy way of rationalizing my decision to take the "bird in the hand" research job for-pay over the "two in the bush" not-for-pay tome on HH.

Now, I have to admit that the research job led me headlong into the Harvey Henderson story anyway, and I can hear the tongue-cluckers out there now saying "so how do you explain that coincidence?" I don't. I admit it was quite a curious thing, but I'm not going to jump to conclusions based on one fluke twist of fate and let it cloud my judgment. I can't afford that as a writer. I know it seems to be a lost art these days, but what passes for objective journalism today is more often than not simply veiled advocacy, a story written to prop up a pre-determined conclusion - distortion of truth intent on shameless persuasion. After all, why do you think they call them "stories"?

Make no mistake, I have a healthy dose of idealism in my makeup. Most journalists, including yours truly, were driven to the profession for that very reason, but, once I decide what my specific arena is for a given story, I put that aside and let my left brain lead the way when I put boots on the ground. Anything less is shoddy journalistic malpractice. Besides, there is no guarantee that the guy in the picture is even my Harvey Henderson and not the guy who had the sandwich named after him.

Three

◆◆

As I approached the CHC, I realized I was actually quite nervous about my upcoming conversation with Karl Schuster. I have interviewed minor drug kingpins, eco-terrorists, skinheads and even the odd tin-horn dictator wannabee, but never had I experienced the butterflies I was experiencing as I approached the diner. I tried to trace the origins of my apprehension. Perhaps it was because I had no idea in what direction this day would take me. I thought that an inadequate cause, but there was no more to consider, as I was now making the final turn and soon the reason would no longer matter.

The parking lot could have easily been mistaken for a pickup truck dealership. A quick scan revealed only five non-trucks in a collection of what must have been over forty vehicles. To be sure, these trucks were truly tools of the trade for their owners, most of whom had to be ranchers or farmers. Besides, I would think the winters in western South Dakota would necessitate reliable wheels. It could actually be a matter of life and death.

Upon entering, I found a very different place from the one I had been frequenting for several weeks. The tables and booths were at capacity. A cacophony of voices, dining room noises and country music were a welcome alternative to the four-hundred and eightieth recycling of the lyric "if you're not into yoga, if you have half a brain" rattling around in my head.

My first order of business was to see if I could spot Karl Schuster based on his football squad picture of seventy years ago.

Doing the math, he would have had to be pushing ninety. That narrowed the field to about a dozen.

"Welcome back, Mr. Preston."

Standing three feet behind me was Wolf Schuster. I wondered how a man of his size could have sneaked up on me without my noticing. Instead of kitchen garb, he was wearing a red western-style shirt with crisp new jeans, cowboy boots and a bolo tie. He had on a tan Stetson with a decorative rattlesnake skin wrapping the perimeter. It was now apparent to me that Wolf was the proprietor and not the kitchen help, as I had assumed the night before.

He was smiling and began walking into the dining area. He motioned for me to follow. We crossed the entire floor to a table in the far corner where three old-timers sat mid-meal. Surprisingly, they all stood when we approached and stayed standing through the introductions. It was a very welcoming gesture and clearly something these men did instinctively. My butterflies flew away. Even before we were formally introduced, I knew exactly which one was Karl Schuster. He had the same powerful eyes and stature similar to Wolf, and though nearly ninety years old, he barely looked seventy. If there were any lingering doubts that he was Wolf's father, they were removed when he shook my hand and sent the needle on the pain meter just below where Wolf had sent it the night before. I sat in the one vacant chair at the table. Wolf said,

"I'll get you some breakfast, Mr. Preston."

"Please, call me Denny."

"All right, Denny it is." He walked away.

21

I realized he hadn't asked me what I would like, but one glance at the delectable food occupying the table, and I knew it wouldn't matter. Anything was going to be perfect. There were huevos rancheros, buttermilk pancakes with REAL maple syrup, thick slices of bacon, biscuits and gravy, skillet potatoes and not a single Belgian waffle with whipped cream and strawberries. This would be a man's breakfast, and I was going to feast on good home cookin' with a side of testosterone.

For the first time in my life, I wished I was eighty-five years old. These men wore it well. They wore it with grandeur. Not once did I hear about this ache or that pain, even though I was sure there were plenty. There really wasn't much talk about days gone by or even last week. It was clear they lived in the moment. They were making plans for the future, and I would wager my left nut, no both of them, that not one of these guys had any idea who Wayne Dyer, Deepak Chopra, or Dr. Phil were.

These were some centered cats, fully comfortable in their skin and going out of their way to make sure I was comfortable in mine - that I was not the odd man out. We were all on a first name basis before long and I wasn't really sure if they even knew why I was brought over to sit at their table, but I was very much part of the conversation.

About forty-five minutes had passed when Karl's companions retired to a room off the dining room saying to Karl,

"We'll get things started. We'll see ya in there."

I assumed they were referring to the gin rummy game. I was leaning back in my chair, lost in post-meal relaxation, when Karl reminded me why I was there.

22

"So, Wolf tells me you knew Harvey."

It actually took me a second or two to dial in and realize what Karl was referring to. I had forgotten what brought me here in the first place.

"Uh..Um…Yeah, well, no. I actually never knew him, at least that I recall."

Karl appeared a bit puzzled. I continued,

"I was a very young child, and I am not even sure if the Harvey Henderson you knew was the one who lived next to my parents."

Still a bit confused, Karl sipped from his coffee cup. I tried to focus a bit more.

"My parents once rented a duplex in St. Paul. Our neighbor, in the other half of the duplex, was a fellow named Harvey Henderson."

Karl nodded as if to say, "Go on."

"I was just wondering if you could shed any light on what might confirm if your teammate was the same Harvey Henderson."

"Honestly, I can't say one way or the other. I lost track of him after high school. We worked together bailing hay the summer after we graduated, then went our separate ways."

"Do you have any idea where he went after that summer?" I asked hoping for anything, a minor trail of breadcrumbs.

"Sorry, son, I really don't. I am pretty sure he was stationed in Germany in the war, but I can't say for sure."

I thought, "See what I mean about 'the gods'? Why the whole picture-in-the-booth thing just to run me down a dead end?" I almost dismissed myself so Karl could get to his gin rummy, but since I was here, I decided to find out more about Karl. I didn't even have to ask.

"I don't rightly know why I lost touch with Harvey. We weren't close friends, but we did do things together from time to time. I grew up in Kansas and Harvey showed up about the time I was in fourth grade."

I pulled a pad and pen from my jacket pocket and gestured to Karl if it was all right to take some notes. He nodded affirmatively while continuing on.

"Our high school was small, and everyone knew everyone, but still, there are friends and then there are *friends*."

"Well, tell me whatever you can, maybe something will click with me," I was looking for anything.

"Hmm..Well, he was on the football team, but he really didn't play all that much, maybe six plays the entire season."

"But, you barely had enough players to play offense and defense as it was," I pointed out.

"Well, he was a small fella and not really that athletic. But we needed bodies, and he was willing, so coach let him suit up. Most of the good players played both offense and defense."

24

"You know, I don't mean to give the impression that he wasn't an important part of the team. He really was. He was the glue. He knew people and how to get them to play their best. Coach had one way - fiery and forceful, that was good for some of us. For those it wasn't good for, there was Harvey. He knew how each of us was put together and translated "coach" into each man's way of thinking. Even though he didn't play much, he was very important to the team's success."

"OK," I thought, "A little insight into HH. But is there a story here?" Karl continued.

"I honestly can't think of anything else really," Karl said shaking his head. "Well, here's my card in case you do. Your gin rummy pals are probably waiting for you. Thank you for your time, Karl."

We shook hands and Karl disappeared into the other room. I collected my things and walked in Wolf's direction while extracting my Visa card from my wallet. Wolf gestured back to indicate there was no charge. I put a ten on the table as a tip and headed towards the door shaking my head in disappointment.

"Oh, Mr. Preston?" came a voice from behind me. I turned. It was Karl who had emerged from the card room.

"I can't believe I almost forgot this. Harvey introduced me to my wife."

I did a one-eighty and headed back towards Karl.

"Come on in. I'll show you a picture." I followed him into the card room which looked to be the cafe's version of a VIP room or

25

something they might set up for a special occasion, party or event. There were three tables of four in the room set up for today's Gin Rummy, but only six or seven players were in attendance. Waist high knotty pine wainscoting was topped by scarlet walls holding more pictures and memorabilia, all illuminated with tiffany fixtures.

I stood next to Karl as he toured me through his life and loves, presented in photo after photo. Some dated back to the photo of the football team era, all the way up to the present and everything in between. Karl narrated, but one needed only look at the photos to know the tale. The leading lady was, without a doubt, Karl's wife, Doreen. Her maiden name was Proudfeather. She was of Native American ancestry, Arapaho, and she was stunningly beautiful with long raven hair, laughing eyes and cheekbones a runway model would kill for.

It's hard to put into words, but even though the photos were all stills and mostly in black and white, her image almost appeared to be in motion, moving while standing still. I flashed on the fact that even though we are all surrounded by solid objects, in reality, these objects are comprised of atoms that are in perpetual rapid motion, a pulsating dance of potential energy - still, but in motion.

Wolf's black hair and chiseled features were now easily explained, clearly a legacy from his mother's side. The name Wolf, I learned, is actually short for Wolfgang - a name which seemed to lend itself to both Karl's German and Doreen's Arapaho heritage.

Doreen succumbed to pancreatic cancer in December thirteen years ago. As devastating as that must have been for Karl, he was all smiles when he talked about her. He never remarried, and I suspect never looked elsewhere. I was sorry that I would never meet this woman, but with Karl's keen memory and inspired devotion giving dimension to the image that was the subject of so many of the pictures hanging here, I knew I would leave feeling like I had.

"So one day after football practice, Harvey says to me, 'Let's go for a soda. I'm buying'," Karl said with a sheepish grin.

"We got in his car and must have driven past four soda fountains before arriving at one about sixteen miles away. I was a bit annoyed, since I knew I'd be late for dinner now and have to catch heck from my parents about that," Karl continued.

"Harvey said, 'Trust me, it'll be worth it,' and it was most surely that and more."

The grin on Karl's face turned to pure joy as he stared intently at one of the pictures of Doreen.

"There she was, sooo beautiful. I had never seen any woman so stunning in all my life and never would again."

He paused, perhaps to relive the moment, perhaps to keep his composure, perhaps both.

"And Harvey…" Karl paused again, "Harvey had no intentions for her except to have *me* meet *her*."

Karl took another pause, but it seemed more from the observation that the full impact of that day so many years ago was finally coming together. That Harvey had somehow wandered to this out-of-the-way soda fountain, then consciously, or subconsciously, decided Karl needed to go there, then kindly kidnapped Karl so he could meet the girl who would be his life-long love.

We spent over an hour and a half sharing Karl's composite of his life story. We shook hands one last time, and Karl assumed his place at the gin rummy table, while I strode towards the front door. I got only a few steps into the dining room, when my attention was drawn to the photos placed on the walls there. I decided to take a closer look at those, since I had only briefly examined them when I first set foot in the CHC. I had a renewed appreciation for the subjects and settings, thanks to Karl's heartfelt presentation moments before.

If I were a romantic, I'd probably reach the conclusion that Harvey was the willing catalyst in the creation of a whole new universe, the architect of a stirring of life that continues to this day of a potent, vigorous, vibrant energy that resonates from his single, simple, unselfish act. And then I would wax on drippy sweet about how we should all learn a little something about ourselves and how it's the little things we do that matter. But I am not a romantic, so I won't.

At about the fourth photo, I felt a presence behind me, recalling an earlier moment in the day. I knew exactly who it was. I spoke without looking.

"These aren't just some random period photos hanging here. These are part of the family album as well, aren't they?"

"You're very perceptive, Mr. Preston," Wolf responded.

"OK, I'm not leaving here until you start calling me 'Denny'."

Wolf chuckled. I continued.

"These are your Mom's side of the family."

"That's right...*Denny,*" emphasizing my first name, "Not a lot of folks know that either. Some of the pictures aren't family, but we've had them for years."

Wolf took the next half hour or so telling me what he knew about the individuals in the photos and where they were taken. The football team picture made sense now. It was not out of place. It was just another family photo. Most of the other restaurant décor was also a collection of family heirlooms, priceless, to be certain. I had to chuckle a bit to myself remembering my day at the storage unit. I imagined how absurdly pathetic the place would look with our family heirlooms as aesthetic ornamentation. I mean not to disparage my family's leftovers and, to be fair, the stuff in the unit was just that, stuff. But the Schuster/Proudfeather legacy wasn't stuff, it was American history.

Wolf and I parted ways, and I swore to him I would return someday. I retired to my motel and booked a room for the night. I had already checked of my room thinking I would be on the road after breakfast, but it was too late to start off for home tonight. I would have to wait until first thing in the morning.

Four

◆◆

He stood before me, a proud tribal chief, a headdress of brilliant white feathers flowing back as far as the eye could see, perhaps even back through time. Why I was here I did not know, but I did know a life-changing moment was imminent. His eyes glowed of transparent turquoise. He raised his bronze, muscular arms and reached towards me. Across his forearms lay a cloak, woven of fine threads, and intricate in pattern.

Without reason, I was now wearing a football helmet (_with_ a facemask, by the way). It blocked my view a bit so I was unable to discern the nature of the pattern, but I felt it was important. Again, I looked in his eyes. His lips began to move. He was about to speak. His eyes glowed more intensely indicating an epiphany may be at hand. He opened his mouth but did not speak. Instead he sang. Strange words, these words…. "Everybody was Kung Fu fightin'….. Those cats were fast as lightnin'"…….

My left arm involuntarily slammed down on the snooze button. My moment of enlightenment had been usurped by Carl Douglas and his 1970's one-hit wonder. I briefly considered had I set my alarm for one minute later, would my life have been profoundly transformed? Easy come, easy go, I guess. At least I knew which song was to be my tormenter for the next couple of days, replacing Rupert Holmes' own one-hit wonder. Who drinks Pina Coladas anyway?

Within twenty minutes I was in the car and on my way, my only companion a twenty ounce black coffee from the complimentary breakfast bar at the motel. I drove into the rising sun which was apropos as the critical journalist in me began shining a bright light on the last twenty-four hours.

The first question, the only question really: Again, is there anything here of journalistic value with regards to Harvey Henderson? Quite honestly the story with legs was the Schuster/Proudfeather story. It was the stuff of Herman Wouk, or James Clavell - a multi-generational, multi-cultural historical tome - a book that would write itself. I still didn't even have any assurances that I had the right Harvey Henderson! And even if he was the right one, was being Karl and Doreen's matchmaker truly a "special" act? That kind of thing happens every day, countless times. Karl and Doreen did all the heavy lifting. Harvey just burned a few cents on gas money and had a soda. I decided to let it simmer and dialed up the "Road Jams" rotation on my iPod which I had playing through the car's sound system.

I made good time to Sioux Falls just a cow pie's throw from the Minnesota border. I stopped for lunch there. With any luck I could be home by dusk on the comfy couch with a beer in one hand and a slice of Teschedi's deep dish in the other. But, while I was thinking of food while eating other food, something was eating away at me. I knew it would only get worse unless I got some concrete substance when it came to THE Harvey Henderson. Where to get that was the rub.

I did some more token searches on my hand-held for HH trying to find links having anything to do with Hays High School in Hays, Kansas, home of the 1940 Kansas Area Championship football team. I found a web site for the high school, a building clearly built after the time of Harvey and Karl. But the rest of the search yielded nothing pertaining to Harvey. Of course, there was no Class of 1940 web site. I was beginning to think if there was Google Mars I might have better luck.

I concluded there was really only one thing to do and that was to go down to Hays and employ my investigative journalist skills to discover once and for all if I was on the right path. So, instead of the four hour trek to St. Paul, I was sentencing myself to at least twelve more hours of driving, which would require another night in a hotel room, most likely in Lincoln, Nebraska. I filled up the tank, motored on and arrived in Hays around noon the next day. I loaded up the GPS on my hand-held, and let it guide me to the high school. Of note, it was Friday afternoon, and I really needed to get something of substantial value, or I'd have to wait out the weekend or just give up the search altogether.

From the web picture it was difficult to tell if the building was a remodel of the original, or a new building altogether. As I approached and entered the front doors, it was clear to me that this was of origin sometime in the past two to three decades, NOT a remodel. This was unfortunate since the likelihood of finding documents or reference material belonging to a time frame of seventy years ago was remote.

It took a couple of tries, but I finally found someone in the administrative office who seemed a reliable source - the principal, Ms. Roberta Brandhill.

"I'm looking for any information you might have on past students, or really anything on..."

She interrupted.

"We aren't allowed to provide any information on former students without written authorization from the superintendant. I'm sure you understand." She seemed a scintilla rude, but it made sense really.

"I see your point, but if I told you it originates from the class of 1940, would that ease the protocol a bit?"

Instead of answering she pointed to a framed newspaper story hanging on the wall. The headline read...

"Hays High Destroyed by Class 4 Twister."

There was a picture next to the article of something that looked like London during the Blitzkrieg. What must have been the high school was now only two unconnected parts of exterior brick walls, which stood among copious rubble. My heart sank.

"Actually the tornado only collapsed about a third of the building, but the boilers were damaged and exploded an hour later, leaving what you see there." She had a certain level of satisfaction in her voice as if to say, "Tough toenails mister snoopy-pants."

All I could say was, "Damn."

She anticipated my next question and added, "Any school records or materials from anytime prior to that were lost forever. It's a sad thing," this time with a tone that seemed to say "It was a sad thing, but you not getting what you want makes the horror and utter devastation entirely worth it."

I was at a loss to understand her attitude. Maybe it was just a Friday afternoon thing.

"So, there is no one who has any information on the school history prior to 1977?" I was hoping for a brief moment of cooperation.

"No," as if to say "aren't you glad you drove 12 hours and slept in a skanky truck stop motel in Lincoln, Nebraska only to get brutally shot down?"

Actually, that was just me thinking that, she really just meant "No".

Defeated, I dragged myself back to the car. I started driving nowhere in particular, got a burger at a drive through and found a parking lot In which to partake in my fast-food feast while I desperately did some more web searching. A few minutes later, I accepted the pointlessness of doing that and sighed. I wracked my brain for ideas, calling on every back-alley investigative journalism device my memory could summon. Nothing came. My senses were frazzled, and to top it off, the aroma of dead skunk was now wafting past my nose as an olfactory commentary on the state of my search.

But then, and if I have a guardian angel, he has an impish sense of humor, it dawned on me that I was actually parked in the lot belonging to the "Westside Public Library". "Old school," I thought, no pun intended "I'll go low tech and maybe get lucky."

My digithead buddy Spence calls them "Book Museums", and perhaps they are becoming a tad obsolete, but right now I was counting on the original hard-copy version of the Internet to proffer my salvation. I entered, expecting a drab, lifeless environ with matronly librarians sporting home-coifed bouffant hairdos and torpedo brassieres. But instead I found myself in a rather hip cyber café. It was a public library but there was a coffee concession brewing every manner of beverage you might find in Paris (France, not Texas), served alongside a formidable pastry selection.

I soon realized that this was actually the source of the dead skunk smell. Funny how context matters, one must admit there is a disturbingly close resemblance to the aroma of a fine coffee house and the reek of freshly flattened skunk, but I digress.

I strode to the main counter in the book part of the library and was greeted by a young lady who was the antithesis of my expectations. No bouffant hair or torpedo bra here. She had straight silken chestnut hair, emerald eyes which sparkled behind the obligatory sexy-smart-girl glasses, and I believe she was wearing a wonder bra which, because it was operating as designed, was offering a challenge to the third button of her crisp white blouse as it struggled to continue operating as it was designed. The top two buttons weren't being employed, so the third was all that remained between a *speculation* and the actual *knowledge* that she was wearing a wonder bra. I was hoping desperately, strictly for purposes of informational accuracy here, that the ten year-old Guatemalan kid was having a bad sewing day when crafting her blouse. I also wondered if I had been on the road too long by myself.

"May I help you with anything?" She said, as if to say "I'm Veronica, and I would like very much to be your very own personal research babe today." ....Definitely on the road too long.

"Yes, I'm looking for information on the Hays High Class of 1940."

"Hmmm..." She looked around.

35

"I know there was a tornado slash explosion that destroyed everything…" I was trying to be of help.

"No, we have stuff here; I'm just trying to remember where."

My heartbeat sped up a bit. Could there actually be something here?

"That's right, follow me," She led me across the library and stopped at a row marked "Local History". She motioned with her hand as if she were Vanna White revealing a critical letter.

"Here you go. We get a lot of stuff donated to us from estates." I assumed she was going to turn and leave me there to rummage the shelf, but she stayed.

"Were you needing anything specific?"

"Well yes, I'm looking for a student named Harvey Henderson, class of 1940."

"Let me….hmmm," as she scanned the shelves. "There we are." She stretched for a high shelf, and before I could offer help, she had grabbed a book.

"Let's start here."

She handed me a Hays High 1940 yearbook. A hard black cover with the word "Mustangs" embossed in worn gold lettering opened to about fifty pages of photos and articles. I eagerly flipped to the senior class student photos. "C" through "E", next page "F" through "J" and there he was. Harvey Henderson. Next to the photo was written "Harvey Henderson: Football 3-4, Debate Society 1-4.

Marksmanship 3-4." That's it. But I had him in hand with a hard reference point. I still couldn't tell if this was the man who handed me "Football Man". After all, this was Harvey Henderson at eighteen years old, and my memories were generated by a two-year old's brain.

"Did you find what you needed?"

"Yes, I did, a starting point at least."

I looked about the page reading some of the well-wishings and "keep in touch" messages penned to the student who once claimed this yearbook as his own. There were even a few phone numbers. Unfortunately, they weren't ten digit numbers, they were written as "Hodgeman 4321" and "Edwards 5212". I had no translation for what I presumed were county names and the modern corresponding area code and prefix. I was calculating the odds that any of these numbers were of any value seventy years later and the investment in time to find the phone company Rosetta stone for the translation. Before I could finish, Veronica got my attention.

"See if this helps." She was holding a ragged white pages from God knows when, open to one of the front pages. She actually found it!! Without my even asking! Like she read my mind, which was good for phone numbers, but not so much for the whole contemplating the imperiled button topic. Actually, she probably didn't need to read my mind to know what was going on in that respect. She had found the county names and the six digit equivalents.

"My God, I could kiss you!" I blurted out, before I could do an internal edit for the creepiness factor that was going to be received on her part. She laughed sweetly as if to say, "as if."

"Let's check out these numbers," she said while walking to a table.

We sat and I read from the yearbook while she found the numbers, which I wrote down along with the names of the students. After four were complete, I reached for my phone and realized I had left it in the car. I started to get up and she said, "I got it," producing her own phone from somewhere. She assumed a mock "I'm all that" librarian macho pose.

"Impressive," I said, "But not quite kiss worthy."

We both laughed as loud as you can in a Library.

"Read me the numbers. I'll dial," she said.

The first number was disconnected. The second was a roofing company. She typed the third and stopped.

"That's weird," furling her brow.

"What?"

"Say that number again," I repeated the number.

"Hmmm...I actually have that number in my contacts. I didn't recognize it 'cause it's on speed dial. It's one of my friends, Julie."

I located the yearbook note which was signed "Lulu". I started scanning pictures looking for a Lulu to gather a last name, hopefully to narrow things down for Veronica.

"Lulu...hmmm... Lulu," thinking out loud trying to spark a memory, "Louise maybe?"

"Yeah," I paged back a couple of pages, "Louise Mickler."

"Oh, my God!" she cocked her head, looked me in the eye and said.

"That's Julie's grandma."

Before I could respond she had dialed.

"Jules, get your butt over here.....No, the 'brary...There's this old guy looking for your grandma."

OK, that stung a bit. "That ought to be worth a compensatory, karmic button failure," I thought, hoping my guardian angel was feeling especially impish and charitable to the one he guards.

".....I know, but come over anyway." Veronica finished her call.

"She's real close. She'll be here in five minutes."

She noticed my bruised ego. She reached out and patted my hand.

"Hey, I *don't* think you're old, we just say that for anyone over thirty. It's like calling a girl, dude."

She smiled and I was healed. I finally exchanged a proper introduction to Veronica and then went to make some photocopies of key pages in the yearbook while waiting for Jules. Back at the table I began organizing things only to be distracted by the approach of a svelte beauty with shoulder length blonde hair, jeans, heels and a subtle salon tan. She stopped at our table. Veronica looked up from her phone. I pinched myself.

"Hey, Jules," She did her Vanna White thing again but this time I was the letter.

"This is Denny."

"The old dude," I said, rising to greet Julie. They laughed.

"He's not that old," Julie said, mostly to Veronica. I felt the years slide right off me. I think I could've dunked a basketball right then and there.

"Thank you, Julie," I smiled.

"Jules, please," Julie insisted. Julie began to pull back a chair to sit. Before she could, I suggested,

"Why don't we all get a latte or something, my treat. I hope that's not a problem while you are on the job, Veronica," I said.

"Not a problem. I'm actually off today."

I looked at her, puzzled.

"I left my phone here last night and came back to get it. I was on the way out when you wandered in so pathetic and helpless, so I reached out."

They laughed, and I rolled my eyes. We found a quiet corner in the café to chat. I took care of the refreshments, and we settled in to our respective choice of beverages and some warm chocolate chip cookies. Julie began,

"So V says you're looking for my grandma?"

"Well, actually someone who might have known your Grandma."

I recounted the whole story; even the football man part of it which they thought was "soooo cute". Unfortunately, Louise Gallagher (nee Mickler) had passed on in the last eighteen months. Julie was the family's logical choice to occupy the house to maintain a presence at the property, since she had no other firm ties or commitments.

The phone number being still active was easily explained. Her Grandma grew up in the house, inherited it and spent the rest of her days there. The phone number, never needing to be changed, was now Julie's. She tried her best to provide useful information. I didn't expect much so I wasn't disappointed. After all, she couldn't recall what she never knew, but she really wanted to be of more help.

I could sense the "Dead End" sign looming as we finished our coffee. While walking out, I profusely thanked the ladies for all their help and sauntered to my car. Before turning the key, I got some things in order, found my phone and checked for messages. I was startled by a knock at the window. I looked up to see Veronica and Julie, powered down the window and Veronica spoke.

"We were wondering if you wanted to join us at Julie's place."

I paused, speechless.

"There's still a lot of my grandma's stuff there. Maybe we can find something there for you," Julie offered.

I was a bit stunned, but gratefully accepted.

"Hop in," I said.

Veronica pointed to a red brick bungalow about six houses down the street.

"Actually, it's the house right over there. We'll just meet you."

They arrived before I did since I found what must have been the only red light in the city of Hays, conveniently located at the intersection by the library. They had already disappeared into the house leaving the door open. I still knocked.

"Do you want a beer or something?" Julie shouted from the kitchen.

"Nnnn..yeah, sure."

Julie returned with two Rolling Rocks and gave me both of them. I was puzzled, but pleased.

"I know guys. You're gonna finish the first one in about three minutes and I'll have to get up again to get you another one."

I couldn't argue with her logic, or her hospitality. "She'll make a great wife someday," I chauvinistically thought, as any man would after a display of such thoughtful foresight. Veronica emerged from a hallway but now sporting a leisure ensemble of baggy, tattered sweatshirt, plaid flannel lounge pants and furry yellow slippers. The glasses were gone too.

My first impulse was one of disappointment, but that settled to relief. I didn't need the distraction. I could focus on the reason I was there in the first place.

"You know, I would completely understand if you guys wanted to invite one or more of the, no doubt, thousands of young men who would surely kill to be over here guarding you damsels from the strange Road Warrior, reporter-dude."

They both shrugged. Veronica put it to rest.

"Not to worry, I teach self-defense classes and Julie has a loaded twelve-gauge."

"Oooh Kaay, soooo maybe *I* need to call someone?"

"It's all good," Julie said. "Take a seat," motioning to the couch.

I settled in. Veronica was straightening up a bit and Julie took a seat to my right in a matching parlor-type armchair. I took a moment to drink in the surroundings which could only be described as estate sale meets college dormitory. Julie noticed me scanning the room.

"The furniture is my grandma's of course," she said apologetically.

"No worries, you should see my place. I decorate in thrift store eclectic," I countered. "Do you live here, Veronica?"

She looked at Julie with a grin, "Sometimes."

They laughed.

"I crash here is a better way to describe it. I live in a dorm the rest of the time."

"No need to explain, I was in college once," I said with fond reminiscence.

Veronica got herself a beer and plopped down on the other end of the couch, a couch that could sincerely be old enough to possibly have once held HH. The couch could easily be in its third generation with Julie, and, if her grandmother was friends with Harvey, maybe he visited a time or two, but there was no evidence that they were even "how 'bout this crazy weather?" acquaintances. As I pondered this, there was a communal awareness of awkward silence. Julie broke in.

"So, there's stuff all about the place in boxes here and there. My aunts and uncles are supposed to come pick it up, but they don't seem to be in a big hurry."

"Stuff?" I thought. I had forgotten why I was in the house in the first place. "Right," I said. "Is there any room that's off-limits?"

"No, go ahead. Knock yourself out."

"We'll give you a hand," Veronica volunteered.

We all spread out in different directions and began rifling through anything that looked as if it might matter. I narrowed the possibilities by naming things that would be most helpful - pictures, news articles, stuff from high school.

After about a half an hour, we had just about been through the lot when Julie piped up from down the hall.

"Hey, I think I might have something here." We gathered in the living room. It was a personal address book. Julie handed it to me, and I made a beeline to the "H" tab. Jackpot! A full page of Harvey Henderson addresses, maybe seven or eight total. It seems Louise and Harvey kept in touch, maybe just Christmas Cards, but it didn't matter. I had Harvey's geographical lifetime in my hand. There were even dates next to the addresses. This was golden. I looked up and proclaimed, "We're done. This is all I need."

We congratulated each other with a round of beers and sat back down in our previous spots to savor the moment. After a bit, I made a proposal.

"Ladies, you have been a dream today. I can't thank you enough, but I'd like to try by whipping up a dinner for the ages. I can cook a little when I feel like it and have the time, and right now I have both, so what say you?"

They looked at each other kind of deer-in-the-headlights.

"Or I could be on my merry way. I *have* used up your afternoon."

"No, I think we were so not expecting that. Put me down for "yeah" on the guy-makes-us-dinner option," Veronica said with aplomb.

"Make it unanimous," seconded Julie.

"All right! Dinner it is!" I replied.

They pointed me in the direction of the nearest grocery store. I added that I needed to check into a motel and make copies of the address book at the library. Julie would have none of the latter two as she told me I was welcome to crash in the bungalow and that I could keep the address book and just send it back when I was done with it. I graciously accepted her offer.

Shopping proved a pleasant surprise. Jasper's market had some superbly fresh produce, organic meat selections and even some game choices. I decided to play it safe and put together a chicken piccata with wild mushroom risotto and some simple field greens tossed with balsamic and olive oil - uncomplicated, easy and delicious. After all, I didn't want to spend all night in the kitchen.

Amazingly, I found a couple of dusty bottles of a 1997 vintage Brunello di Montalcino hiding on a nearby liquor store shelf for a steal of a price. Not the perfect wine for a piccata dinner, but hey, 1997 Brunello was good enough to actually BE dinner.

The liquor store proprietor seemed glad to get rid of them since they had probably been sitting there since Veronica and Julie were in grade school, oblivious to the fact that they were probably worth several hundred dollars. I grabbed a Pinot Gris for a starter to go with some imported olives and cheeses while I prepared the main course.

I couldn't recall the last time I cooked for a woman let alone two. The culinary arts used to be my "entrée" (pardon the pun) into women's hearts, or at least to get their attention a little, not like I was a "Playah" or anything, casting spells on unsuspecting women, finding my way to the promised land by way of the palate. I was a shy lad back then, and a fine meal was a good show, and a grandiose prop to disguise the fact that I was a tad boring and scared to death! I still like to cook here and there, and mostly for friends, but it's for the food and the making of good memories, not as a distraction for my social clumsiness.

Ninety minutes after leaving the bungalow I had shopped, cooked, and upon returning, cleaned myself up. Dinner was on the dining room table which had to be cleared of two weeks' worth of mail, text books and some unfolded laundry. It was evident that Veronica and Julie hadn't had a proper sit-down dinner in some time, and certainly not without a television on, and/or a texting apparatus in hand. They appeared slightly disoriented for a while, but once we got to eating, drinking and talking they found a rhythm and thoroughly enjoyed themselves, as did I.

We talked about what you might expect, the standard Q&A, banter and jibes friendly strangers use to discover each other. Unfortunately, things gravitated to them doing a lot more of the Q and me doing a lot more of the A which found us talking about my career and events leading up to that. I'm not big on self-aggrandizement. I'm a journalist. I find others more interesting than myself, but they were sincerely interested, and I did appreciate that. There was not an inkling of patronization or feigned curiosity from either. I was a bit surprised since they were born of the WiFi, A.D.D. generation, and not predisposed to lengthy conversation, but they were, so I obliged their choice of topic.

They insisted on doing the dishes, but when that would happen was unclear. They moved straight to the couch, wine glasses in hand. We were now into the last bottle of Brunello. I was trying not to keep track of time, but that was unavoidable given the ever-presence of technology. I had to think back a couple of times, but realized we had talked for two and a half hours at the dining table. I landed in the armchair, and Veronica manned the remote control surfing for something to watch. She stopped when she arrived at one of those twenty-something, non-network, primetime glamour soaps. There may or may not have been vampires. I didn't pay that much attention. I relaxed in my chair just "being". All critical thinking had been shut down in the mind of Denny Preston. I was just hangin', sipping superb wine, and enjoying the best company I had known in at least a couple of years.

Veronica didn't last long. A sound not unlike an un-oiled, industrial chainsaw resonated from her nasal passages as she drifted into slumber. Julie and I remained silent, but there was too much comedy in the moment, and we both broke out laughing spontaneously. Julie rescued her friend from further embarrassment, gently roused "V" and carefully guided her into one of the bedrooms.

It was just Julie and I now. After a few minutes, the seating arrangement seemed awkward, and Jules insisted I move to the couch. We kind of watched TV for a bit, but then Julie spoke up.

"I kinda didn't tell the truth earlier. See, I'm not a Business major." This had been part of the dinner conversation.

"I'm actually a Journalism major." The pitch of her voice rose at the end to indicate she was in confession.

"Why would you say you are a Business major?" I questioned.

"Oh…I don't know…I guess I was a little self-conscious about the fact that I'm just this undergrad and you are….well…"

"Not smart enough to find another line of work?" I joked.

Julie laughed nervously, which puzzled me.

"No, it's just that I know…knew…I remembered some of the things you wrote…." Julie struggled for the right words. She tried again.

"I just admire your work a lot."

Now I was really confused. She continued.

"You're a good writer. I've even saved a few of your pieces and read them over again."

"My God," I thought to myself "I've actually met one of the seven people who bother to read my stuff." I didn't know how to reply except to say "thanks". I leaned forward to take another sip of wine and when I leaned back again, before I could even think, I was in the throes of amorous embrace. Julie was kissing me, and not like, "Thanks for dinner" more like "I'm dessert".

The strangest thing was that instead of every last pleasure center in my brain firing at full tilt drowning out all reason and intellect, I experienced a sort of out-of-body, personal inventory, free-association, winner-take-all throw-down starring the full cast of characters that make up the psyche of Denny Preston. It went something like this….

"What the?!! OMG!"

"I can't believe I just used a text shortcut during a conversation in my head."

"Julie! I LOVE you!"

"Let's see, I could probably get most of my stuff in a 24 foot U-haul and be moved in by the middle of next week."

"Oh, she's a GREAT kisser."

"Lips Like butter."

"Crap, did I put too much butter in the piccata?"

"Man she was on me faster than that crab thing that attached itself to John Hurt in "Alien". Not to imply she's like an alien crab creature or anything."

"Denny, she wasn't even alive when "Alien" first came out."

"Shut up, Dude, this is a once in a lifetime opportunity."

"She doesn't know what she's doing. She's star struck. She's been drinking."

"So, she's HOT!"

"Hot? I think I left the stove on. Her GRANDMA'S stove! Her GRANDMA'S couch! It's like I'm making out with her GRANDMA now."

"Hang in there, dude. Breathe through it. The hot blonde will be back shortly."

"She's gonna hate herself and ME!"

"You'll be gone tomorrow, screw it."

"She's gonna hate HERSELF! She'll quit Journalism."

"Then you're doing her a favor."

"That's not my call."

"Speaking of "call", remind me to call the Darwin Institute to inform them there may be a few flaws in the whole desire-to-mate-takes-precedent because I think I'm talking myself out of the Big Bang."

"Dude, you suck. Sure, now you grow a conscience."

"Shit! Shit! Shit!"

And there I was, lip-locked with a beautiful, young, willing, fantasy come to life. And contrary to my own expectation of how I would react in this situation, I instantly grew-up, made the adult decision, the right decision. A decision I would probably cry like a baby about later, but nevertheless, I did what I did, I took the high road.

This conversation took all of just three seconds believe it or not. I gently, reluctantly retreated, ending the kiss. My primary concern was now Julie's interpretation of my reaction. She was vulnerable, and I didn't want her to remember this as "The night that old creep Denny Preston rejected me".

She looked down and away, slightly embarrassed. I softly touched her cheek and turned her head back to look at me. When our eyes met I said.

"Sweet, beautiful Julie. I would feel a horrible person to take advantage of you, and I would be doing just that."

"But Denny..." she protested. I continued.

"I've been here before and know exactly what would happen. After tonight we would never speak again."

"That's not true, I..."

Calmly, I kept on.

"Right now this evening has been perfect. I want to keep it that way."

She sat thinking, almost speaking a couple of times, but then wrapped her arms around me with a big platonic hug. I breathed relief, bittersweet to be sure. Taking the high road is gratifying, but it's a path paved with a lot of "No", and that can leave a little sting. And even though my mind persisted in sorting through scenarios that resulted in a lifetime of bliss and harmony with Julie, I knew they were just hopeless inventions.

Julie began in again on how connected she felt and what it was about my work that had captured her admiration. She wasn't gushing though. This was almost a professional critique. I made a promise to help her with her work and getting a start after she graduated, which would be just a few months away. I let her know my door was always open. I also congratulated her on being my one and only groupie, which elicited a laugh and a big happy smile. We talked some more, enjoying one of those rare, pure moments where all the usual things that matter like gender, age, setting, status and physical proximity, were non-existent. Just two people being people with one another.

At about ten minutes post-kiss, I noticed my legs were going a bit numb. This was because Julie was still sitting, facing me, her knees at my hips, my legs as seat cushions. I also began to notice, the softness of the skin on her lower neck, the subtle floral aroma of her golden hair, the gentle roaming of her slender fingers on my bare arms, the almost whispering tone of her voice and her smiling blue eyes.

Note to self: Cancel the call to the Darwin Institute.

I politely interrupted Julie from whatever she was saying (because as you can see, at this point I was in no way hearing a word of it) and requested she move to a seat on the couch. She paused for a moment to process that, took note of the exquisitely uncomfortable situation I was in and then lithely unwrapped herself from me, finally resting on the couch beside me at a safe distance.

"I fear my newly discovered chivalry, in the long run, is no match for your charms my dear. Best not to tempt fate more than it has to be."

She accepted the indirect compliment, and if she harbored any remaining doubts that my rebuff of her advance was in any way related to the quality of her femininity, they were most assuredly obliterated. Her self-esteem was fully restored. She knew I was desirous, was barely maintaining my composure and would be left wanting. The natural order of things had been restored.

We both decided to call it a night. I began to arrange the couch for my night's sleep, but Julie stepped in.

"Oh no you don't, you're sleeping in my bed."

My heart leapt, I felt a healthy shot of adrenaline discharge down my spine.

"Oh My God," I thought. "She's incorrigible."

Julie took a breath.

"Wow, that didn't sound right did it? I meant, I will sleep with Veronica in the other room, and you can sleep in my room."

I nodded, once again both relieved and disappointed all at the same time. As I began to drift off, I remember thinking Julie might recall this night as the night Denny Preston became her lifelong friend and mentor. What a perfect day.

Five

◆ ◆

I awoke to the distant sound of kitchen noises. I tossed my clothes on from the night before and stumbled my way towards the din hoping a piping hot fresh pot of coffee waited for me. My eight-hour slumber had reset my senses to their defaults so I was defenseless and unsuspecting of the visual assault that ensued the moment I turned into the kitchen. You see, Veronica was doing the dishes…

Let me pause here to explain something before I continue…

I know by now, as a reader, you are having serious doubts about my priorities as a storyteller since I have spent a good deal of ink here lately on prurient observations. But, if you will indulge me, I would be most grateful. For my intention here is not to titillate, but to provide an honest accounting of my state of mind, experiences and observations, and I would be disingenuous, and it would seem quite incredulous actually, if I were to simply write…

"I walked in the kitchen where Veronica was busy doing the dishes. I took note that her outfit was rather unconventional for the task as she had chosen some gym shorts and a junior size t-shirt, which appeared to be hand cropped. Her hair was up, and it seemed she was being rather sloppy with the soap suds."

That's one version. But honestly, you don't want to read that, and it doesn't tell the story anyway.

Let's try again...

My eight hour slumber had reset my senses to their defaults so I was defenseless and unsuspecting of the visual assault that ensued the moment I turned into the kitchen. You see, Veronica was doing the dishes...

Quite involuntarily, my eyes went straight to her short, sapphire, silk boxers. Her shirt was just a T-shirt, perhaps a size less than manufacturers' recommendation for proper fit. The bottom part of the T-shirt had been unceremoniously ripped away, leaving about half of what one would expect in a normal T-shirt. Everything else in sight was strictly Veronica as she was... shapely, bronze, Veronica.

Her hair was up, Sarah Palin style, with a few wisps trailing down her cheeks and neck. Some of the soap suds had found their way from the sink to light randomly as decoration across skin, clothes and hair. I paused for a few seconds to collect myself and piped up,

"Good Morning."

No reply. I now noticed the iPod and earphones.

"GOOD MORNING."

Still no reply. Do I tap her on the shoulder? Step into her peripheral vision and wave? Yell louder? Either way there was a good chance she was going to be scared to death, and I would learn the hard way how good a self-defense instructor she was.

I chose the tap on the shoulder which of course startled her, causing her to flinch. A glass squirted from her soapy hands into the air splashing water down the front of her shirt. It wasn't a lot, but it was enough. Fortunately, I was able to catch the glass before it shattered on the floor.

"Well, it looks like I made it in time for the floor show," came a voice from behind me.

It was Julie who was carrying a to-go tray of library coffees. I can only imagine what was going through her mind seeing me with a water glass and Veronica with a wet T-shirt. Julie turned to me with an impish grin.

"But if you've already paid for the lap dance, I can leave you two alone for a while."

I knew everything was good, but still felt the need to offer some explanation.

"No, I haven't paid for the lap dance."

"Well you sure ain't gettin' one for free," Veronica chirped, feigning outrage.

"No, I meant there is no lap dance...And this glass...the water..." It was no use, they were both howling with laughter.

"That's right, there is no lap dance," Veronica added, "you couldn't afford me anyway."

More howls. I retorted.

"How about washing my car in slow motion? What would that set me back?"

Julie had to set the coffees down so as not to spill them while she wriggled and giggled.

I decided to push the comic envelope...

"Christ, I feel like I'm in an episode of "Three's Company".

Silence..... and then in unison the girls replied,

"Three's Company? What's that?"

Ok, should've stopped with the car wash joke, I thought.

"Yo, dish-wench, why don't you go put some real clothes on," Julie dressed down Veronica.

Veronica grabbed a coffee and strutted out of the kitchen. Julie and I sat at a table in the kitchen nook.

"I got you black coffee. That's what you had yesterday so..."

"Thank you."

"Don't you think for a second that wasn't all for your benefit," Julie said, slightly perturbed.

"What was for my benefit?"

"That little Lolita-meets-cheerleader-gone-wild costume. Let me tell you what happened. You woke up to the sound of her washing dishes, which she did loudly enough to be sure you got up. Am I right?"

"Yeah."

"I love the girl but she is a salacious tease. We go out to bars, and it's just cruel the way she lures these guys in and then crushes them. It's like a sport for her."

Julie sipped from her coffee and continued.

"Not that she was trying to lure you in and crush *you*, she just wanted to watch you drool a little."

"I didn't drool."

She tilted her head down in admonishment.

"OK…yes… but not much."

"I'm just afraid she's going to tease herself right out of a real good thing one of these days and regret it. She's lost a couple of great guys because she can't help playing her games."

Julie changed the subject.

"So, I suppose you're going to be taking off, not staying another day?"

"You suppose correctly, but if I could get in a quick shower, I would be most grateful."

It wasn't like I didn't consider staying another day, another week, forever. But, what needed to happen was for me to continue on and the college girls to go to college.

"You better come back and visit or I'm gonna kick your ass. Remember, I got a loaded twelve gauge, and I will find you," Julie commanded. We laughed. I began to walk away. Julie spoke.

"Late seventies sitcom."

I turned, puzzled. She added.

"John Ritter, Suzanne Somers, Joyce Dewitt."

"You DID know, you little scamp."

I showered, got my things together, made sure to grab the Mickler-Gallagher address book, and Julie walked me to my car. Veronica came bounding out of the house.

"You weren't going to leave without saying goodbye were you?"

Veronica had changed clothes all right, but she now had on workout garb, all skin tight. Julie and I looked at each other and smiled. I pretended to wipe drool from my chin.

We all exchanged obligatory farewells, and then Julie surprised me again, wrapping her arms around me and planting another big kiss on me. Before I let myself get carried away again, I realized it was mostly meant to shock Veronica, in which case it was a direct hit. I played along.

"Thanks for last night Jules; you're amazing."

Veronica's jaw hit the pavement. I coolly got behind the wheel and drove off into the sunset...well, about seven hours before the actual sunset and in the opposite direction really, but you get where I'm coming from.

Before long, Hays had disappeared from my rear-view mirror and so did the afterglow of a rather heady twenty-four hours. I was still a bit bewildered about Julie's admiration. Sure, it is flattering, and maybe it's just that I'm not used to people remembering, or even noticing my work, but out of the expansive universe of feature writers, how does a college senior in Hays, Kansas imprint on me as her writing guru? Even more curious, how does my journey lead right to her door? I reserve judgment. You know, the whole objective observer as a reporter thing again.

My heading now was due east, straight down Interstate 70 to Kansas City, Missouri. The most recently dated address for "H. Henderson" in the Mickler-Gallagher address book was just about four hours away. Unfortunately, there are no phone numbers in the book for Harvey, only addresses, otherwise I would have taken a shot at a phone call. This indicated Harvey and Louise were probably content exchanging Christmas cards and no more.

As I approached K.C., I hit some traffic, at least "traffic" as defined by the locations I had taken residence in over the last ten to twelve weeks. For the citizens of Kansas City, this was probably just a light, Saturday afternoon on the roads, but I was aware of some slight tension on my part, which I traced to a sensation of claustrophobia, or perhaps even agoraphobia. I was reminded of the disorientation observed of indigenous peoples of the Amazon when exposed to an open air environment without the benefit of the forest canopy. They are unequipped to comprehend distances, and the relational size of objects near and far, as they have never known anything to be more distant than what the density of the rain forest they inhabit would allow them to see. I was sure my experience was nowhere near that of an Amazon tribesman, but still, this was a new sensation for me.

My GPS brought me to the downtown skyline, and then had me veer due South for roughly five to six miles. I found myself

61

cruising a modest 1950's era middle-class suburb, judging by the residences that were scattered about the gently rolling landscape. The fading green lawns of summer were contrasted by a robust backdrop of rich, flowing autumn hues.

Each house sat on at least an acre of land. No fences were needed due to the dense bordering of maple, elm, ash and the occasional fruit tree, which separated the mostly well-kept properties.

I took note that my heartbeat was quickening as I approached the actual street, and then counting down the individual address numbers. My destination was 14567 Leewood Lane. 14561, then 14565, 14569 and 14575...No 14567? I backed up and checked again, but sure enough, there was no 14567. A moment of panic set in, I checked the address book again and all seemed in order, except there was no 14567. I parked the car and looked to see which residence might be occupied so that I might get an assist with the address find. The winner, with two cars in the driveway, was 14569. I rang the doorbell and knocked, but no reply. I waited for longer than I thought was needed (which was about three minutes). I almost left a note but thought that might seem strange. Instead, I decided to go round up a room for the night and return later. Before I got to my car, a woman who had emerged from 14565 and was standing on her porch stoop, got my attention.

"Can I help you, sir?"

"Yes, thank you, I am looking for 14567 Leewood Lane."

"Oh, right, you're not going to find that from where you are. Follow me."

She walked around the side of her house and headed into the woods behind her backyard. I thought this was a bold move on her part since she didn't know me from Adam, but then I considered the wood chipper scene from "Fargo" and decided I might want to be the one on guard here.

I had caught up so that I was about twenty feet from her. She motioned again to follow, and disappeared into the tall trees. Just thirty feet in was a small house. It couldn't have been more than nine-hundred square feet. It was one story with a small front porch, and perfectly square. The roof was in need of repair, and some of the wood siding was curling at the edges. It didn't look occupied. The woman, now at the entrance to the house, spoke again.

"It needs some work, but that's why the price is so low. It's a fixer-upper."

I joined her on the porch.

"Is there another way back here? Can you get a car back here?" I asked.

"See, over there," she pointed.

"It's grown over, but through there is access to Temple Street, about a hundred yards or so. It should only take a day or two to clear, no big deal really. Would you like to see the inside?"

I almost declined, but decided she might change her mind if she knew why I was really here. I agreed. She unlocked the door, and we crossed the threshold.

I began snapping pictures with my cell phone camera, but there really wasn't much to see. With the exception of a single bedroom, the house was essentially one room. The kitchen area was off to the left, there was a fireplace to the right and nothing in between. There was a single bathroom which was only accessible through the bedroom. There were no furnishings.

This didn't bode well for a one-on-one interview with the man himself. If this was the last address in HH's life, then he was no more.

"And what of the previous resident?" I asked.

"He passed on several years back, seven I think."

That about cinched it.

"And it's been vacant ever since?" I asked.

She reluctantly replied "Yes," suspecting it might suggest the property was more neglected than appearances would let on. I decided to come clean.

"Was his name Harvey Henderson?"

"Why yes, how did you know?"

"I'm actually not looking to buy, I am a writer who..."

I proceeded to fill her in on the details. She introduced herself as Dorothy Trombley. She and her husband owned both 14565 and 14567 and were selling off the latter to cover some college costs for their second born. I asked her for any information she had on HH, and she invited me to 14565 for a cup of coffee and a sit-down chat. On the way, in my own thoughts, I grieved a little as I knew now I would never actually meet the man, well, meet him again. I knew the odds were slim to begin with, but just the same, now it was official.

We chatted small talk for the few minutes it took Dorothy to brew a pot of coffee. Once settled in, I didn't even have to ask a question before Dorothy began a steady flow of the last year or so of Harvey's life. To begin at the end, Harvey actually passed away in 14567 in the Spring of 2003 at age 81 in his sleep. The cause of death was undetermined, but Dorothy described it as if his heart had just stopped. It wasn't a heart attack, but she said the unofficial ruling was: one moment his heart was beating, and the next it wasn't. As if the last grain of sand in his hourglass had finally fallen. How that was determined she had no idea, but it was good enough for me. I wasn't writing a murder mystery here, and I didn't want to get sidetracked on a subject matter post-Harvey.

Dorothy summed up Harvey's final days as one might expect an eighty-one year-old's final days to be. He was in good health and sound mind until the end which afforded him the "luxury" of being able to avoid any time in a senior care facility. She said Harvey was grateful for that. She recounted that he was a simple man, a man who pretty much kept to himself, and if he had visitors, she wouldn't have known much about that since there was no view of the road to his place from her house.

I took copious notes and read between the lines a little, but when she was finished with her recollection of Harvey, I realized there wasn't much "sizzle" there. Everything was very ordinary and unspectacular. But, as they say, be careful what you wish for. I didn't have to wait long to get some "sizzle", and then some. Unfortunately, the "sizzle" was the actual burning of my own soul as Dorothy answered my innocent, parting question on how she and her family happened to find their way to Leewood Lane.

Six

◆◆

The Memphis Summer of 1995 was an especially sweltering one. The heat arrived in early May, and with the rare exception of a day or two scattered here and there, it was a relentless pressure cooker. Following suit, I and my then brother in arms Carson Rodgers, were turning up the heat on a motley collection of slimy characters scattered about the wide power spectrum of Politics, Industry, Union Leadership, Televangelism and everything in between. We had unearthed the makings of a monumental story. It was stuff of legendary proportion, a career maker, and we were riding herd with a vengeance.

It's not as if this is breaking news to most anyone reading this. It was one of the most talked-about scandals of the mid 90's, but in case you were in a coma or too young to remember, let me rehash the basics for you.

It was called "Baker Bridge", named because of the August 23, 1994, collapse of a small two-lane bridge dedicated to a local Civil War notable, about thirty-five miles north-northeast of Fayetteville, Louisiana. On the surface it looked as though it had a story-life of two, maybe three, news cycles and then a three-paragraph follow up whenever the official investigation was completed.

There was a certain amount of tragedy as six unfortunate souls were traveling the bridge at the critical moment, including a grandmother of eight, a future basketball phenom and a woman seven-months pregnant.

The official inquiry concluded that the bridge failure was the result of inferior material and manufacture of the "adjoinment and abutment integration devices". For those of us not versed in engineer-speak, that means the rivets broke. Technically, rivets AND bolts, but the rivets that failed were alone sufficient to have caused the disaster.

The tort lawyers swam like sharks to the chum, stirring up the public venom to make the "responsible parties pay dearly" for the appalling loss of life. The press followed in their wake, wanting no more than to parasitically milk, and market, the frenetic emotions of those most grieved by sticking cameras and microphones in their anguished faces, asking them the generic "how do you feel?" question to elicit a reaction and then shamelessly saturation-broadcasting these most vulnerable moments as sweeps fodder.

Carson and I, in our initial surface scratching, kept uncovering inconsistencies which only prompted us to dig deeper and deeper and then deeper again uncovering an intricate labyrinth of entrenched corruption.

The specific subject matter was rather unsexy, centering on industrial rivets, bolts and the like. In fact, had the illegalities involved only sub-standard quality and overpricing of infrastructure hardware, the story would have died a quick death. After all, who wants to read about metallurgical tensile ratios, and p.s.i. thresholds of threading densities? That's right, no one!

What made the story run was good old fashioned greed, unbridled immorality and the brazen arrogance that metastasizes when the relied-upon policing mechanisms have been systematically compromised. The nature of the corruption wasn't even that complex. It only amounted to simple overcharging, undersupplying and shoddy oversight all reinforced by payoffs, favors and incestuous patronage. In reality, it was decades in the making, a multi-generational erosion of standards and practices fueled by complacency, and a collective dependency on a sacred cash cow.

On the surface one might wonder how much graft could really be had selling nuts and bolts, but when it becomes apparent the enormity of scale involved in supplying every nut, bolt, rivet, screw, nail, staple, and push pin used by Federal and Local governments, the mind boggles at the possibilities. To be honest Thatcher-Crowne, the corporation at the epicenter of the scandal, wasn't the sole provider, but for all intents and purposes, they might as well have been.

The scandal had everything: blackmail, envelopes of cash changing hands at 3 A.M. in a Dunkin' Donuts, code words, informant nicknames like "Hound Dog" and "Blackjack", prostitutes (both male and female, some of whom were both), "Investor" groups made up of professional athletes, TV personalities, college presidents and on and on. More detail is irrelevant to the direction I'm headed for the moment. If you need more, there is plenty of archival material available.

What is important is the unavoidable transformative force and gravitational energy something of this magnitude can wrest upon mere mortals such as two haughty, up-and-coming

69

investigative journalists named Denny Preston and Carson Rodgers. You see, crusades always look good on paper, but the externalities that result from the actual execution of them become the Devil's playground.

Carson and I had been hired as staff reporters the prior seven and four months respectively for a magazine called Reliable Source Weekly. You may recognize that as the Hollywood tabloid rag (mostly web based now) that it has become, but in 1995, it was a fledgling news operation. The culture there encouraged a claws-out, take-no-prisoners then burn-the-village, journalism style. Neither of us had really established a signature style of our own yet, which was one reason we were hired. We had cut our teeth as small-town newspaper writers from different pockets of the U.S. - Carson from East Texas and me from Wisconsin. We were moldable talent, raw clay in the hands of an ambitious feature editor, hell-bent on sculpting us into mighty reporter-warriors and fired with white-hot embers stoked by left-wing, anti-corporate, power-to-the-people politics.

Currently, this same editor still works at the magazine, is part owner, has been the architect of layoffs totaling over 2,000 and counting, while cashing bonus checks in the meantime. So much for ideology.

The teaming of Carson and me on the Baker Bridge story had no deeper reason than we were just the two guys standing at the water cooler within earshot of our editor's desk at the time he needed a couple of reporters. I have to admit, his instincts were keen. He smelled a story where no one else had, and a huge one at that. And whether it truly was his instinct or just politics driving the decision, professionally it was a shrewd call.

Carson and I penned three extensive articles scattered over two months, the last two being cover stories. We were becoming noticed in journalism circles, even garnering some Pulitzer buzz, and the quick rise was intoxicating. We were a rare breed passing two unofficial watermarks as newsmen: Reporters being reported on by other reporters and unearthing a scandal grand enough that its moniker didn't need to end in the word "gate".

The trilogy of articles was more than enough to satisfy any standard for quality informative reporting. We had cast a bright light, and the cockroaches scurried leaving an alphabet soup of bureaus and departments to clean up the mess, as it should be.

But greed is not limited to rivet and bolt makers. The magazine wanted more. Carson and I had a book deal dangled in front of us, but before that could come to fruition, we were strongly "encouraged" to deliver two more installments on Baker Bridge for Reliable Source.

We were all too willing to cooperate. It wasn't just the book deal either. We were enjoying the spoils too much to think about how we were going to come up with another 20,000 words worth of meaningful material. We were dazzled by the perquisites of elite status celebrity cocktail parties, Sunday morning news show appearances, first class accommodations and even a few autographs along the way.

And why should we worry? We were full-fledged reporter-warriors now - wordsmithing wizards. We could have written 20,000 words on a jar of bean dip, and ended up with a dozen indictments and a full confession. Or so we thought. Instead, we struggled for an angle, for anything new to expose. We got to where we were perilously close to our deadline, and that fabled jar of bean dip was looking, well, like a jar of bean dip.

In subconscious desperation, as we were too full of ourselves to admit our predicament, we fell back on good old-fashioned, self-righteous, rabble-rousing. We catered to the snarling, craven desires of populist bloodlust. The big dogs had already been tossed into the meat grinder, and all that was left to topple were iconic symbols, and the most primary was Thatcher-Crowne itself.

It was an easy target. In fact, we got plenty of support to do whatever was necessary to take the company down hard, which is still applauded by a disturbing number of our own colleagues to this day. But we both knew in our heart that it was totally unnecessary. We even had numerous corporate analysts and financial experts objectively advise us during our investigation that Thatcher-Crowne was a vibrant company, a stalwart American corporate model. With the surgical removal of the cancerous elements that had conceived and executed the illegalities, there was no reason the company couldn't recover its reputation and remain one of the few lasting legacies of the once majestic industrial manufacturing foundation that built this country.

We chose to ignore the experts. Given the environment in which we were earning our living, it was easy to dismiss their analysis and write it off as transparent corporate shilling by Wall Street types. Rather than carefully adding contrast to the subtle shades of gray, we slathered our literary canvas with broad brushstrokes of black and white, casting only heroes and villains in terms of melodramatic proportion. The greatest villain of all was the monolithic, but mute, corporate giant.

Indeed, it was our talent as writers that enabled us to draw a trusting readership to direct all of its trumped up indignation at the one entity unable to defend itself. We peppered our prose with innuendo and loaded rhetorical questions. It was all based in truth. We didn't make things up, but we knew how to skew the angles enough so that light and dark fell just where we wanted it to over the landscape.

So, inevitably, we had stirred enough bile into the soup that the public sentiment would only be satisfied by a public execution. They got all that and more. Thatcher-Crowne was toppled, disemboweled and dismembered right in the public square. Our reporting prowess was such that the company's value plummeted, causing the stock price to tumble to risky depths. Shrewd arbitragers rode in and mounted a hostile takeover, parted out the assets and pimped out the specific departmental entities. The result was a whole bunch of rich people getting richer and a net loss of just over 17,000 jobs, averaging over 12 years of service. Nearly 3,800 of those dismissed had been with the company at least twenty years.

Even to this day I had no idea the extent to which I had rationalized the eventual outcome to myself with sanctimonious agitprop. I had so thoroughly indoctrinated myself to believe that the only way to save the village was to burn it, that I had been able to insulate myself from the true carnage that had been leveled on innocents. Thousands of lives had been turned upside-down, people doing no more than living the best they knew how were just so much collateral damage. And now, fifteen years later, I was sitting at the kitchen table of one of those very innocents.

The Shaker style chair on which I sat in Dorothy Trombley's kitchen had now become like an electric chair for my execution. I desperately hoped the years that had passed would at least mean she would not remember my name as one of the two scoundrels who so callously bulldozed her career, and who knows what else. That was all I was spared though.

Dorothy recounted the series of events that led her and her family to Kansas City. She was a VP of Human Resources for Thatcher-Crowne, bringing home a tad more than eighty-five grand a year with sparkling benefits, which was a handsome package in 1995. She was the sole breadwinner at the time, because her husband had begun a custom cabinetry and furniture business using recycled deadwood from diseased trees. They had invested twelve years worth of savings to get it off the ground. She showed me some old brochures, and the finished products were stunning. When she lost her job, Frank (her husband) had to abandon the business just five months into the endeavor because it was not yet turning a profit. They needed immediate income so he returned to work as a diesel mechanic. So, I killed his dream too. The collateral damage was not limited to the employees of Thatcher-Crowne.

I wondered how many others had to adjust their lives even though they never worked a day there. It was really immeasurable. Since Dorothy was a VP of HR, she was primarily the one who was tasked with coordinating the dismissal process. All 17,000-plus! She provided summarized accounts of dozens of specific cases off the top of her head. It seemed she had to be as much a grief counselor as a VP - Grown men sobbing in her office, single mothers who not only lost their income, but the day care benefit the company provided. Most of them worked there and stayed there for that reason alone. The glut on the regional job market created by the massive layoff meant middle-managers were working as janitors and fry cooks. Families had to uproot to new locales leaving behind important friendships.

As she progressed, a vivid image of Baker Bridge froze in my mind. I soon realized it was not Baker Bridge. It was a construction of my own making, a bridge I had built fifteen years before in my psyche to provide a hasty retreat back to the side of "the people's right to know" from the side of "knowing what's right for the people". The chasm it traversed was my conscience and innate sense of right and wrong. With each heart-wrenching story, the rivets I had manufactured from the raw material of hubristic rationalizations began to give way.

After what seemed like ages, Dorothy ended the litany of Thatcher-Crowne sadness. What remained of my soul was a curdled mess, but I was certain I could sort it all out over time, a good amount of time, but with an eventual restoration. My bridge was in bad shape, on the brink, teetering, but it appeared an ultimate collapse had been averted. It was a short-lived certainty though. Dorothy had one more story.

"Oh, I almost forgot, Harvey."

"What about Harvey?" I sheepishly uttered.

"He had a good deal of his retirement invested in Thatcher-Crowne stock. He lost half his net worth."

Pop! Creak!

The last rivet gave way. I sat devastated, trying not to look devastated. Dorothy continued on, but her words were so much background noise to the frenzied, scrambled conversation in my head. A cacophony of desperate pleas to try to rescue myself from this horrid situation. Eventually, I returned to the environment of Dorothy's kitchen to hear her finishing up about Harvey.

"...I can't recall him ever cursing his fate or complaining in any way. He just accepted where he was and how he got there."

I didn't feel any better. I felt worse actually, but not sure why.

She continued.

"He used to say, "What kind of idiot has half his wealth in one stock at age seventy-three?" But, he wasn't an idiot it was one of the most reliable firms of the twentieth century. Thatcher-Crowne was THE definition of blue chip, virtually every stable mutual fund out there had some portion invested in TC."

She was right, of course. Now, I had the weight of nationwide retirement losses piled on top of the already crushing burden of job loss and family upheaval. I began to feel strange, made up an excuse as to why I needed to leave, and did so. I probably shouldn't have been driving, but I did, and I kept driving. I had planned on a hotel stay in K.C., but I knew exactly where I needed to go, and it wasn't a hotel. It was home. I was about seven hours away, which meant roughly a ten P.M. arrival, maybe sooner. There was no need to stop for food, I couldn't eat anything anyway. I needed to see someone, the only someone who could offer me any semblance of absolution. Mom.

Seven

◆◆

My thoughts leaving Kansas City were ironically similar to those when arriving. I was feeling a kindred spirit to those Amazon jungle dwellers and their acquired inability to judge the distance to the horizon. The difference was the horizon I was unable to see was that of my own redemption. I would never have the chance to restore the damage I had leveled. The man was dead, and I had made his final years much less than they should have been. My penchant for rationalization was still alive and well though, as I tried to salve my wounds with empty denials.

"Yeah, what kind of idiot *does* put half of his retirement nest egg in one stock no matter its reputation?"

And

"How many unseen forces have damaged my own life - life's a bitch right?"

And

"Given the scandal, how do you know Thatcher-Crowne wasn't going to crash and burn anyway?"

I stopped myself before I got much past these, realizing there was no currency in my lame stabs at revisionist proclamations. I resolved I would just have to own it. Ultimately, I would just never know. I understood there was no escape from my choices years ago. The die was cast.

I decided to leave my continued pursuit of the Harvey Henderson project in a state of "we'll see." I knew I didn't want to continue on out of a sense of guilt. That course would most certainly yield something decidedly unworthy and would be a pathetic act of groveling to the specter of self-indulgent contrition.

I took a pause from the churning of my thoughts to realize the world outside my car, travelling past me at seventy miles per hour, was actually now dark. Somehow, I didn't notice the sunset, and somewhere along the way I had even turned on my headlights, but could not recall when. I took a peek at the dashboard clock and calculated I had been driving for nearly four hours, and had somehow managed to make my way halfway through Iowa without even being aware of it.

It's not like there were a lot of twists and turns. Kansas City to Minneapolis/St. Paul is a straight shot up I-35. Somehow, I had managed to make my way through Des Moines and past Ames without a coherent recollection of either town. I counted my blessings and decided I should pull over and stretch my legs, find a restroom and grab a caffeinated beverage (or two) to get me the rest of the way. The next most convenient place for that was Story City.

Story City lies just a mile or so west of I-35. A convenience-gas "oasis" allowed me to accomplish all three of my assigned tasks plus a couple more. My appetite did make an appearance finally, so I indulged in a rotisserie hot dog to accompany my tidal wave-sized cola, and I decided to top off the gas tank as well. I took a moment to gaze at the clear night sky. I found Orion and the Big Dipper. I estimated the actual light energy that was hitting my retinas was sent out long before humans were even, well, human. I embraced the synchronicity of the moment, one where an energy from long ago was having influence on and direct participation in the experience of the present. It gave me a strange but delicate sense of relief, as I saw my dilemma compared to the enormity of the cosmos. I climbed in the car again and drove back towards I-35.

Unfortunately, the way back to I-35 Northbound was detoured down a frontage road. I followed the signs and drove for ten minutes, zigging here and zagging there. It soon became apparent that something was awry. I could no longer see the highway, and the thick woods around the road made it impossible to see any lights from Story City or anywhere else for that matter. I pulled over to get my bearings.

Stopped, I consulted my GPS for some direction. Strangely, it was having problems homing in on my location. I rebooted it and still nothing. I couldn't put a finger on why, but my impression was it sensed I was at more than one place at the same time.

There was nothing else to do but turn around and retrace my steps. I began a U-turn, but misjudged the proximity of the drainage canal. The edge of the shoulder gave way, and my front-end was instantly under about two feet of water. The car was high-centered, so my front-wheel drive was unable to gain traction in the mud below. I shook my head, uttered an expletive, opened the door and carefully extracted myself from the car.

I looked to see if I could McGyver my way out of this predicament. The immediate assessment was a firm "No". I walked about to get any sort of viewing angle through the trees that would give me a hint as to where I was. I even looked up to locate Orion and the Big Dipper as reference, but I couldn't seem to find them.

Finally, I was aware that I didn't hear anything either. There was no other traffic noise, no noise at all really. I gingerly sat on the rear bumper for a minute or two, a bit concerned, but more frustrated really.

From up the road I saw a single light moving toward me. It seemed to take a while longer than I would have thought, but eventually engine noise became audible. Finally, the vehicle slowed down and then stopped. Amazingly, it was a tow truck. The single light was due to one of the headlights being out. The driver stuck his head out of the window.

"Looks like you got yourself in quite a pickle."

"To say the least," I replied.

"OK, I'll go on up the road and call someone for ya."

He began to drive off, which got me off the bumper post-haste.

"Hey what about?...."

He stopped and backed up. He was laughing up a storm.

"Oh, I love that one. Gets 'em every time. You should have seen your face!"

He laughed some more and then rolled the truck into proper position to employ the winch attached to the back of his rig. He parked and got out.

He couldn't have been more than five feet, four inches tall. Tom Cruise could have called him "shorty". He looked to be at least seventy and had the weathered look of someone who had been through a lot of life but in a good way. He wasn't weary looking or used up. He was just vintage. He probably could have fit in perfectly in Fortune, South Dakota circa 1877. He sported a slightly unkempt, full, gray moustache and beard. He wore a tattered straw cowboy hat, and his oil-stained, faded denim coveralls hung drape-like on his slight but sinewy frame.

He spoke as he pulled the winch hook towards the rear of my car.

"You got yourself good and lost back there didn't you?"

"Well, I thought I was paying attention to all the signs. Maybe I missed one or two."

"Oh, at least one or two," he said with firm certainty. He finished hooking up the winch.

"OK, get back behind the wheel again and drop it in neutral with your foot on the brake. Release the parking brake, and when I give the signal, take your foot off the brake altogether."

I did as commanded, and in a matter of seconds, all four tires were resting on dry pavement again. I got out to thank him.

"So what do I owe you? I hope you take plastic."

"Please, no," he said.

"Look, I would have been out here all night if you hadn't come along, let me give you something," I implored.

"Well, there is one thing. Give me your undivided attention for about thirty seconds."

I nodded.

"I'm going to tell you what you need to do to get back on the proper path here. It would be a mistake to go back where you came from. You'd just end up right back here again."

He pointed down the road ahead.

"This is the way you want to go. For a while it's going to seem like it's going nowhere, but, once you are out of the forest, you'll begin to see it. Beyond that, there will be a couple of signs, but they will be harder to see than the ones you missed earlier. They are not as well lit. Soon after that, you will know exactly what you need to do to get back on the correct road ahead. Got it?"

"Absolutely, sir, but should I be aware of any distances or time involved? I don't want to get lost again."

"Not really, you'll know when to do what you need to do. Just pay attention!"

I offered to pay again, but he refused more vehemently and sent me on my way. I headed up the road and within a mile was approaching Story City again. This made no sense, since I was certain Story City was behind me. Also, I saw not a single sign on the way, but I did know where I was now, so I didn't care. Across the way was the "oasis" I stopped at before. I noticed the road signs were still in place approaching the North-bound on-ramp to I-35, with the exception of the detour signs. As strange as that was, I decided it wasn't worth the brain damage to figure it out, and I proceeded to the on-ramp. Just seconds later, I was back to seventy MPH, headed North on I-35.

I drove for about ten minutes, was just getting myself back in the rhythm of the road, when I saw a bright sign in the distance. It was the kind you only see out in extremely rural areas. A regular sized sign, but on seventy foot standards rising high into the night. I recognized it but couldn't place it until I got close enough to see several tow trucks in front of the building. The sign was for "Angelo's Road Service", the very towing outfit that pulled me from the ditch not a quarter of an hour before. I took the off ramp, parked and entered the front door. Two beefy fellows, in red logoed shirts greeted me from behind a counter.

"Can we help you, sir?"

"Yes. I was just rescued by one of your drivers about fifteen minutes ago, and he refused payment. I'd like to see if I could pay here."

They looked at each other sort of incredulously.

"Uh...oh boy...I hope I didn't get him in trouble or anything for not charging me. He was very helpful..."

"No sir, it's nothing like that."

"So, can you write up an invoice?" I asked.

"Well....you see, sir.....we haven't had a call all night, it wasn't us."

"Seriously, this guy was driving one of your trucks."

"Couldn't have been, all four of ours are right out front, and have been since four P.M.."

83

"No really, he was a short, older fellow. He looked like he could have been an old-time prospector or something."

Again, they looked at each other. The second guy piped up, laughing a bit.

"If it would make you feel better, go ahead and pay us."

The first guy spoke again.

"Honestly, we can't even do that. Unless we have it in an official driver's log entry, we can't charge for it. Sorry."

I thanked them anyway, left and was back to seventy MPH in less than a minute. I was confused to be sure, but I decided to focus solely on getting home. I was getting tired and I still had at least three hours of driving left to reach St. Paul.

I reflected back on the day - one I could have lived without - but I decided was worth the experience. Words like "humbling" and "transformative" kept rattling around in my brain. I took a mental journey back to the shack in the woods where Harvey spent his last days. Did he really blame himself for his financial misfortune? Did he finish out his days thinking he was the architect of his Spartan existence? I truly hoped Dorothy Trombley was speaking truth when she said Harvey had reached full acceptance with his circumstance. Not that it was any measure of absolution for me if he had.

Then there was the mundanely surreal visit to Story City, the disappearing detour, the temporary GPS failure, the phantom tow truck driver. There were probably logical explanations for all of these, like maybe a strange hallucinogenic chemical reaction to the

84

rotisserie hot dog. The events were bizarre for sure, but what meaningful purpose did it all serve except to add fifteen bewildering minutes to my trip home.

All in all, the day left me with the strange sense of euphoria one feels after spending a day that possesses more impetus than most others, as if you are part of something discreetly purposeful, but not privy to the details behind the discretion, leaving nothing to take from it but wonderment.

Exhausted, I finally turned the key to my place in St. Paul at 10:18 P.M.. I hadn't crossed the threshold in over two months and was looking forward to some down time on the comfy couch. I grabbed a beer and settled in. Within forty-five seconds it was as if I had never left. My brain had successfully reloaded the cable station roster, and my right thumb was quickly restoring its muscle memory relationship to the universal remote's button array.

Soon, the beer was empty, and as I got up to get another, I had two thoughts. First, that I should have remembered Julie's (from Fort Hays) beverage axiom regarding guys and beers so that I wouldn't have needed to get up again, and second, that even though I was getting a beer from my own fridge, I had this odd feeling I should be getting permission from someone to help myself to one.

I made it back to the couch, and the feeling intensified finally gelling as a subtle overall sensation that I was not "home". It was my place, but I was not home. It was quite unsettling. I worked through that while sipping from beer number two. I wrote it off as fatigue and went to bed.

The next morning, refreshed and aware, I was no different. Actually, it was worse. I was flooded with questions. Why did I feel this way? Had I been on the road so long I was conditioned to being a nomad? Had I really undergone some cosmic transformation? Did I leave myself behind? Was I more myself than I had ever been?

There were no answers. Even the questions seemed out of place, in a way. They were highly inadequate. The more I thought about it, the more confused I became. The bottom line was I didn't feel like I was home, and I didn't feel like anywhere else was home. I was a stranger in my own apartment and maybe even in my own life.

Eight

◆ ◆

"Maybe you've just outgrown the place, honey," my mom suggested as a possible reason for the strange disconnect I was experiencing regarding my living quarters. "I recall feeling that way a couple of times myself," she continued.

"I suppose, but I've been away longer than this before and never had this happen, not even close," I responded while arranging the various lunch items I had picked up from Nick's Bistro, now scattered about Mom's kitchen table where we were seated.

"Well, has anything changed for you lately? What are you working on right now?"

It immediately dawned on me, while dishing up some curried chicken salad and tossed greens, that across from me was an immediate source whom I had completely overlooked, a trusted eyewitness to a defined period of time in Harvey Henderson's life.

"Well...," I hesitated, for some reason feeling I needed to develop a "pitch" to explain my latest project to my own mother.

"Can you recall your very first memory, Mom?"

"Hmmm. No, not really."

"Well, I discovered I do, and I decided to use that as the starting point for a sort of human interest yarn to explore if there is some cosmic significance or deeper meaning to *the* very first point in my life that has a memory attached."

"And how's that working out?"

"So far not too bad, but it's still very much a work in progress."

"So, without hemming and hawing, what about this project has you reassessing your own life so deeply?" Mom said in an all-knowing Mom sort of way.

"Why would you come to that conclusion?" I tried to deflect.

"Dennis dear, please, don't try to put one past your old Mom, OK?"

I capitulated, telling her about HH, where it had led me, culminating in the Thatcher-Crowne business and the personally traumatic encounter with Dorothy Trombley. She paused a bit to gather her thoughts while sipping some of Nick's special Creamy Tomato soup.

"Look, Denny, I'm not going to lecture you again on the whole business at that irksome magazine where you worked." She was referring to Reliable Source Weekly. "I had my say on that years ago, and it would seem life still has you harvesting some bitter fruit from that episode. Frankly, I don't think I could teach you more than karma is so generously dishing up for you at this very moment anyway."

I nodded. "So, would you conclude my strange disconnection is a good thing?" I asked with a tone meaning to lead her to an easy, "Yes."

"Sure, it seems obvious to me."

"So, what's your sound, motherly advice for this contrite prodigal son?"

She leaned back in her chair, dabbed her mouth with a napkin and thought about it for a moment.

"That depends."

"On what?" I asked.

"If you picked up any "Nickerdoodles"?" "Nickerdoodles" being Snickerdoodle cookies from Nick's.

"Of course I did."

I pointed to a bag which she immediately commandeered with a smile. She plated one of the cookies and then said,

"Go in the guest room and in the roll-top desk you'll find an old Whitman's Sampler Chocolate box. Bring it back here. I have something for you."

I did so and set the box on the table in front of her. She opened it and sorted through some papers, the sheer number of which you would think could never fit in a box that size.

"Here it is!"

She handed me a green 8 1/2 by 11 sheet of paper folded in fourths. It was one of those year-end Christmas message letters people send out with their holiday cards. It was dated 1983.

"Take a look at the bottom, Denny."

My eyes found the signature. It said "Harvey".

89

"Maybe this will help you. I don't know why I kept it all these years. I ran across it just last week while getting my ducks in a row for sending out Christmas cards this year. It isn't that far off you know..... Go on, read it."

Mom got up and proceeded to clean up the lunch dishes. I read.

December, 11, 1983

Greetings All,

Joy and good tidings from the western coast. I wish you all the spectacular blessings this sacred season can bring. Nineteen Hundred and Eighty-Three has been a year of discovery and awakening for yours truly. In the event you did not take notice of the postmark, I have found my way to the charming hamlet of Mendocino, California.

The air sings with sea breezes, and life abounds in a patient, thoughtful way. The arts thrive here, and I have taken my place among the artists, finding talents I did not know I had. I am reborn to a world of color and light and now proud to call myself a "painter".

I have found so many who appreciate what I can bring to their life, and simply through the judicious application of fine pigments. It is energizing that something which comes so naturally and so effortlessly to me can inspire and amaze others.

By day, I paint. In the evenings, newfound friends and I share food, drink and laughter. It is good to shine among them. I pray all of you will find your own version of this delightful existence.

I think of all of you often and do sincerely hope you can soon find your way to my door and spend a while with me enjoying the goodness I have found here.

With Love,

Harvey

"I thought it would be good for you to see a different side of Harvey besides the sad old man you invented living in a shack in the woods. This letter is the real Harvey."

"So, he became an artist? Did you ever see any of his work?"

"No, I didn't."

I began to search the chocolate box, but Mom anticipated what I was doing.

"That's the only letter from Harvey I have. As a matter of fact, that's the only Christmas letter he ever sent. I guess he wasn't much for writing. I think the main reason I kept it was because he was so happy. He was always a delightful man, but it was inspiring to see he had found his bliss."

"It is that," I said.

"I think you should go."

"But, Mom, I've only been here twenty minutes."

She laughed. "No, I think you should go to Mendocino, see what you can find out. If you don't find anything, then at least you will enjoy a beautiful vacation. My treat: an early Christmas present. You just have to promise to be home by Thanksgiving." I thought about it. "Sure," I said. "I feel out of place at home anyway."

"Oh, by the way, I saw Katie the other day."

"And how is she?" I replied calmly.

"Good I guess, the kids are already twelve and eight. She's still running that non-profit thing she started so long ago."

"The Grandheim Foundation."

"Yes, that's it."

"Otherwise she's doing well? Still married to Tom?"

"As far as I know. I said hello for you."

"Thanks, Mom."

"You know it wouldn't be out of line to just send her an e-mail or something, say hello yourself."

"Mom…..It would be weird."

◆ ◆

I insisted on paying my own way. I decided it was a trip that needed to be taken, and driving was not an option. I booked a bargain name-your-fare flight, and in two days I was at a cruising altitude of 37,000 feet - destination Mendocino, California. I landed late morning at the closest airport in Santa Rosa, about eighty miles away. I rented a car and made my way to The Bayhouse Bed and Breakfast.

The cause of Harvey's Christmas letter exuberance was overtly apparent. The town of Mendocino is a destination, scenic coastal community. It rests some forty to fifty feet above the Pacific Ocean separated by sheer cliff faces. The land which holds the main population center juts out into the ocean, leaving a bay formation on either side. I say "population center" in the loosest sense since Mendocino itself boasts a permanent population of less than 1,000. The dwellings consist mainly of Victorian style homes, interspersed with cottages not unlike those one might find in a seaside community of Rhode Island or Massachusetts, but with a West Coast feel.

I was met halfway up the walkway to the front door of the Bayhouse by a young man named Dylan. He assumed the burden of carrying my bag in and then took a place behind the counter to complete my check-in.

"So what brings you to Mendocino, sir? Wine tours? Relaxation? Good food? All of the above?"

"Well, I was hoping to get some of that in."

"If you need anything, just ask."

He filled me in on the desk hours, breakfast time and the local activities. I zeroed in on a lunch venue and headed that way after getting settled in my room. I decided to walk as my chosen dining spot, The Pelican, was just four blocks away.

The short walk was peaceful. I walked slowly, stopping a couple of times to take in the character of some of the homes, appreciating the views and surroundings, trying to get a sense of what Harvey might have used as inspiration for his paintings. One would have to think landscapes would be the primary subject of choice.

Because I wasn't super hungry, I noshed on a fruit and cheese platter partnered with a crisp chardonnay. While waiting for some post-lunch coffee, I took a few moments to stretch my legs and walk around the dining floor to get a closer look at the paintings adorning the restaurant walls on the off-chance lightning might strike twice - the same lightning that struck once before in the Crazy Horse Café with a certain photo of a football team. None of the paintings was signed by Harvey.

My meal complete, I strolled back to The Bayhouse and surrendered to an Adirondack chair situated on a common deck area facing the Pacific Ocean. The sun was warm and inviting, with an occasional salty breeze. I briefly drifted off, then groggily perused some promotional pamphlets for wine tours, spas and the like. Dylan from the desk came out to check on me.

"Can I interest you in a glass of wine, Mr. Preston?"

"What time is it anyway?" I asked.

"It's four thirty-seven, sir."

"Really? I guess I drifted off longer than I thought."

Dylan handed me a wine list. I thought it over. "Let's see, how about a glass of pinot noir, something local, whatever you recommend."

"I'll be right back."

Within a minute, I was savoring the complex notes of a wine bottled five years before, not ten miles from where I was sitting. Dylan advised he was adding the charge to the room tab, which was fine by me. I was so relaxed, the thought of reaching for my wallet was exhausting on its own. I was able to muster the strength for a question of my host though.

"Dylan, I was wondering if you know of anyone who might be schooled in the local art scene circa 1983?"

"1983? Hmmm, well let me think. There are a few galleries within a half mile of here. They might be open until seven or so. You should probably start there. Personally, I am not really an art buff."

"No, that's fine. That is a good starting point, but I think I will pursue that tomorrow."

Dylan handed me a blanket. "You might need this in a bit. It can get a little brisk when the sun starts to go down."

I took it as a courtesy to his attentiveness, but since I hail from Minnesota, I doubted I would need it. I sat quietly, slowly sipping pinot noir for a couple of hours in my chair. I even attempted channeling the spirit of Harvey Henderson for inspiration, guidance, and whatever else to transport myself back twenty-seven years to Harvey's own epiphany regarding his artistic talents. Was it the place? Was it where he was in life at the time? What had shaped Harvey's life such that he found his bliss at age sixty-one, so far away from the mid-western environs he had inhabited years before and would eventually return to years later. Whatever the reason, this was an extremely pivotal point in Harvey's life. There was something different about this place. I could feel it myself, not necessarily a spiritual thing for me, but I could see how one might have it be that.

From all indications, given what I had gathered so far regarding Harvey's makeup, a transformation to "artist" as career was a quantum leap. Granted, there was much about him that I had yet to learn, but to discover a natural talent for art in his seventh decade is a paradigm shift worthy of ink on a page. I was reenergized. I could now be assured that I was writing for the reasons that inspire me to write and not because I felt I owed it to someone whose life I had impacted negatively by gutting his retirement nest egg.

I rose from the Adirondack chair, found my room again, took a warm shower, had a burger from the bar menu in the Bayhouse Pub and turned in early. I wanted to get to tomorrow as soon as possible. My project was now a different, more vibrant animal.

Nine

◆ ◆

The eager morning light peeking through the gaps in the window curtains, along with the tantalizing aroma of freshly baked blueberry muffins paired with applewood smoked bacon wafting up from the kitchen below, was all the motivation I needed to set foot on the ground and assume vertical position. I also had a distinct sense that today was going to be different from a great many that had preceded it. As I was grazing the superb buffet spread of victuals in the dining room of The Bayhouse which amply fulfilled the latter promise in the contract: Bed and *Breakfast*, I set my expectations for a day of enlightenment and breakthrough.

My first destination of the day was The Easel, an art gallery that specializes in showcasing local artists. It was located in a cluster of other galleries covering a wide range of style and price point. The journey was, once again, an easy hike, just three blocks further than The Pelican.

My entrance was heralded by small wind chimes that were activated by the opening of the door. A lone employee, the proprietor I presumed, greeted me.

"How are you, sir? How can I help you?"

I decided to just blurt it out. "Do you have anything painted by Harvey Henderson?"

"Hmmmm...I'm afraid you have me stumped."

"I should mention he was a Mendocino resident way back in 1983, perhaps a few years more after that."

"Ummmm....I'm still drawing a blank, and I've been here since 1977. Back in 1983, the most prominent names around here were Flagler, Stransford, Plessinger, Lozano, a few others, but I am not aware of Henderson. A pseudonym perhaps?"

"No, I seriously doubt that."

I tried every memory jogging trick in the book, but there was no inkling of any artist named "Harvey" or "Henderson". I had this same conversation six more times at six other galleries. I was disappointed but not discouraged. It was looking as if I was going to have to delve deeper into the culture of Mendocino to uncover the lost art of Harvey Henderson. I decided to regroup for a plan B personal brainstorming session over lunch.

My heart was set on sampling a bistro I had seen in my room's promo literature, even though it was a good mile walk. I decided to go for it. As I walked, I noticed differences, differences in me. I had been here for less than twenty-four hours, but my demeanor had already changed. I considered the seven straight art gallery rejections on the matter of Harvey's artistic whereabouts. Normally, I would have been a bit perturbed, but instead I remained decidedly optimistic. I was even considering picking up some art supplies and giving it a go myself.

I began noting a measured pace to my steps, patient breaths, a cavalier but healthy attitude with regard to the awareness of the passage of time. It was intoxicating, meditative. My stillness was suddenly broken by a scraping metal-on-metal sound, followed by a, "Whoa Shit!" I turned to see a man hanging precariously from a second story gutter downspout. A ladder teetering on one leg was starting to topple in the opposite direction. I yelled to the fellow to hang on and resituated the ladder so he could find a foothold. The man made a hasty retreat to solid ground, while I made sure he got there by steadying the ladder.

"Jesus! That was close."

"Are you OK?...uhhh."

"Chester. Chester A. Arthur. I am just fine, thanks to you, sir. And you are?"

I couldn't resist.

"Taylor, Zachary Taylor."

"No Shit!"

"No...Shit...I am Denny Preston."

"The Dude's messin' with me, I dig it. So, I once met a James Polk, but a Zachary Taylor would have been a trip. I think you saved my life, brother. Thanks!"

"No sweat."

Now that the adrenaline was wearing off, my powers of observation kicked in. The man standing in front of me possessing a presidential moniker much more resembled a member of the Grateful Dead than a dead president. His face boasted more hair than visible skin. The hair, with traces of gray, was peppered with pastel colors making it look like he had recently had Skittles or M&M's randomly glued there. What skin was visible was weathered as if he had spent a good deal of time outdoors. But in a strange way it all worked for him. He was frumpy and unkempt, but in a way that didn't speak to slobbery. I had now put the pieces together as to why. The ladder, the colored specks - the man was a house painter.

Before his near demise, he was touching up some trim on a two-story Victorian home. Per tradition, the house was adorned with scalloped woodwork, rosettes, turned railing supports, etc. each wearing some different color of the rainbow. Although, not the colors I would have chosen.

Victorians seem to get a pass when it comes to crossing the house paint equivalent of "fashion disaster". Any other home sporting Lilac, Key Lime, or Daffodil Yellow would merit a speedy intervention visit from an HOA covenant committee and a possible psych eval for the homeowner. But make it a Victorian, and it's fodder for a magazine spread and a style award.

"You aren't familiar to me. Are you visiting for a few days?"

"Yeah, sort of a work-vacation thing. I was going to grab a bite down the road here, Chester. Will you be all right on your own, or do you need me to hold the ladder for you? Would you like to join me for lunch?"

"No thanks on both counts. I should be OK. I just get so focused on the details sometimes I lose track of where I am, especially when restoring an original Henderson."

"OK, you take care"......I paused, and turned back around.

"Did you say Henderson?"

"Yeah."

He motioned to the house. I continued.

"Not Harvey Henderson."

"Yeah!! Hot damn! You know about Harvey Henderson?!!"

My brain seized while my current version of the Harvey-as-Mendocino-artist story fell off its own ladder crashing to the ground.

"Dude, Harvey's the man. Don't get me started, or I'll never get back on the ladder, and I gotta get this one done today."

I was speechless, incredulous. It never dawned on me that when Harvey wrote in his letter about being a painter, that he ACTUALLY meant he was a painter! Not an artist, not the guy down by the oceanside with easel and folding chair, replete with goatee and beret administering careful, considered brushstrokes to virgin canvas. No, he was an ordinary schlep, slopping buckets of candy colored latex on older layers of candy colored latex for eight bucks an hour.

I mumbled, "Take care Chester, nice to meet you," while turning down the road, walking a bit quicker pace with each step. Lunch became an afterthought as I had lost my appetite. I just kept walking. The road turned into a path, turned into a stairway and eventually became a beach. I was now trekking the cool, wet sand with no purposeful destination in mind.

I should have seen it coming. I wanted so badly to have this be a transcendental event in the telling of this man's life. I had projected so much onto Harvey just from those few words in the Christmas letter, but I forgave myself some modicum of the blame based on the fact that no ordinary human being would derive such monumental delight from simply painting houses.

Not to cast aspersions on the work of the many fine tradesmen who earn their living from painting, but I seriously doubt any of them find it as any measure of completeness of self, with the exception of a means to pay the bills, so as to announce it triumphantly to the world in one's only lifetime issuance of a Christmas missal.

I began to question Harvey's sanity. Perhaps his excitement was merely over-exuberance at finding a new, vibrant circle of friends and finding it necessary to justify his standing among artisans by overinflating the importance of his own occupation. If so, that was a sad thing really. It might explain why he didn't stay in Mendocino. Eventually, maybe the false pretense wore thin, and when faced with the reality, he moved on.

I resolved it was time I move on too. I would return to The Bayhouse, pack up and check out. I still had two days left before my return flight. Perhaps a stint in wine country would be a good diversion.

Dylan was manning the front desk, and as I approached he got my attention. "Mr. Preston, someone left a note for you."

The note said, "Meet me here at 5:30 this evening. You really need to see something."

It was signed "The Prez" and had an address. I assumed it was Chester, because I knew the real President was in South America for a trade summit. I shook my head and climbed the stairs to my room. I packed my bag with the full intention of ignoring

Chester's note. After all, what could he possibly offer me but further disappointment. Nothing against him as he obviously had an affinity for Harvey, and I'm sure he had his reasons, but from my standpoint it would simply mean another drab coat of paint on my wobbling hovel of a story.

I had the packed suitcase with handle in hand ready to lift from the bed, but I caved and decided I at least owed it to Chester, based on my abrupt departure earlier this afternoon. For some reason he felt the need to take the time to track down where I was staying and leave a note. That had to be worth something.

I still had a couple of hours until 5:30. Dylan was able to arrange a massage on a moment's notice, so I indulged in an in-room deep tissue to work out the kinks from the last several hours, followed by a twenty-minute power nap. I was now ready to face more disappointment, if that was indeed where I was headed.

Once again I strolled to where I was going. Except this time I had a different eye while scanning the dwellings one-by-one as I passed. "Was this one a Henderson? Was that one a Henderson?" It sounded so ungainly. I even said it out loud and it was worse.

I arrived at "Chester's Abode" at 5:33 P.M.. I really didn't need the address as it was obvious it was "Chester's Abode", because the mailbox stand actually had a hand painted sign that read "Chester's Abode" written on it. Of course, it was a Victorian.

Before I could reach the door, Chester came bounding out and met me halfway. "I knew you'd show up, man!"

He shook my hand with a big smile. Chester was all cleaned up from his day of painting and actually looked rather dignified. His wild hair had been tamed, now pulled back into a short pony tail. His beard was combed and perhaps trimmed a bit since the afternoon. The drops of paint that served as decoration earlier had vanished. He wore a loose, crisp, white, cotton shirt, some slightly crumpled khaki slacks and woven leather sandals. He accessorized with a yellow "livestrong" wristband. He invited me inside the "abode" stopping in the front-most room.

"Well, Denny, here it is," his arms open to the room before him. "I can call you Denny right?"

"Most certainly. Here is what?"

"Harvey's masterpiece."

"He painted this room?"

"Dude, he painted the whole house. About half of it is still the actual paint he applied by his own hand. I had to touch up here and there, mostly outside stuff though."

Whatever it was Chester was seeing was lost on me. It looked nice, but a bit mismatched perhaps. I confess to having absolutely no eye for décor, so maybe it was the bees' knees, and I just didn't get it. He walked over to a buffet cabinet and grabbed a bottle of wine and a couple of big Bordeaux glasses handing me one.

"I was so sure you were coming, I cracked this open."

He showed me the bottle angling it so I could read the label. It was a 1984 Cabernet Sauvignon Reserve. I was impressed that he held me in such high regard as to open a twenty-five-plus year old bottle on my behalf with no assurances I was even going to be there.

"A gift from the man himself."

"What man?"

"Harvey."

I was even more impressed.

"Harvey gave me a case of this as a going away present back in 1987. It was our traditional celebration wine. I have three bottles left, including this one. I only break the seal on one when I get a strong Harvey vibe, and you saving my ass, and then it turning out you actually knew Harvey, well, that's providential right?"

"Sure, why not."

I had to admit to being touched a bit, but mostly I was trying to catch up to everything that was going on in front of me. I was standing in an original "Henderson", about to sip wine from a bottle hand-picked by HH and then learn something "inside" about the man himself. Chester poured a small amount in each glass, handed one to me and began swirling the glass. I followed suit. He stuck his nose up to the glass and took a long, deliberate sniff. I again followed suit.

"Oh my God!!! That is incredible!" Chester proclaimed with a gleaming smile.

I had to agree. It was magnificent. He held the glass up to offer a toast.

"To Harvey," he said.

"To Harvey."

We sipped. Chester grew another huge grin on his face. I imagined he was flashing back to a celebratory moment he once shared with Harvey.

"Hard to believe this is just grape juice."

He paused to savor the wine a bit, then snapped to as if he had a purpose.

"OK, we have to get down to business or we're going to miss the moment. You will need to sit there."

He pointed to a well-used, ragged, upholstered chair. I would rather have had a seat on the couch, but he insisted it had to be the chair, so there I sat. He brought the wine over, filled my glass to a proper amount, then his, put the bottle on a coffee table between us, and then took a seat to my left on the couch.

"So, tell me what you see."

I was settling into skeptical, but for now we were just sitting and drinking amazing wine, so I didn't complain.

"Hmmm...I see before me a large picture window framing the Pacific Ocean. The sun is beginning to set on the horizon. In the foreground I see a seating area in a living room, adorned with a scattering of interesting but unmatched furniture and accessories which probably have deep meaning to the occupant of the house, which I presume is you, Chester."

"Right on all counts, but you are missing something very important."

I looked around and then around some more.

"The walls man, the walls...." Chester implored.

I looked around again.

"Suuuurrre....Hmmmm....Hey Chester, I'm sorry I don't get it."

"Look at the colors, man."

The three walls in sight, were three completely different colors. My internal thought was "So Harvey decided to use up three odd cans of paint so they didn't go to waste." Then I recalled Harvey's Christmas letter, his mention of being "reborn to a world of color and light". I reconsidered, gave the moment the benefit of the doubt and settled back in my chair. I took another sip of wine and then decided to let another part of my brain take over. Chester noticed my change of posture.

"Cool, there you go, just chill and enjoy the show."

My initial description was correct, but incomplete. The Pacific Ocean was indeed the subject matter of the large picture window that lay directly in front of me. The sun, probably twenty-five minutes from disappearing into the water, was a pale yellow egg yolk against an accompanying backdrop of white clouds that served as the whites. The sky was its usual robin's egg blue, but more intense than the blue I remembered just five or six minutes before while walking over. I realized the increase in intensity was the effect of the eggplant hue covering the wall directly in front of me that surrounded the window. That, and its dark cherry wood frame, gave contrast to the scenery outside, brightening and enhancing the natural colors of the sunset. Chester was observing my contemplative nature.

"It wouldn't work the way it does unless he had added the coat of navy blue under the eggplant."

I noticed shortly after that the foliage, mostly green plants and bushes just outside the window, was coming into its own. Due to the subtle change in light from the continuing setting of the sun, the hunter green wall to my right was now vibrantly dancing with the plant life outside, having the strange effect of pulling it closer to me, as if it were growing before my eyes.

"Are the plants growing yet?" Chester said with a knowing smile.

As if someone had begun turning the balance knob on the color stereo, a short time after that, I became aware of the left side of the room increasing in "volume". The left wall was crimson but had a textured look. This wasn't actually due to texture, but to thin veins of gold that had not been noticeable until now, as the yellow sun began turning orange.

The clouds were becoming a molten fiery reddish orange with plum trimming that was quite agreeable to the crimson wall. The room was now like a cauldron. The crimson wall almost seemed like a lava flow as the metallic gold streaks took on a shimmering appearance like running liquid. The sunset was alive, reacting in concert with the pulsing space surrounding me. The eggplant wall, which had been fading to black until now, came back into play. The reddish tones in the eggplant which previously had been muted by the dominant blues, were now being drawn out. The blues had had their moment and taken a bow. Chester, acting as though he were a *color* analyst, explained this was because of the reflection from the crimson wall.

"You see the red now instead of blue. It comes out of the purple because it is vibrating with the reflected light from Mr. Red Wall back here. The light is such that the blue in the eggplant and the navy cancel out, causing the red to be the only wavelength left active on the front wall."

The show ended with the orange sun vanishing into the Pacific Ocean amidst the burning embers of red clouds. The room grew dark, and Chester lit some candles, which he explained was necessary because, "immediately turning on the light switch would be offensive to the eyes and the gods."

I sorted out what I had just experienced. To say the least, I had no idea such formidable sensory stimulation could be had from the convergence of wall paint and the departure of the last light of day. Indeed, it was like static performance art. It was alive, but nothing moved except the normal rotation of the Earth, spectral wavelengths and my brain synapses, but what a performance it was. I took the last sip from my glass and looked at Chester with approval.

"Yeah! You get it now, don't you? This was Harvey's gift. He could look at a house or sit in a room and know what it wanted to say, and then he'd give it a voice to say it through color."

Chester's words sounded so stonerific, and had I not just experienced the phenomenon myself, I would think him a bit "off the reservation". Chester carefully turned on the house lights, poured me another glass, and began to lead me around the house to catalogue the other subtleties characteristic of Harvey's repertoire as an artist (yes, I said "artist") things like how he always used downward brushstrokes on the exterior scalloping to ensure that water would channel off the woodwork to the ground. Horizontal brush strokes would tend to retain water and thus encourage decay and rot.

Harvey's attention to surface prep, taking more time sanding, filling and priming than he did to actually paint was a trademark. Chester estimated that of the forty-seven houses Harvey had painted in Mendocino, over seventy percent were still using the same color scheme, and over half still had some amount of original paint as applied by HH. That was saying a lot given the salt air of the seaside environment. Apparently, Harvey had his own proprietary blend of additives that he included in his paints which gave them superior bonding and protective qualities. So, even my supposition that he was using simple latex was incorrect. He had to be using petroleum based paints.

Harvey could have probably made a small mint off patenting his formulas had he pursued it further, but Chester said Harvey wasn't interested in "wasting ten years of his life running the legal obstacle course to get a few dollars he'd be too old to enjoy". I thought to myself, "besides he would have lost it a few years later anyway after investing it in Thatcher-Crowne stock."

It was becoming clearer to me that what motivated Harvey was something altogether different from most of the rest of us. I recalled my initial thoughts upon learning Harvey's painting was that of houses and not of canvas were "no ordinary human being would derive such monumental delight from simply painting houses". Indeed, these words were true, but not the way I meant them. Harvey was most certainly NOT an "ordinary" human being. To me he was looking most definitely like an exceptional and unique one, and it was abundantly clear there was one fellow who inherited Mr. Henderson's understanding of how one goes about life, and that person was Chester.

It was now approaching 7:00 P.M.. The doorbell rang, followed by a "Hello" and footsteps. A couple in their fifties bearing bottles of wine and some type of appetizer dip entered. The woman spoke up.

"Hello, Chester. It is the second Saturday of the month. Is the party still on?"

"Absolutely, Marlene," said Chester. "I'd like you to meet Denny Preston. He's writing about Harvey."

"Henderson? It's about time somebody did. It's a pleasure to meet you, Mister Preston."

Bit by bit, friends, neighbors and even a handful of tourists found their way inside Chester's Abode. It seems Chester held a standing invite for the second Saturday of every month for a BYOB party. Over the course of the evening, I met many people, some of whom had met Harvey or had him paint their house or paint their parents' house. Harvey's legacy was well intact and sure to be carried forth by his protégé, Chester.

After midnight, I said my goodbyes and leisurely staggered back to the Bayhouse after a healthy share of food and drink. It was another rollercoaster ride of a day, but what a ride, what a day!

I decided to stay another day longer than I had initially planned, leaving three days to myself. I spent one day touring wineries, another on spa and relaxation and a third day helping Chester paint a house "Henderson" style, sort of the Mendocino version of raking the Zen garden, giving honor and tribute to the man that brought me here and spending a day in his shoes.

Rested and renewed, I headed back to frigid St. Paul. Staying the extra day involved some logistical gymnastics. I had to add another connection to my flight which put me on three separate aircraft, on two different airlines, with a four hour layover in Detroit. But, doing this allowed me to accommodate my Mom's request to be home for Thanksgiving.

I really didn't mind that so much. Airport layovers are good catch-up time for writing, and I really needed to get some thoughts collected and typed out. The last ten days or so had really been a whirlwind, and by my estimate, I had over fifty pages of material backed up in the old gray-matter hard drive. I also wanted to give some thought to my next destination. Quite frankly, I had yet to really plot out a defined course in the continuing search for all things Harvey. Until now, my decisions had been pretty much seat-of-the-pants decisions about where to go next, but I felt I really needed to prioritize my destinations, if for no other reason than managing my travel costs. I decided to set aside some time to map a timeline of Harvey's life based on the Mickler-Gallagher phone book entries for Henderson addresses.

It seemed to me that, using the locations, the dates of the entries, and the length of time between them, I would be able to get a sense about critical periods in Harvey's life. The addresses themselves would be a valuable commentary on the state of Harvey's existence based on the circumstances of his living conditions.

Leg one of my trio of flights landed me in Phoenix. I got nothing done in the air, as I dozed off just ten minutes into the flight. Leg two was three hours to Detroit. I crafted a few pages on the plane, but my laptop battery grew weary an hour in, and I resorted to music and the stock airline magazine crossword puzzle. Awaiting my second leg touchdown, I located the departure gate for my final leg, found an electrical output for the PC and set up shop for a long wait. I polished off a six-dollar slice of air terminal pizza, and began typing away in the virtual silence of an ever-darkening cluster of departure gates.

In the quiet meditation of assembling the events of the last few weeks in narrative prose, I had finally concluded there was a story here worth telling. Granted, there was still a degree of guilt about the Thatcher-Crowne effect on Harvey's life, but I was interested enough as a journalist to see this play out to its ultimate conclusion. There was still a decent chance that the life of Harvey Henderson might not prove read-worthy in the end, but I was interested enough, and that's all that mattered. "Onward and upward," I thought. "I'm in this for the long haul."

The anchor flight of my airline relay to Minneapolis/St. Paul arrived an hour before the weather, which was just enough time to get home before the big flakes started sticking to the stairs I had to climb to reach the front door of the home that still didn't feel like home.

Ten

◆ ◆

Thanksgiving at the Preston condo-munity is earlier than most. Mom likes to start serving by noon so she can take the rest of the day to relax and enjoy her company. Company this year consisted of my sister Karen, her husband Jim, son Jeremy, and younger daughter Kristi, along with a couple of solo friends/neighbors of Mom, and me. I brought pies, wine, and beer.

After discourse on the snowstorms past and present, proper turkey trussing techniques, which cranberry sauce was preferred by whom (the gelatinous cylinder still displaying the imprinted ridges from the can finished in first place), and a memory straining session on where a certain casserole dish was purchased, the table conversation inevitably turned to Harvey and my project, mostly because Mom asked how Mendocino was. I relayed the events piece by piece. The confusion about Harvey being a painter and not an artist got a gleeful rise out of the gathering. Mom wasn't too surprised, though.

"Harvey was different that way. He was good people, though. I can't say I ever heard anything bad about him, or even recall him in a bad mood. Extraordinary, really," Mom reflected.

I asked about the two years he lived next to us in the duplex, hoping Mom could dust off some significant recollections that might provide any insight. She drew a blank. It was over forty years ago, so I wasn't too surprised by the lack of response.

114

Jim, the kids, and neighbors took off for alternate pursuits that centered on football and video games, leaving Mom, Karen and me at the table. I asked about the storage unit boxes, and Karen replied that she had managed all of that within two weeks of my delivery to her garage. Mom piped up.

"You know, I think there was a box or two of Harvey's in all that mess."

My eyebrows rose, stunned at the news.

"There was real life Harvey Henderson stuff in that storage unit? How?...Why..?

"I think there was, unless your dad disposed of it."

"Dad? Dispose of anything?" Karen quipped.

"When Harvey moved from the duplex, he had a number of people help him out. In all the confusion, a couple of boxes got left behind. When the new residents moved in, they left the boxes with us. We wrote Harvey several times to remind him, but he never picked them up."

"Karen, are you absolutely sure you...."

"Absolutely Denny. You know me, I didn't inherit that pack rat gene from Dad."

My heart sank a bit. It was only a second or so of hope and exhilaration, but it was enough to realize even a tad more disappointment.

"Sorry, Denny, I didn't know."

"No apology necessary," I said.

The three of us cleared the table and managed the dishes, taking the time to catch up on some small talk in the kitchen. All the while my thoughts were still on the fact that I had actually briefly held some of Harvey's history in my hands the same day I reacquainted myself with Football Man. The fact is, had I opened every box in that storage unit and rummaged through them, I still wouldn't have known which boxes were his or the significance of the contents. The gods do love to tease.

"I think we actually had Harvey over for a Thanksgiving back in that old duplex one of those years," Mom said with a slight sense of confidence.

"I think you're right Mom," Karen added.

"C'mon how old were you, five?" I chided.

"So, you can remember getting a doll at age two, but I can't remember Thanksgiving at five?" Karen retorted with the compulsory tone of condescending older sister.

"Point made," I conceded.

"I remember we played hearts, or at least Harvey showed me how to play, or tried to. It's a complicated game for a five-year old," Karen remembered.

"It's *still* a complicated game for *you*," I jibed, as my own contribution to sibling rivalry.

"Whoa, mister. I will clean your clock anytime, anywhere."

Karen was actually a very good hearts player, and usually came out victorious as I recall, but I couldn't resist a little trash talk. I would never concede her skills openly, of course. Besides the gauntlet had been thrown down, and any concessions would only serve to tilt the confidence scale in her favor when cards were in hand not soon after the dishes were dismissed.

"You know, it was actually twice," Mom broke in.

"What was actually twice?" I answered.

"Twice we tried to give those boxes back to Harvey."

She paused, scraping her memory for details.

"As it turned out, it was the last time we saw him. He came here for a couple of days back in 1998 on his way through to Kansas City, and your father recalled Harvey's belongings. He even spent a couple hours digging through that storage unit for those boxes. He found them, gave them to Harvey, and then Harvey took off and left them behind again, so your dad put them back. "

"Why didn't you ship them out to him after all that, get it over with?" Karen offered as managerial input.

"He said he was coming back through in another month or so. He never did. We all forgot about it and that's that."

Eleven

◆◆

I've put this off long enough, procrastinating because there is a certain amount of emotional pain associated with it, but, without it, this narrative would fall way short of complete. So, despite a dose of personal anguish, I feel I must introduce Katie. You may recall a brief mention of her in a conversation I had with my mother just prior to my Mendocino trip.

Katie was the entirety of my world at one time in my life. I don't claim to believe in "soul mates" personally, but if there was one for me, it was she.

It was 1993. A recent graduate from Journalism school, I had accepted my first writing assignment as a staff reporter for a small weekly newspaper in Madison, Wisconsin. To call it a newspaper is a bit misleading though. I'm sure the term "newspaper" evokes a traditional, sectioned out, "World", "Local", "Sports", "Business" construction that is tossed from bicycles by 12-year old entrepreneurs onto neighborhood doorsteps before 6 a.m. each morning. Instead, picture a rack at the entrance to a campus coffeehouse or trendy urban ethnic restaurant stacked with folded, tabloid formatted copies consisting entirely of investigative screeds headlined by pithy puns, all laid out side-by-side with advertisements for tanning salons, martini bars, and glorified booty-calls masquerading as personal ads. Our demographic was primarily progressive-thinking college types, urban dwelling professionals, and the curious, but bored, patron waiting for his latte or babaganoush platter.

It sounds small time and was especially so when it came to monetary compensation, but it was a good place for a wet-behind-the-ears fledgling reporter to cut his teeth, have a scrap of journalistic freedom, and avoid the traditional cub reporter starting track of penning obituaries (which seems ironic, starting with the end) and working up to feature writing in five to ten years. One of my assignments had me conducting fact-finding interviews on a potential scandal involving a recycling operation and their suspected dumping of a portion of collected recyclables in nearby strip mall roll-off dumpsters. Granted, "scandal" has much larger connotations than one might normally apply to stealth, after-hours rubbish disposal, but when you're a fledgling reporter, that's how you brand it. As it turns out, there was dumping going on, but the recycling operation was not involved. Despite that, I did uncover a true gem - not a story mind you, but Katie.

I first spotted her while I was information-gathering around the recycling operation. She was a volunteer working by herself on the line, sorting bits of rubbish brought in by the collection fleet. She stood outside at the side of a conveyor belt separating rubbish into plastic, glass and paper, and guiding each to their proper destination. She wore a powder blue, full-body, hazmat suit, protective goggles, a yellow hardhat, thick canvas gloves and work boots. Her face, suit and boots were smudged with random grime. She was quite irresistible, really.

Despite not being able to see her face much at all, or anything else really, there was something attracting me. I walked over and began a lame attempt at reporter questions. At about the third question, she shut down the conveyor, walked over to me, and removed her goggles and hardhat revealing deep chocolate brown eyes set off by brunette curls. I was a basket case from then on. She could have answered the question (one I can't recall anymore) with...

"Sure I dumped trash.... sell crank to ten year olds, own a non-profit puppy mill, am orchestrating a coup in three separate South American countries, run an old growth forest clear-cutting operation for the fun of it, and use incandescent light bulbs exclusively."

And I would have said.

"That's nice."

I couldn't think of anything else for several days after our brief encounter. I decided to ask her out, so I ventured back to the recycling plant, and while hidden, I placed a single rose on the conveyor belt with a note attached. I watched intently as the rose made its way towards Katie. She was sorting so fast she missed the rose, but it didn't miss her. The thorns stuck to her glove. She tried to shake it off, but it refused to release. Eventually, she had to stop the conveyor. She read the attached card. "Offering refuge from your refuse," it said. She raised her goggles and looked around the recycling yard. I emerged from my hiding spot. She laughed appreciatively.

Fast forward two years to us living together. She was working as a paralegal and considering law school. I had accepted the position at Reliable Source Weekly, and the months that followed had me embroiled in the Thatcher-Crowne scandal - on the fast track to becoming a journalism rock star. Unfortunately, the heady intoxication that accompanied that period also served to cloud my heart.

I talked myself into believing I had outgrown Katie. I found someone else more important to me, more seductive and intriguing, more worldly and profound, and that person was me. I was swept away with the person I thought I was, the one everyone was telling me I had become - the great slayer of corporate dragons and weaver of prosaic yarns serving as fervent inspiration for the righteous and stern warnings to the heathen.

Katie wised up. I returned from one of my many trips to Memphis to find she had moved out of our apartment. Instead of seeking reconciliation, I compounded my sin by choosing to wait her out, certain she would return. I wrote off my delay and inaction to the need to focus on Thatcher-Crowne, and to some extent that was true. By the time the dust had settled on Thatcher-Crowne and gravity had caught up to my meteoric rise, six months had passed. At a party, I inadvertently learned in that short span of time, Katie had found another and even married him.

Including the Thatcher-Crowne business and all that accompanied it, if I could redo only one thing in my life, it would be losing Katie. I still don't know why I hesitated to make things right, but I do know it wasn't for a lack of loving her. I lost her because I put myself first, but she still meant the world to me.

The devastation hasn't been served up in one big lump either. It has been a death of a thousand cuts since then, a thousand and still counting, really. It never ends. My heart walks a perpetual memory minefield - emotional explosives lying in wait across my path every single day to disrupt and unsettle. They come in the form of movies, food, casual phrases, smells, numbers and songs, so much so, that I have altered my behavior to limit my chances of exposure to potential encounters that will evoke the worst of them.

I haven't had an omelet in fifteen years. That was our signature homemade Sunday breakfast. I can't listen to Counting Crows - it was our "road music". The word "intrinsically" has been removed from my vocabulary. There was a way she said it that was kind of sexy.

Locating her is not the problem. I know where she works. My mom has her home address and still talks to her from time to time. Why I have never contacted her mystifies me. It would be easy to dismiss it as simple cowardice, but that's not it. I suppose it's more out of a twisted sense of respect. I know that sounds strange, but for some reason it seemed then, and still does, that presenting myself to her as the far from perfect person I have become compared to the good wife and mother she is, would only serve to remind her of the almost three years she wasted on me and the poor choice she made at one time in her life. For my part, I would walk away having rehashed once more that I screwed up in grand style. It's a lose-lose situation and best left alone.

Since Katie, I've had a couple of short, meaningless relationships. There will never be another Katie. Despite the emotional minefield and subsequent altered lifestyle, life is good. I'm still writing. More importantly, you're still reading, and there is a story still waiting to be told.

Twelve

◆◆

Fall turned into winter, then into spring. Travel costs and other expenses had put a serious dent in my rainy day funds, requiring me to take some non-Harvey related work. To be honest, had I been able to pursue the Henderson story I wouldn't have gotten far anyway. I did take some time to do some home-based inquiries using the information in the Mickler-Gallagher address book which essentially turned into dead ends. I mostly encountered vague recollections and hearsay accounts that were unreliable. Still, I hadn't given up on the story, and fortunately the story hadn't given up on me either.

Thump! Thump! Thump!

I awoke.

It took a moment to collect myself. I checked the clock. It read 2:14 A.M.. I managed a "What the f..."

Thump! Thump! Thump!

"Just a minute!" I yelled. With my right hand, I grabbed my jeans from the floor and, with the left, found my Harmon Killebrew Louisville Slugger, which I keep under the bed. I managed to squirm into my pants while negotiating the stairs to the main floor below. I peeked out of the peephole viewer in the door to see two men in black suits sans ties. A closer look revealed telltale curlicue wires leading from their left ears and disappearing into their shirt collars. Assuming they weren't here to raise money for the hearing impaired, I concluded these were standard issue for someone in their line of work, whatever that was. They were also wearing sunglasses which almost seemed comical given that it was dark out. Briefly the thought occurred to me, "Men in Black?" I dismissed that. Then, and this is where a reporter's curiosity is a bad thing, I opened the door. I did make sure they could plainly see the baseball bat though.

"Preston? Dennis Herfelter Preston?" One of the men questioned.

"Hey, not so loud with the middle name, people treat you differently when they find out something like Herfelter."

Possibly in mortal peril, and I'm cracking jokes, but you wouldn't know it from my audience. They didn't move a single facial muscle.

"Wow, tough crowd. I tell ya' I don't get no resp..."

"We have been instructed by our employer to escort you to a secured location where you will be questioned as to a matter of utmost importance."

"Excuse me...your employer?"

My mind was on rapid fire search mode rerunning every story I had written or thought of writing in the last twenty years. About five or so came to mind, but if it were one of those I would probably have been dealt with years ago.

"We want to express emphatically that this is a request and not a demand. You are free to refuse, but our employer is quite certain you may benefit substantially by cooperating with us."

"Benefit? How? Who is this...this...employer?"

"That's none of your concern, Mr. Preston."

"Well, of course, how rude of me. I'm being selfish thinking I should be looking out for my own well-being. Tell your employer no dice....And next time he wants to get Dennis Herfelter Preston to do his bidding, he's going to have to send more than a couple of glorified boy scouts to do his dirty work...... like maybe a buxom, saucy blond and a mysterious, scantily clad girl, preferably of Asian descent ....just a suggestion."

These guys must have had a sense of humor somewhere behind their stoic demeanors, otherwise I would have been a pile of broken bones and plasma by now. I began to close the door, when one of them blocked the door with a hand the size of a t-bone steak.

"Mr. Preston, our employer wanted to make it crystal clear that your attendance is really quite imperative, and our returning without you would be a matter of extreme disappointment...."

"And?...."

"And...we would strongly recommend you come with us."

"Or what?"

They responded with silence, a long silence, then I couldn't stand it anymore.

"Say, *please.*"

They looked at each other, as if seeking approval from the other.

125

"Please, Mr. Preston."

"Can I at least put a shirt on?"

In a minute, I was back fully dressed, minus one baseball bat. A short walk to a limousine and we were off.

The hired help sat in the front seat. The silent one drove.

"Help yourself to a beverage, Mr. Preston."

In front of me was an impressive collection of top-shelf booze, some beer on ice, and a couple of wine selections. I thought about it and passed, not because I was concerned about something funky in the liquor, I just don't usually *start* drinking at 2:30 A.M.

I'm sure you're wondering why I so cavalierly allowed two strangers to de facto kidnap me when I could just as easily have been back in bed finishing a good night's sleep. The thought did cross my mind too, but this wasn't the first time I had been in a situation similar to this, and it just didn't set off any of the usual alarms.

First off, if this were a true kidnapping they wouldn't have "invited" me. If they had wanted to kill me, they would have done so already, and muggers don't walk around in suits with earpieces. Sure, the thought of some organ harvesting operation crossed my mind, but then why the stocked liquor supply? And frankly, you'd have to be pretty desperate to harvest the organs of Denny Preston. I stretched my legs out and got comfortable for the ride, once again pondering who might be orchestrating this elaborate invite. I still came up blank.

126

After about a thirty-five minute ride, the car stopped at what I quickly determined was a small private airport. In fact, we were parked just fifty yards or so from a Lear jet in idle, or whatever they call it when Lear jets are running while parked. We boarded, and, in five minutes, we were wheels-up headed somewhere I could only venture a guess at. I decided to ask.

"Hey, either of you gorillas know where this crate is headed?"

I know the "gorillas" thing was pushing it, but whoever was employing these guys had, no doubt, emphasized a gentle approach. So their hands were tied when it came to retaliation....or maybe not. The other gorilla, the one who had not spoken a word yet, got up and walked over to my seat. I straightened up. He came to a stop, pulled off his sunglasses, placed one hand on each armrest, looked me in the eye, and said.

"Mr. Preston..."

"Please, call me Denny."

"Mr. Preston, you know, we're human beings too...have families...sometimes even cry at movies. Words can be hurtful. Is common courtesy out of the question?"

"Uhhhh....Of course not, um...," I extended my hand sheepishly.

"Dirk," He shook my hand.

"And you are?" Looking at the lead gorilla.

"Grainger."

"Rhymes with danger," I nervously chuckled.

They even cracked a slight smile. Grainger took off his sunglasses too and said, "You might want to kick back and grab some shuteye, we're going to be a while."

Dirk showed me the seat controls which included a full recline. There were some earplugs and an eye cover, which I decided would be a good move. Surprisingly, I drifted off rather quickly despite the last hour's excitement and the unfamiliar surroundings.

◆ ◆

I awoke to the fiery light of the rising sun which had just pierced the distant horizon as framed by the oval window nearest my seat in the jet. My eyeshade was a bit askew allowing the orange glow to peek through to my eyelids, which was enough to stir me. "Still in the air," I thought. The sun was ahead of us, we were heading east. Below us were mostly clouds, but what weren't clouds was most assuredly open ocean. Someone tapped my shoulder. I fully removed my sleep gear and noticed it was Grainger.

"Mr. Preston, would you like some coffee? Something for breakfast?"

My first instinct was to say, "No", but when the next opportunity for a meal was going to be was uncertain, and besides, there was a push cart with the most glorious looking croissants, butter and jams, a coffee carafe, and fruit. The serving set was silver with real china cups and saucers.

"Well, if you insist. By the way, feel free to kidnap me anytime. Is there a signup sheet or something?"

"Mr. Preston, I'd like to remind you, you are here of your own free will. You were not kidnapped."

"Agreed. I was joking. Jesus, lighten up Grainger Danger," I jibed as I made my selection from the cart using sterling tongs.

A minute later I was sipping the most superb cup of coffee I had enjoyed in ages, followed by the magnificent unraveling of thin, flaky layers of elegant puff pastry against my palate.

Any last worry that this was a nefarious undertaking had been extinguished, but now a new curiosity began brewing. Why the royal treatment? Who goes around clandestinely nabbing people only to pamper them and burn mass quantities of jet fuel to do who knows what? I thought "Reality Show", but this was too elaborate even for Hollywood. Maybe a remote island cult looking for a human sacrifice? I took another succulent bite of croissant and decided I could live with that.

I looked out of the window, and the cloud cover below had dispersed. All that could be seen was water in every direction. I did the math, and the only possibility was that we were over the Atlantic Ocean, our destination was foreign soil.

"Yo, Danger, where are we headed anyway?"

"That way," he pointed to the front of the plane smiling. I guess Danger had finally lightened up.

"Very clever, smart guy," I said "But, seriously, maybe a hint or something?"

"Our employer insists ...."

"Yeah, right, I get it. Say no more."

There was no sight of land before I had completed two crosswords, read three magazine articles, and played cribbage with Grainger - nearly three and a half hours in total. Judging by the coastline topography, we were over Europe, most likely France. I had more information, but even more questions. Who in France needs to see Denny Preston? Wouldn't a phone call get the job done? Who do I know, good or bad, that has the kind of money to do international errand running? I came up blank - not even a maybe.

We began our descent not too long after crossing land. A half-hour later, we had touched down on a small runway amidst an agrarian rural paradise. My neck craned as I tried to take in as much of the surroundings as I could through the few windows viewable from my seat. I could see some signs, the language of which confirmed we had landed in France. The plane came to a stop. Dirk and Danger unbuckled and did some quick post-flight tasks. I sat for a moment or two, then unbuckled. Dirk motioned for me to remain seated. They opened the jet door, mulled around a bit, and then motioned for me towards the door. We continued down the steps straight into a vintage Bentley.

This time there was a driver, so my bestest new buddies climbed in the back with me. Grainger handed me some sunglasses.

"You need to put these on."

I did so, but they weren't sunglasses, they were really just a fancy blindfold. They had solid black lenses and wrapped around so even my peripheral vision was blocked.

"Really guys? Are you kidding me? Are we going to Goldfinger's lair or something?"

"I'm afraid we are under strict orders from...."

"I know, your *employer*."

I donned the black lenses. I heard two taps on what must have been the glass between the driver and us, and the car began moving. We rode for twenty minutes or so at fairly low speed, stopping several times, apparently ambling our way through country roads, crossing a couple of small bridges along the way. Judging by sound, we paused at a security gate, moved ahead, and stopped for good about a minute later. I thought to myself, "That's one serious driveway."

My primate escorts helped me out of the car and led me on a short hike, eventually landing me in a plush armchair.

"You may remove your sunglasses, Mr. Preston."

"It's about time, Danger. Christ, I..."

The sunglasses were now off. I noticed Grainger had adopted a more serious visage and posture. His expression was telling me to shut up. His eyes motioned to the far corner of the room. I say "room", but there was a thought that perhaps the car ride was unnecessary since the plane could have actually landed within the four walls which now contained me. The gorillas, and a figure at the far corner facing away from us. The figure spoke. The voice was that of a woman.

"Mr. Preston, I presume."

"Goldfinger? You look much different in person."

Grainger reflexively placed his hand on my shoulder as a gesture to cool it.

"I'm afraid I am at a loss as to the meaning of your, no doubt, pithy, blasé, jest. I'm sure it would give Grainger's nephews a rollicking cackle though. A pity it was wasted on me."

She had an accent, not French, more the make of stuffy, erudite, Northeastern United States, old money.

"I do apologize for all the cloak and dagger, but I needed you here, and a more formal invitation might have met with delay. It is not in my interest to wait for anything."

"Quite all right. I'll just have to call Trump and push our lunch out to next week," I blurted.

"Do you mean *Donald*? Not to worry, I will have Grainger reschedule for you."

"Well, that's not really..."

"You know, Mr. Preston, I have a rather practiced dry wit myself."

I nodded.

"You do realize that if I wanted to, I could get Don on the phone at this very moment, wherever he is."

"I'm sure you could."

"I could have him on a plane in twenty minutes and sitting right next to you in less than six hours, if I chose to. I wouldn't because I find him boorish and a troglodyte. I just want to give you a sense of gravity about whom you are dealing with here. I am a serious woman, Mr. Preston. Bullshit has its place, but this is not one of those times. Do I make myself clear?"

I looked up at Grainger as if to say "Is she for real?" He was stern and stiff. His eyes motioned for me to answer the question.

"Yes, perfectly so."

She turned and began walking gingerly towards us. Her measured pace was quite evidently due to her age which seemed to increase ten years with every ten feet she grew closer. She walked with a cane. I took the time to give the room a good once over. Its functional purpose was not eminently apparent - perhaps a library, given that there were enough books to keep an avid reader occupied for a solid decade. The furniture was classic and timeless. There were tapestries draped down some of the walls which reached twenty feet in length. Huge picture windows, and marble were everywhere. It was like being in one of the turn-of-the-century mansions in Newport but without the velvet ropes. She finally was standing in front of me. I estimated she had travelled ninety feet, give or take.

"Mr. Preston, I understand you are currently working on a project of utmost interest to me."

My brain churned away trying to make sense of that. "She must be mistaken," I thought. Maybe she meant Thatcher-Crowne, but that would mean she was way late to the party or possibly quite senile. The expression on her face must have tipped her off to my confusion.

"You know, Harvard."

"Oh Boy," I thought, "Is she going to be disappointed." I tried to construct a lie in my head. I didn't know how she was going to react to being wrong about this, but nothing jelled. All I could say was...

"I hate to tell you this, but I can't recall ever working on anything related to Harvard University, ever."

She shook her head in disgust.

"And you call yourself a reporter? You're working on this project all this time, and you're going to try to tell me you don't even know his first name?"

"Who's first name?.....Do you mean Harvey? His name is Harvard?"

"He was born Harvard Wilson Henderson."

"Honestly, this is news to me. Everyone I've met that knew him called him 'Harvey', so you'll have to cut me some slack on that detail, Miss?..What is your name anyway?"

"I suppose you're right, Mr. Preston."

"I don't know this for sure, but I'm fairly certain, based on what I know about him, he would have preferred Harvey anyway."

134

"What you know about him, I'm sure, is a trifle," she scolded.

"Well, enlighten me then?"

"It is against my better judgment to offer you anything at this time regarding Harvard. I'm not quite sure I trust you, Mr. Preston. I don't trust journalists, and given your track record with matters of accuracy and professional judgment, I would be a fool to consider otherwise."

"So, let me get this straight, you haul my ass out of bed at two in the morning, taxi me by private jet across the Atlantic Ocean costing probably ten grand, to basically tell me his name is Harvard, not Harvey, and that's all you're gonna tell me, and good day Mr. Preston? You know you could have just called me for that, maybe splurge a little and do it by singing telegram."

There was a slight pain in my right shoulder which was generated by Grainger's hand which merely began as another non-verbal cautionary notice, but escalated into an involuntarily clutching as he began expressing his extreme tension at helplessly witnessing what must have been a rare occurrence - a stern admonition of his employer. She took one step closer, her eyes aflame.

"Mr. Preston, you will hear me on this, and you will do what I tell you. You will cease ALL manner of investigation and reportage in the matter of Harvard Henderson. Any continuance will be met with strong repercussions."

I tried to stifle a laugh, but the situation seemed so absurd that one got out. It was the exact wrong place for that, but it was my honest reaction. I thought, "Harvey Henderson? Really?"

"Have a good chortle, Mr. Preston. Take this lightly and find out how determined this old bitch really is. That's right, I can haul your ass out of bed at two in the morning and taxi you by private jet across the Atlantic Ocean costing *twelve* grand actually. Next time I might not fly you ALL the way across."

I think I had just been threatened. She continued.

"So ask yourself, 'if she's willing to do all that to have a five minute conversation with me, what is she willing to do if she wants to make my life truly miserable?' Believe me, Mr. Preston, you don't want to know."

She turned and ambled back to the corner whence she came. On the way, she uttered,

"Grainger? You know what to do now, correct?"

"Yes, Ma'am."

"Let me know when you have concluded your business."

That could have meant a lot of things, one in particular had me a tad worried. But if that meant there were some sort of harm in the offing, I would have suspected the previous conversation to have been completely unnecessary, let alone the jet ride and all that came before it. Grainger and Dirk led me back to the Bentley. The driver was no longer there. Dirk was going to drive, and Grainger would ride in the back with me. The sunglasses reappeared, and I donned them, leaving me nervously in the dark in more ways than one.

"So, Danger, Remember way back at my front door in the good old U-S-of-A. when you promised I would substantially benefit from this excursion…Well?"

"I'm sorry, Mr. Preston. I think if you would have been a little less combative things might have gone better for you."

"Look, Grange, my man, I think I was a pretty patient pup considering….Do you think you could at least tell me who she is?"

"I'm really not at liberty to divulge that. I'm sure you will learn that soon enough."

"I don't take her for an idiot, and maybe she just doesn't grasp the resolve of a grizzled investigative reporter, but she has to realize a challenge to cease my efforts is really just a call to action for a man like me."

"I can't speak to that, Mr. Preston."

"She has to know threats and bluster only serve to pique my curiosity that there is a story in all this, a big one."

"Look, Dennis, listen to me. Don't mess with Mrs. Trentsworth. She's destroyed many with fewer resources than you."

"Now I'm *Dennis*? Wait….Trentsworth? *Lillian* Trentsworth? That's Lillian Trentsworth!"

"This conversation is over, Mr. Preston. Just don't say I didn't warn you." Grainger was trying to cover his disappointment with ardent bravado at his letting her name slip. I'm sure it was an accident. I hoped that wouldn't come back to haunt him with his employer.

So, Lillian Trentsworth, THAT'S Lillian Trentsworth, widow of the late Gordon Trentsworth, heiress to the Trentsworth empire, the tentacles of which stretch far and wide across thirty-seven countries, spanning just about every industry one can think of - manufacturing, energy, telecommunications, retail, shipping and so on. Never in my wildest dreams had I imagined a lark concerning a stuffed doll would lead me face-to-face with possibly the most powerful woman in the world - perhaps the most powerful *person* period.

God knows where Harvey Henderson fits in, though. How in the world does a man as seemingly innocuous as he come to know a woman of Lillian Trentsworth's ilk, let alone cause her, at the mere delving of this reporter, some apparent measure of undoing years after his death? And how in God's name did she find out I was delving?

My train of thought was interrupted by Grainger's voice.

"This is it. Pull over here," Grainger directed to Dirk. The car pulled to the left and came to a stop. The door opened.

"Get out of the car, Mr. Preston. Leave the glasses on."

I obeyed.

"Now, walk forty paces directly ahead."

I gingerly tread step-by-step counting out loud. I thought to run but decided that might be what they were hoping for – me dashing blindly towards a cliff, perhaps just thirty-five paces ahead.

I heard a loud bang, which made me flinch, but I realized it was only the car door. I expected footsteps next, but instead heard the car accelerate and drive off. I waited what seemed like a reasonable time, and removed my sunglasses. Adjusting my eyes, I saw a cloud of dust which was the result of the Bentley heading away on a dirt road. I looked around and was immediately aware I was standing in a pasture of cows - no gorillas in sight. One of the bovines was no more than ten feet from me. She looked at me with one eye, carrying a jaded expression that seemed to indicate the depositing of humans in this cow pasture was a common occurrence.

"So, now what?" I thought. It looked to be about 2:00 in the afternoon. I had on jeans, a T-shirt and tennis shoes with no jacket. I had no passport, spoke no French, and in the excitement of last night's abduction (Yes, I know it wasn't an abduction), left my handheld back in St. Paul.

Given my predicament, one could probably have done worse. As far as the eye could see were small farms, vineyards, a majestic estate spread or two, all interwoven by winding two-lane dirt roads bordered by stone walls and rustic wood fences. It was like a photograph right out of a travel guide. "Come frolic among the picturesque beauty of….of….somewhere in France." it would read. So, where the hell in France was I?

I realized I needed to relieve myself. I found the nearest cow and blocked myself from the road, facing away. I was mid-stream when I heard a car pull up and stop by the side of the road. The engine remained idling. I finished my business and resituated my garments as discreetly as possible.

"Pardon monsieur, pourquoi sont vous tenant dans la pâture de vache?"

I tried to ignore the voice. The way this day was going, this would probably not be good.

"Vous faire a besoin de l'assistance?"

I understood the last word…I think…I turned around.

"Hello, I'm sorry I don't speak Chinese."

I was joking of course. The car was a topless jeep, probably twenty-five years old or so. The same could be said of the driver, except for the topless part, which was unfortunate since she was a comely female. She answered.

"I am speaking French, not Chinese."

"Actually, that sounds like English."

"Of course, but I *was* speaking French. Now, I am speaking English," she responded, but with such a thick French inflection, it still sounded like French.

I began walking towards the Jeep.

"I know. Thank you for asking…and for knowing English."

I had reached the Jeep.

"Bonjour, I am Danielle."

I introduced myself. She was French, to be sure, but her look was more Eddie Bauer than anything. She wore a red tank top and taupe shorts with the legs rolled up a time or two showcasing her toned thighs. She had on hiking boots with rolled down socks. Under a baseball cap matching her shorts, her curly brown locks found a home. The overflow extending down her neck and back through the opening in the hat back.

"Are you lost?"

"I suppose, yes." I replied.

"Do you need a ride? You seem rather confused and disoriented."

"Yes, I am, and I would love a ride. I just don't know where to."

Now, she looked confused, thought for a moment, and then said,

"Well, get in then. There's nothing useful about standing in a field full of cows. If you don't mind, I have some stops to make. Maybe you can help me."

I wondered what that might mean as I climbed in the Jeep, which was easy, since there were no doors. We continued down the dirt road. There were a few minor bumps in the road which elicited some noise from the back area of the Jeep. I glanced to see shovels and rakes, along with some buckets and such.

"So how does an American lose his way in a meadow full of French cows?" She asked with a grin.

"It's a long story, really. Let's just say I wore out my welcome."

"Let me guess. Lillian Trentsworth."

I looked at her stunned by her clairvoyance.

"She's famous for that. You aren't the first one I've found out there. I think I once even rescued Donald Trump."

"I'll have to give old Don a ribbing about that one," I said, playing along.

"That would be funny. Tell him Danielle said, 'Hello'."

"You have my word on it. As soon as I see him I will tell him that."

We had driven for about ten minutes, when Danielle pulled into a residential driveway and parked. It was a small spread, certainly by comparison on a Trentsworth scale. Danielle got out and began grabbing tools from the back.

"Do you mind helping me?"

"I'm all yours."

Famous last words. We finally called it a day after visiting five different locations to perform a variety of duties for Danielle's chosen vocation which turned out to be landscaping (Although, it might as well have been slavemaster). Quite surreptitiously she adopted the role of foreman, while I one of indentured servant. I pulled weeds, dug holes, pulled up bushes, planted flowers, and shoveled manure, all while Danielle stood by, directing the action in her ever-pristine canvas work gloves. I began to wonder what she did the other days when I wasn't available wandering aimlessly in a cow pasture.

It seemed to me a distinct possibility as to why she had stumbled upon me so off the beaten path. She probably goes by there everyday, hoping to snatch up Lillian Trentsworth's discards as free labor. I wondered if "The Donald" had met with a similar fate. Still, if one had to be enslaved, I can't think of a more pleasant slavemaster than Danielle. She had a way of saying something like "You know, on second thought, those two tons of granite stone looked better where they were the first time. Move them back," and you would do it with a smile.

The sun was creeping close to the western horizon. The two of us and the tools were all back in the Jeep. Danielle entered some notes on a pad of paper, then apologetically asked,

"So, you must be famished. I owe you a lot for helping me today. I can offer you a place above my garage and a good meal. Would you like that?"

"Sure, as long as I don't have to actually build the garage or kill the meal," I sighed.

She laughed.

"I'm sorry, I worked you to death. I get carried away, and you were magnificent. Thank you so much, Dennis."

Danielle put the Jeep in gear, and we sped off arriving at her place twenty minutes later. In short order, she had me set up as her guest in accommodations above the garage, which sounds like a ramshackle arrangement, but it was really quite nice. There was a small kitchenette, and a full bathroom, a queen sized bed, clothes that fit, and even satellite TV. I didn't even mind the daisy print on the bed sheets. I got cleaned up and headed downstairs and across the short stretch of yard which separated the main house from the detached garage. Before I could reach the house, Danielle met me halfway carrying two glasses of red wine. She handed me one of them.

"I presume you drink wine, Dennis?"

"You presume correct."

"This is a local Bordeaux. You can't get it in the U.S."

It was delicious. Other factors were at play to make the moment enjoyable as well. The sun was setting in the distance, stretching shadows across the rolling countryside. The perfect temperature with a slight movement in the air gave the unseasonably warm evening intermittent crispness. The afternoon of physical work left me sore and a bit sunburned, but my body was buzzing with endorphin response from the day's work. And then there was Danielle, who had shed her tomboy work garb for a sundress and sandals. Her freshly washed brown curls, now released from the confines of the baseball cap, served to elegantly frame her faintly freckled, angular face.

"I hope you don't mind leftovers. I didn't have time to prepare a full meal."

"I'm sure it will be superb. Here's to...well....an interesting day to say the least," I raised my glass and she met it with hers.

"So you met Lillian Trentsworth."

"Briefly so."

"Is she as much of a bitch as people say?"

"Well… Let me put it this way. She didn't give me any evidence to the contrary."

"How do you mean? Why did you meet with her?"

"I'm working on a project that she apparently has some sort of connection to, and she informed me that it did not meet with her approval."

"So what are you going to do?"

"I have no choice. Her threats made me even more curious."

"Aren't you afraid of her? She is very powerful, you know."

"Afraid? No."

I said this more out of ignorance than bravado. Some of my best work in the past had been done while proceeding where, had I known the risks involved or chosen not to remain ignorant, I would have put the kibosh on right away. If I had outlasted execution-happy, African tinhorn dictators, I could weather a ninety-year old woman, no matter how much influence she had. I continued.

"Look, I don't really know the first thing about her. She's got her own agenda I guess, but with this project I'm working on, I have no intentions of dragging anyone through the mud publically. It's not that kind of project. Given the subject matter, she might even come across looking peachy from a public relations perspective, when all is said and done. From what little I know about her, she could use a little positive image work anyway. Don't get me wrong, I'm not going to sugar coat things, but I'm not out to smear her either. However it plays out is how it will get told."

145

"That's all she should expect," Danielle chirped, supportively.

"I'm hoping so. She must have some intricate network of feelers out there. I'm so off the radar I don't know how she even knew I was working on this."

"From what I know, she's got people everywhere. I think you will be all right though. You seem like a good man, Dennis."

"Thanks, dear."

I raised my glass again, and Danielle responded in kind.

Leftovers turned out to be Coq au Vin. If this was "leftovers", sign me up for leftovers for life. Tender chicken pieces braised in red wine with savory herbs, aromatic vegetables, and mushrooms. It was the best I had ever had. She served it in shallow white china dishes, with fresh baguette, butter, and tossed greens served with an olive oil and lemon dressing. Greens from her own garden, of course. We dined al fresco and chatted past dinner and into the evening by torch and candlelight. We worked our way through to a second bottle of Bordeaux, sipped, and dialogued about cultures, writing, food and gardening, something Danielle was quite learned in. She revealed she had recently completed a PhD in Horticulture at Cornell - the one in New York.

When we got to the subject of gardening, the floor was all hers. I volunteered a self-assessment that I was possibly the worst enemy of all things green, given my track record with house plants. I even once tried a Chia pet and couldn't even get it to sprout. She walked me over to another side of the house where stood her formidable vegetable garden in full glory. The garden area was essentially a greenhouse setup but also convertible to allow full open-air exposure using large removable sections of window panels, should she choose to do that. There was every kind of vegetable you could imagine - not just the token zucchini and tomato plants, but bok choy, and leeks, even asparagus and a couple I had never seen before.

"You know your craft, young lady. What's your secret?"

"So many people think it's the seeds or the amount of water or nutrient blend, but it's all about symbiosis."

I nodded as if I knew what she was talking about.

"What makes things grow and flourish happens in the places you don't see, the 'mycorrhizosphere' we call it."

"The what?"

I couldn't fake that I knew anything about that. I couldn't even pronounce it.

"The soil contains a complex community of its own. The microscopic fungi and bacteria are the real champions of a beautiful garden. By doing their thing, they provide a rich environment for the plants to grow and flourish. Specific species of fungi and bacteria are complementary to specific species of plant life. You have to know which ones go with which directly or in general."

"So it's all about the little people, the nameless masses," I offered lightly.

"I suppose you could say that. Yes! Isn't it always?"

There was a slight pause as we drank that in with a little more wine.

"It's like the vegetables and flowers are the movie stars...the Nobel scientists...and the fungus and bacteria, are the commoners, who go through life unpraised and unrecognized, but they are the unsung heroes," I waxed my wine-soaked philosophy.

"So, for every Lillian Trentsworth there is a....a...

"Harvey Henderson," I blurted reflexively, finishing Danielle's sentence.

"That's it," I thought. Not to imply HH was a fungi. We have all known someone of that character. From what I knew he seemed to be a catalyst. One of those rare people who was as comfortable among the hoi polloi as with the glitterati, able to be himself regardless of the social environment, unfazed by wealth or status. That certainly sounds consistent with the accounts of the man I have been privy to. Of course, this was speculative, but it made sense.

Why would that cause so much distress to Lillian Trentsworth? Sometimes the powerful, the uber control-freaks, those not used to being questioned or corrected, become strangely enchanted by anyone possessing the wherewithal and self-confidence to be immune to position and magnitude. It drives them nuts, and they find themselves irresistibly drawn to that indifference and purity. After all, if you're surrounded by sycophants and gold diggers, whom can you trust for a frank opinion, except someone with no agenda, one who honestly speaks his mind? Someone like that doesn't even have to be deep thinker. To the contrary, much more prized than schooled analysis is a genuine gift for no-nonsense wisdom.

Somewhere along the way in the whimsical twists and turns of Harvey's journey through life, he encountered Lillian Trentsworth. Whatever his influence on her, for good or for bad, she has been left wanting since his death seven years ago. Perhaps she had closed the books on this chapter in her life until fresh news of an investigative reporter, hot on the trail of a person she thought was dead and buried, reawakened a desire, or maybe a concern, that something hidden might be revealed. Given the sphere of influence of a woman of Lillian Trentsworth's stature, the nature of her concern could be almost anything.

"Harvey Hen...Who?" Danielle broke through the silence.

"He's...well...he's the project."

"I don't understand."

"He's why Lillian Trentsworth brought me to France."

"I am so confused, Dennis."

I paused while she processed.

"Do you mean some fellow named Harvey He..Hender...Hen."

"Henderson."

"This guy is what all the fuss is about?"

"Bingo."

She looked at me, puzzled.

"That's right, Harvey Henderson," I rephrased.

"She should fly Mr. Henderson, not you."

"Except he's long since dead."

Danielle scratched her head and still looked puzzled.

"I know, it sounds weird, but there it is."

It was late, and the crazy events of the day (or was it two? given the time difference) was finally catching up with me. Danielle suggested I retreat to my digs above the garage, where in less than ten short minutes, I was fast asleep.

Thirteen

◆◆

The soft patter of voices wafted into the open window of my garage-loft crash pad bringing me back to consciousness from eight straight hours of undisturbed sleep. I was groggy but refreshed. The voices were distinctly three: two male and one female. All were speaking French. I contorted myself so as to try to get a peek outside without actually having to assume vertical position. No such luck. I gathered myself, slid into the pants from the previous evening, and turned to look down to the yard below. Whoever it was had gone into the main house, but the automobile parked in front was a dead giveaway. I couldn't believe it. I ran downstairs and burst into the kitchen of Danielle's house.

"Are you kidding me?"

Silence, and blank stares were all I received in return. Of course, the female was Danielle, the other two were Grainger and Dirk.

"Good morning, Mr. Preston," volunteered Grainger as if the day before hadn't happened.

"Good morning?....Good MORNING!? As if!"

"You seem to have fared pretty well, Mr. Preston, if I do say so myself."

"Yes, and no thanks to you! And how have you come to ruin today for me? Maybe deposit me amongst a herd of free-range chickens? Cover me with honey and tie me to an anthill?"

"I don't think chickens come in herds," Danielle corrected.

"Yes, I think rather a brood," Dirk chimed in.

"I've heard it called a run. You know, a run of chickens," added Grainger

"On the more obscure end, I've heard it referenced as a clutch somewhere, I think," Danielle responded.

"My grammy called it a peep, a peep of chicks," said Grainger emphasizing the "peep" an octave higher than the rest of the words.

"Why not flock?" Dirk questioned.

"FLOCK? What the FLOCK!" I broke in, which brought the chicken conversation to an abrupt halt.

"Seriously, Grainger, what trouble have you in store for me today?"

"We've come to take you home, Dennis."

"And home would be?"

"Across the Atlantic."

"ALL the way across?"

"Yes. The plane leaves in an hour."

"How did you find me? Did you implant a microchip on the flight over while I was sleeping?"

"We asked around. A man fitting your description was seen in the custody of a fetching young landscaper girl."

"I've done some work for the Trentsworth estate," Danielle confirmed. "They know me."

"I can't believe you left me out there in that cow pasture. I could've been trampled to death," I protested, taking one last pathetic shot at victimhood. That elicited robust laughter from the assembly.

"Trampled? By those cows? More likely cats than those cows," Grainger managed to utter between belly laughs.

They all seemed pretty much in agreement on that.

"Well, you can't blame a guy for trying. I thought I'd try to *milk* it for all it's worth."

That shameless pun brought forth mighty groans. I grabbed some coffee, got myself cleaned up, and in a half hour we were off. I jested for Grainger to grab my luggage upstairs, which he almost fell for. I was spared the sunglasses while the vehicle ambled down country roads on our way to the airport. The scenery was captivating and relaxing, and despite the circumstances which brought me here, I was sorry to be leaving so soon. Something told me I'd be back though, perhaps under more duress, or possibly in pieces as soon as Lillian Trentsworth discovered my zeal for the HH story had redoubled.

We boarded the Lear and were off in a jiffy chasing the sun to America. I resolved to let the HH matter lie while in the air, and it seemed Grainger and Dirk had their mind set on maintaining an unspoken truce as well. I knew I wouldn't be able to sleep, so it looked as if we were all in for a marathon cribbage tournament. We did that and still had time to screen "Lawrence of Arabia", which was probably from Lillian Trentsworth's "New Releases" selection.

Given the Lear's airspeed and the advantage of walking off the plane straight to the limo, I was home just a few hours later St. Paul-time than the time was in France when we left. It was mid-afternoon, and I was full of renewed enthusiasm for the project. Ms. Trentsworth's venom had awakened a sleeping giant. Once again, I went back to the only touchstone I had for all things HH, the Mickler-Gallagher phone book. Maybe I had missed something earlier that newly charged eyes would reveal.

I turned the pages back and forth hoping something would jump out at me. It didn't. I got frustrated, escalating to irritation. I was being blocked by something, and it didn't take long to realize what it was. It was the unmitigated gall, the presumptive arrogance of that woman, Lillian Trentsworth. If there's anything I find more audacious and infuriating than brazen, elitist conceit, I don't know what it is. The more I thought about it, the more the whole thing really got my dander up. She actually threatened me. My mind was made up. The course of my investigation was no longer going to be Harvey Henderson, it was Lillian Trentsworth, at least, for the time being. Of course, this did not mean HH was out of the picture. To the contrary, my best lead to him was through her, at this point anyway. Harvey's trail was cold, and I knew pursuing Lillian Trentsworth would eventually lead me to another doorstep into Harvey's life.

I began with the Internet. The subject of Lillian Trentsworth was quite the opposite of Harvey Henderson. Searches came back with anything and everything. The problem was finding useful information. It was a case of paralysis by information overload. Her name peppered all manner of corporate quarterly reports, and subsequently the exponentially abundant analysis documents from every stockbroker, hedge fund manager and banking consultant choosing to speculate on the meaningfulness of every twitch of Lillian Trentsworth's left eyebrow.

There were articles on charity auctions and yacht races, historical societies and dedications of new wings for medical research facilities. She figured prominently as the devil in numerous anti-corporate hate blogs. It really was quite amazing how so much mention could yield so little usable information for my purposes. I stuck with it for most of the afternoon.

Eventually, I was rewarded with a diamond in the rough on Page 36 of my fifteenth search, and it was quite literally a diamond. I almost passed it off as hokum, but some detailed reading, additional research, and careful discernment on my part brought me to the conclusion that this was a genuine article. The diamond was a marquis item for an auction list belonging to a defunct Hollywood props supplier. Where Lillian Trentsworth (nee Lillian Richter) tied in was in the item description:

Solitaire teardrop diamond, 1.75 Ct, with serpentine necklace, worn by actress Lillian Richter (Trentsworth) in "Palisades Remembered".

There was a black and white photo from the movie featuring an angular beauty in formal evening attire wearing the diamond. I was taken aback at the radiance and sophistication of this woman. I stared for a lengthy time trying to age her face through sixty-plus more years to conclude whether or not this was indeed the woman who had verbally accosted me just one day before. It was inconclusive. It might have been, it might not have been.

The auction was long past, dated February 17th, 2006. I phoned the auction house and waited an eternity while they researched the buyer whose name I was fully expecting to be denied. Since it was a commercial dealer though, there was no restriction on releasing the information, which was listed as Tanner's Collectibles in Dallas, Texas.

I found a web site for Tanner's, got the phone number, and gave them a call. I got an answering machine and left a message. Finally, taking another first step towards progress had given me a reason to relax. My shoulders sank involuntarily, as I realized how truly fatigued I was. I decided to grab a shower, figure out a dinner plan and try to stay awake at least until 10:00 P.M., so as to get myself back in sync with Central Time.

I settled on Chinese, because I wouldn't have to leave my place, and I wouldn't have to cook. I use the term "cook" loosely since it was pretty much a choice between frozen dinners or ramen. I moved operations to the comfy couch, grabbed a couple of beers (per the Julie rule) and typed "Palisades Remembered" in my browser's entry bar. At the top were the usual film industry reference and catalogue sites.

I found more photos and some film history buff blog sites waxing nostalgic about the era of post-war cinema. The only references to Lillian Richter were pertaining to "Palisades Remembered". Her film career was decidedly short lived, not quite a flash in the pan, but short at best. Finally, the day had taken the last of my energy, and I decided to call it a night.

Morning came, and after the usual rituals of coffee and some light stretching, I noticed I had a phone message. I didn't recall the phone ringing, but the caller ID said it came in around 11:00 P.M., and I was in stage 4 REM at that time, so I slept right through it. The message was from Ainsley Tanner of Tanner's collectibles. The diamond necklace was still in his possession, but he was adamant that it was not for sale, even though I had not mentioned wanting to buy it.

I dialed back, and moments after the 3rd ring, he was answering questions about Lillian Trentsworth, and in a rather detailed way. It was all Hollywood stuff, which is what I was looking for. After twenty minutes or so, I concluded a trip to the Lone Star State was in order. He didn't just have information, he had stuff - pictures and hardware that really needed to be seen and held.

Because of earlier assignments, I was not unfamiliar with the Minneapolis-Dallas connection. There was a non-stop that was not much more than a two hour trip leaving at 2:16 P.M.. I got my things together and was in Dallas by dinnertime.

Tanner's opened at 8:00 A.M.. I arrived an hour later and was greeted by Ainsley Tanner himself. He was a stout five-foot-three, with a short-cropped towhead. His face was round and highlighted by blushed tones and rosy spider veins in his cheeks. He was delightful and clearly in his element amongst the tokens of grandeur that graced his establishment.

"Mr. Preston, I took the initiative to bring out ALL my Lillian Richter items, so you could get a good look. I just love sharing my obsessions. They're over here on this large table."

We sat. There were three plastic file type boxes and a couple of cardboard boxes. The vast majority were photographs, but there were also wardrobe items, legal papers, signed screenplays, even cigarette butts with lipstick on them meticulously preserved in vacuum sealed plastic display cases. I carefully rummaged through everything, while Tanner recited an abridged history of Lillian Richter's brief stint in Hollywood.

"'Palisades' was actually her third movie, but in the previous two, 'Homebound' and 'Wayward Inn' she was only in bit roles, not even credited. She only appeared in four movies."

"Not much of an actress, I guess," I commented.

"To the contrary, I think she was very underrated, but once she met Gordon Trentsworth, all bets were off. There was no thrill Hollywood could provide that the wealth and prestige of being on Gordon Trentsworth's arm couldn't trump three times over. They met during her fourth film, 'Soft Landing'. He was the money. A brash young overnight millionaire trying to slough off the dreary scales of the 'Industrialist' moniker for something with a little more panache, like that of 'Movie Producer'. The movie was a flop from a cinematic and box office perspective, but a huge hit otherwise since they fell deeply in love during the shooting of the film. They quickly outgrew any further desires for Hollywood fame. Of course, you know his story, the first ever billionaire on the planet, and she right alongside, schooling herself on the rare skills her husband possessed, eventually to become his heir apparent. They practically invented the concept of the power couple. He died fifteen years ago, and she has continued on valiantly."

That got a raised eyebrow out of me. There was nothing valiant in the Lillian Trentsworth I encountered. I kept my mouth shut and let him continue. Shortly thereafter, I was left to my own devices as Tanner attended to some clientele. I carefully examined each photograph taking the liberty of snapping some cellphone photos of ones I thought I might want to look at again later. With barely a dozen photos remaining in the stack, I came across what I was looking for.

It was an original eight by ten, black and white print with a red, rubber stamped cataloging marker. It read:

Property of Life Magazine

copyright 1946 - All rights reserved

Photographer: GTW

913-4567-889674-YNP July, 10 1946

The photo was star studded, featuring twelve people. It was a candid shot of a grouping of Hollywood celebrities in some sort of outdoor setting amongst pine trees and large boulders. They were facing one other individual - a man in some sort of official uniform. He was holding a cantaloupe-sized rock and apparently passing on some sort of vital information about its origins.

The celebrities included three or four that I recognized, but couldn't name. Then there were Clark Gable, Olivia DeHaviland, and of course, Lillian Richter, and sure enough, the man holding the rock was the one and only Harvey Henderson.

I stared at the photo, examining every last detail of body language and facial expressions, trying to read any apparent recognition or connection between Lillian and Harvey. There wasn't any that I could see, but I reminded myself the photograph was just an instant captured in time and not to read too much into any perceived emotion that might be trapped there. There wasn't any anyway.

Not to miss the forest for the trees as it were, I did note the significance that here was hard evidence that they knew each other, although apparently not well.

"Ah, the Yellowstone photo."

Tanner had returned to the table.

"What do you know about this?" I asked.

"Well, after the war, there was a lot of sentiment from the powers that be towards recharging the spirit of the American people. This photo was part of a promotional newsreel short to promote the national parks, specifically Yellowstone, in this case. The movie 'Wayward Inn' was shot in Jackson Hole, and the cast and crew spent a weekend in Yellowstone capturing good footage on the park and its beauty. The project was government-funded and paid for half of 'Wayward Inn's' budget. It was a win all around."

"And this guy in the uniform? Any ideas?"

"Him?...A park ranger, I presume - just a nobody. He wasn't in the movie, if that's what you mean."

Part of me felt a sting at the "nobody" remark. HH was not a nobody to me, but as far as Ainsley Tanner was concerned, Harvey Henderson was exactly that. He didn't mean anything personal by it, but I noted to myself that I took some measure of umbrage. The front door chime rang, and Tanner left again. I did some analysis.

It was a curious thing that the man who knows all things Lillian Richter-Trentsworth had no idea about Harvey Henderson. That could mean his role in her life was brief but impactful. Maybe he witnessed something on that Yellowstone weekend, something that would be personally devastating to Lillian or Gordon Trentsworth's image even sixty-five years later, something she was afraid I would stumble upon and expose. That seemed the most reasonable scenario. But what?

An affair? But she hadn't even met Gordon Trentsworth yet. 'Wayward Inn' was her second movie, and they met during her fourth. Perhaps a murder? Some crime with no statute of limitations? That sounds so "Agatha Christie" though, so "McMillan and Wife", so "Lillian-Trentsworth-in-the-library-with-the-candlestick". "Implausible," I thought, but it couldn't be completely ruled out. It had to be something big in order to cause LR-T to feel it necessary to carry out a pseudo-kidnapping of yours truly.

The bad news was I was abruptly at another dead-end. There was nothing about the photo that would lead to a next step. All I could conclude was at the moment the shutter fell in that camera decades ago, producing the photo I now held in my hands, it was clear they were complete strangers, she a rising Hollywood actress and he a common park ranger chosen to guide the glitterati through their Yellowstone weekend.

◆ ◆

My plane touched down in Minneapolis just a few minutes before it had two days ago on my return from France. I decided to stop into a coffee shop and sort through my cell photos from Tanner's collection while sipping a latte. One by one, I titled them and filed them away for later reference. A hand grabbed the other chair at my table, pulled it out, and before I could look up, the seat was occupied. A voice announced the arrival, and it was a familiar one, but from a long time ago.

"Denny? Oh, my God! How are you?"

I looked up and was immediately speechless. A brief moment of panic washed over me accompanied by a compulsion to find an exit. All this before the thinking part of my brain could catch up enough to my fight-or-flight programming to register the identity of the person now seated in front of me. She was Katie. One final moment of processing had me analyzing why the visceral reflex to run was so powerful. The root of it was shame, and I hoped my facial expression was not one to betray my feelings.

"Hi, Katie," I uttered while mustering the most heartfelt expression of joy that I could. (Not that part of me wasn't leaping, it was) She was the love of my life at one time, and those feelings never fully dissolved. But my selfish actions fifteen years before still had a powerful grip on me, and it was shrouding any excitement with a pall of disgrace.

I looked at her, so close to me now, actually closer than in nearly a decade and a half. Time had been good to her. She had the inevitable crow's feet, yet most likely in her case etched from a lifetime of genuine smiles and hearty laughter. She was always the bright light in the room, and today was no different.

She was in fantastic shape as always - a testament to her unflagging dedication to a life of positive activity. She appeared to have just completed some manner of daily workout regimen. She was a bit flushed and dressed in workout attire, but instead of looking tired and sweaty as most would be, she wore it as a vibrant glow.

"I saw your mom the other day. She said you were working on something a bit….well… different."

"Yes, something more personal, less mercenary I guess a..."

I had glanced at my phone again for that part of my response, but looked up mid-sentence to stop at Katie's brown eyes, windows to a soul greater than mine. I stuttered briefly as I foolishly pondered some means to adorn my response with postured importance, thinking I needed to impress her in some way. It only served to show me how far I had fallen.

When we were together, I never needed to impress Katie. Being myself was all that was needed. I knew of no other way. I was brash, confident, and even caustic at times. And even though those were the qualities that contributed to our undoing, that was the mojo that captured Katie's curiosity and ultimately her heart. I felt none of that now. Katie detected my lengthy pause as more than just part of my conversation, so she jumped in again.

"Your mom said it was a book. That's kind of exciting. What's it about?"

She was genuinely interested and also trying to jump-start me back into the dialogue. She even sounded impressed, and I hadn't done a thing...."That's probably why," I thought.

"It's hard to describe, kind of a blind search for origins, a random call to the universe to show me something extraordinary."

She smiled, and yes, it sounded as over-archingly pretentious to my own ears then as it does when I see it again written here.

"So, it's a light subject then.." she smiled and laughed again.

"I know, I just made it sound all 'Chopra-by-way-of-Kerouac', but it's really just a deeper look into....well...something more personal."

"Deep and personal is fine." She looked at me and smiled her support, then endearingly said, "And It's about time, Denny."

She reached out and touched my hand with hers. My shame left me. How could she do that? How much grace can one soul have? Here, in this rare opportunity to purge every harbored furious emotion with the unabashed zeal of a woman scorned, she instead chose to use the moment to empower me.

"What a fool I was," I thought....yet again.

We spent another twenty minutes at the table catching up, but in the guarded way of two people being overly cautious so as not to tread callously beyond the established neutral territory of common politeness. It was nice but ultimately very sad. Here we were, two souls who used to share possibilities, dreams and delicate intimacies now relegated to sterile dispensers of life-data, the busy-work, checklist reportage of career plans, kid's soccer camps, the married, the divorced, the successful, the sick, and the dead.

All I wanted was to say I was sorry, to look deep into her eyes, into her soul and heal her, but this urge was quickly rebuffed by a dozen-fold reasons why that would be a bad idea and ultimately a selfish act, since I was really the one wanting absolution and healing. She was doing just fine and the last thing she needed was an absurdly late, groveling, hail-Mary pass of an apology to ruin her day and provide the impetus to write me off completely for the rest of time.

The data exchange was complete, and Katie voiced she had to collect her 8-year old from school, then on to soccer practice. We hugged, and I watched her exit and drive off. I returned to my seat and tried to sort out the mess of feelings and thoughts now stirring in the whirlpool that was my psyche, eventually concluding there was no tidy sorting to be had, just the living with them until something of more gravity could arrive. I picked myself up and returned home.

I decided to take the rest of the day off from the project to take care of some personal matters. I took another day, which turned into a week, which turned into two. "Personal matters" means sorting and filing stacks of procrastinated paperwork, cleaning my condo, thinning my wardrobe of long unworn items and dropping them in the Salvation Army bin, going through the pantry to purge expired food. It took me that long to realize that I was simply externalizing my inner turmoil. I was converting the energy of my confusion into the simple certainty of predictable, menial work-a-day, organization tasks.

My reaction to the trigger event - the coffee house encounter with Katie - was unexpected. I had rehearsed what would be said and how it would play out at least a thousand times in any number of locales, including a coffeehouse or two. And frankly, my anticipated encounter wasn't too far from what actually happened. What threw me was the unexpected watershed of emotions I had thought had long since been dealt with. I expected closure, but instead, Katie's presence unleashed a spectrum of random feelings and scattered bits of unresolved yesterday. She set in motion a compulsive comparison of "what is" versus "what was supposed to be".

"So this is how a mid-life crisis feels," I said to myself. I had arrived at the point in time in my life where I compare earlier expectations with present day reality, expectations set by the idealism of my youth where I was unaware of the impending friction that ordinary life would exact on the kinetic forces of spirit and desire, not to mention the full-on roadblocks that would crop up along the way.

Katie's appearance only served to reanimate the expectation part of my equation, which had been rendered dormant years before when she had moved out. I thought it had left for good when she did, but it seems I had secured it all in a vault of my own making only to be unlocked again by Katie's return.

And just when I had finished working through the past versus present thing and the litany of shortcomings and underachievement unearthed by that process, the remainder became grounded in a measured cautiousness, the paralyzing hesitation to make any promise at all to myself, to even begin to undertake anything of modest import or to set any goal, no matter how innocuous. My mind's eye could now actually begin to focus in and see the end of the road, and I certainly don't want a repeat performance of shortcomings later on, except this time while taking my final breaths.

Finding the right balance, and where to set the bar is a tricky thing. I resolved there isn't a lot of time left for second chances at this point in my life. This is the place where I had to realize every moment counts, which can be a blessing, but for me, life just became about quality, and not quantity.

My catharsis complete, I decided to set no expectations but to get rolling again in some productive way. I stared into the emptiness that was the Harvey Henderson project, and the big sign that read, "Now what?" I waited and waited. For three days I chased dead ends, then three more days. I decided to indulge myself with a game of golf. On the eighth hole, my patience was rewarded.

Fourteen

◆ ◆

It was a hopeless cause. I was already into a second sleeve of golf balls, and I wasn't even halfway through my round. The dense woods left of the fairway of hole number eight at the Lakeshire Club had claimed another victim. I was sure somewhere on the original golf course design schematics were hazards marked "entrance to an alternate universe". There were most certainly large piles of unclaimed golf balls (many once belonging to me) now resting undisturbed amid the fantastical landscape of some alien habitat residing on the destination end of these wormhole-like hazards.

While fishing in my bag for the next candidate for inter-universal travel, my handheld began to vibrate. I thought maybe it could be my last ball communicating from beyond to advise me of its whereabouts, but no such luck. It was a bit cryptic - one I ignored and almost deleted since it was out of context. It said "E. Pasternak" then a phone number, and then, "Bon Chance, G."

I played on. It took until I bladed my chip shot across the 14th green to realize the origin of the text. The key was the French phrase for "good luck" followed by the letter "G". It seemed unlikely, but there was no other explanation. The text was from Grainger. It was risky given his employer's disdain for the recipient, and I thought to reply but didn't want to risk a reply falling into the wrong hands no matter how low the probability. The text was a curious thing since I couldn't recall ever giving my contact info to anyone in France. I didn't have any personal technology with me at all when I was there, so how was it possible.

168

With just a first initial "E", I knew any sort of web search for background material on the name would be pointless. I did search the phone number, and it yielded a response of "unlisted number". I was left with no option but to make a cold call. The golf course was certainly no place to proceed, so I called from my place later that evening.

What I did know about the phone number was that it was somewhere in Washington state. The phone rang three times, and then a man answered.

"Evan Pasternak here."

I suddenly realized I had no response. I couldn't say I was referred by Grainger. I didn't want to lead with Harvey Henderson. There was a real chance he had no idea who Harvey Henderson was. I stuttered and fidgeted. The voice spoke again.

"Hello? Can I help you?"

I decided to go big.

"Mr. Pasternak, my name is Dennis Preston. I'm a writer and currently working on a piece with ties to the life and times of Lillian Trentsworth. I was hoping you could help me."

There was silence. I couldn't believe the words that came out of my mouth. Leading with Lillian Trentsworth? If there were ever a recipe for having a phone slammed in your ear, that was it. After all, what person in his right mind with useful knowledge about Lillian Trentsworth would give a random writer the time of day knowing the consequences.

169

"What do you mean by a piece with *ties* to Lillian Trentsworth?"

This time, silence on my part. "What the hell," I thought.

"Oh..well...shit.. Mr. Pasternak, have you ever heard of Harvey Henderson?"

"Sure, that goes back a ways, but I once knew a Harvey Henderson."

That was a blessing. I was afraid my bold frankness might end up exposing Grainger down the line. But that didn't happen. I detected no suspicion coming from Pasternak. I continued.

"Mr. Pasternak, I was given your name by a friend. I am indeed a writer and have actually been pursuing a story on Mr. Henderson."

"Well, I'll have to dust off my brain cells a bit. I'll give you what I can. A story on Harvey? Now you have my curiosity. Maybe I should be interviewing you, Mr. Preston."

"Well, Mr. Pasternak, this isn't an interview per se...And why do you say you should be interviewing me?"

"Well....I don't know....Harvey wasn't really the kind of individual that intentionally drew attention to himself. Don't get me wrong, he was a GREAT guy, but he didn't really generate a lot of buzz, if you get me."

"That's kind of why I'm pursuing this, Mr. Pasternak. I think everyone has a buzz. It's just some broadcast it at a lower frequency."

"Well put, Mr. Preston, and yes, Harvey wasn't a buzz seeker."

We carried on our introductory banter for about ten minutes or so when Pasternak decided to extend an invitation to have me come visit for a couple of days. He said it would be worth my while - much more congenial and in the spirit of Harvey to meet in person. We agreed on the following Tuesday, I booked a flight and a car, and was on my way to suburban Seattle, just off Puget Sound.

Pasternak's home was tucked among the heavenly, timbered landscape resting between the Olympic and Cascade mountain ranges, all reflecting off the pristine mirror that was the bay of Puget Sound. It was a sunny day which made it even more rare given the Seattle area's notoriety for frequent rainfall.

The home itself was constructed of hewn stone in the manner of a small castle, although probably no more than 3,500 square feet in total. Behind the house, a few hundred feet away, and further into the woods, was another structure of the same finished look, about twenty feet high. It appeared to be an observatory of some kind.

I pulled into the drive and got out, gave a stretch, and pondered the sight of Mt. Rainier in the distance. It rests a dormant volcano now, but as we all found out not so long ago with Mt. St. Helens, a sudden violent upheaval is always possible.

My thoughts were interrupted by Evan Pasternak stepping out the front door. His lithe frame gracefully crossed the cobblestone drive to greet me. He introduced himself, firmly shook my hand with a smile, grabbed my bag without asking, and began

171

walking towards the house inquiring the obligatory post-travel questions such as "How was your flight?" He poured some eighteen year-old single malt into two glasses and toasted our meeting, and as tribute to the man who brought us together - Harvey.

Before I could get out a question, Pasternak beat me to the punch.

"So tell me, How did you know Harvey Henderson?"

"He knew my parents. I was a small child. I really didn't know him."

"Hence the search."

"Exactly."

"So, how's that going?"

"Hmmm...that's a good question..."

"Not what you expected, but that's to be expected right?"

I laughed.

"Exactly," I repeated. It was my turn.

"And where was Harvey in your life?" I asked.

"I was a child too, but older, from age fourteen to sixteen."

Pasternak looked to be about late fifties, early sixties, so this dated his tale to the mid to late '60's, which would place Harvey in his later forties.

"My family lived in Kansas. My father worked for the railroad. It was a desk job. He coordinated shipments and scheduling and such, at least for the majority of his forty-three years there. He traveled a lot though, leaving a great many nights of my formative youth to quiet nights alone with my Mother, who was usually pretty worn out since she was a school teacher. I was an only child. At fourteen, I noticed our neighbor, Harvey, who actually lived a mile away, starting a walk just about dusk almost every night into a secluded glade over a small hill. He was always gone for several hours. I decided to follow him one night and then another. All he did was spread out a blanket on the ground and stare at the night sky for hours. Eventually, my curiosity caught up with me, and I just flat out asked him one day what the hell he was doing out there at night. I actually used the word "hell" and said it with the somewhat annoying tone genetically encoded in every boy at the onset of puberty. Harvey said, with matter of fact assuredness, 'Why, I'm just looking at the magnificence of God, young lad.' Well, that was not what I expected."

"Unexpected seems to be a common theme when Harvey's involved," I quipped.

"He invited me along, with my parent's approval of course, to observe what he was so dedicated to. So I went, carrying with me a healthy dose of skepticism and, I suppose a bit of youthfully arrogant condescension. I didn't vocalize it though. My curiosity outweighed my doubts about what could actually exist in a random field in Kansas that was even close to representing the 'magnificence of God'. To me, at that age, Kansas was as godforsaken a place as could exist."

"So what was in that field?" I asked anxiously.

173

"Nothing really…in the field that is…it was the sky above, the brilliant night sky that shone forth as an undeniable testament to the greatness and awesome wonder that only an infinite conscious being could design."

"The stars?"

"Oh, much more than that I learned. Harvey explained how each pinpoint of light was a transmission that began its journey millions of years ago, just passing through to tell a story or be part of another."

"I don't follow." I really didn't.

"The light itself tells us the nature of its origin from a scientific standpoint, through Doppler shifts and the gravitational forces acting on it as it travels millions of light years to find planet Earth. And then there are the stories and personalities we assign to them through their participation in a given constellation or as a navigational aid. Mankind has been in communion with the stars above for centuries…well, until recently."

"Until recently?"

"Think of this. Before television and radio, electric light and advanced scientific discovery, for thousands of years, the stars were our guides. They were even gods to some. They led us both literally, as navigational points, and figuratively, through horoscope and mythology. Lives were lived, battles planned and fought, kingdoms toppled and reborn, all around the messages and cycles that mankind perceived to be coded into the collective canopy of flickering dots - flickering dots, by the way, that are, in reality, gargantuan, raging infernos of nuclear fusion. Mankind's attachment to the heavens has outlived and predated uncounted long-lost religions and civilizations. I'm sad to say mankind's gaze has been diverted from the wonder and imagination that lies above to the dreary business of banal earthly pursuits here below."

"Sounds bleak, Mr. Pasternak."

"Please, call me Evan."

"Sounds bleak, Evan."

"I suppose it does. Don't get me wrong, I am an optimist at heart, but I do note this a seminal era, this age we live in. The heavens have become mere overhead decoration to most rather than revered territory."

"So how long did you two share your stargazing?"

"Off and on for a couple of years."

"And then?"

"Well, Harvey moved away, I entered high school, and my evenings were spent on teenage pursuits. But it's all still with me. I utilize something from those years quite often."

"Please explain." My curiosity piqued.

"Well, in my work I sometimes employ the mythology of the constellations."

"What do you do?"

"I'm a corporate consultant. I help growing companies find their identity. I'm a kind of cultural analyst for companies."

175

His answer put to rest a growing curiosity I had about why Pasternak so verbosely described his life and experiences as a well-structured narrative. He was a presenter, a man who spent a lot of time in front of groups and captive audiences.

"That sounds intriguing, a cultural analyst?" I asked.

"Sometimes, when companies grow, especially rapidly, they have a hard time fitting into their skin. A startup enterprise is defined by an idea, getting that idea out there and growing a client base. Once all that is established and the company is flourishing, the next important step to grow further is to discover its culture and persona."

"You mean like an image."

"Not exactly. An image is a façade, a projection. I'm talking about the collective unconscious."

"Like Groupthink?" I said as a playful jibe. Pasternak mustered a bit of a smile knowing it was a joke, but he was clearly in the zone and not willing to be distracted by a pithy aside.

"No. Groupthink is a derogatory label that some use to describe what they *think* corporations want to achieve. Good companies want to do just the opposite - create an environment where individuality thrives for the good of all. I know that sounds contradictory, but it isn't. Strong, growing companies are populated with dynamic individuals, not mindless robots."

"But there has to be some semblance of obedience and common vision, or you'll have chaos. Correct?" throwing in my two cents worth.

176

"Yes, anarchy is the extreme case of individuality without cohesive structure, but there is a happy medium."

"And where is that place?"

"That depends on the company, what they sell, whom they reach, and the makeup of the people trying to accomplish those goals."

"So how do the constellations fit in?"

"All those stories in the sky are the external representation of our internal archetypes - archetypes that reflect the shaping of cultures from all over the world. I don't limit myself to constellation mythology, there are others I employ, but there is plenty of worthy material in those stars."

"I'm not putting this together in my head. Can you dumb it down?"

"Have you ever read Joseph Campbell?"

"A little," I was telling the truth.

"How about Jung?"

"Carl Jung? A little," again, the truth.

"Then you have a basic understanding of archetypes."

"I think you'll still have to refresh my memory."

"There are certain universal characters that represent iconic models for our cultural existence. Movies, books, and television are all filled with them, and every culture that has ever existed long enough to make a difference had them too. The stories may be a little different here and there, but we all know about the hero, the warrior, the savior, to name a few."

"OK, so how does that translate to a corporate mission statement?" I challenged.

"Good question. I take a deep look at the management team, the product, the people in the trenches….everything. I gather histories, long and short term goals, corporate morale, customer feedback…again everything, and I begin to piece together an analysis looking at the whole picture in allegorical terms. Almost without fail a picture emerges that echoes a story that has already been told."

I was motionless. Either this man was a complete con artist or a pure genius. I told myself.

"So, then what happens? Role play with tunics?" I said, laughing a bit.

"I advise them on which course to take, which leaders are best for their story, as it were. You see, these archetypes are universal and arguably encoded in our DNA. Finding the storyline that best matches the company persona will send them ahead on a successful path of least resistance. The players will transmit the destiny they want to inhabit, and the most apt template is one that already exists in their collective psyche. When I present my final proposal, they can almost always finish it for me, because they already know what it is. All I really do is take a mirror and shine it back at them. They do the rest."

"Wow.....so they don't balk and resist when you start talking about Greek myths or Mayan legends and how it applies to their corporation?"

"No..well...I don't actually present it to them that way. I don't reveal that part of the process to them."

"Like a trade secret?"

"No, it comes across as more than a bit strange. Unless you've spent a good deal of time studying archetypes, it can seem rather eccentric, to say the least. Besides, I don't want them trying to make the translation. It's my job to present the conclusions in terms they understand so they can execute them properly. It's definitely not a 'trade secret' thing. I doubt there are many out there who could do what I do, the way I do it."

That sounded really pompous, but given the complexity of his method and the knowledge base needed to command it the way Pasternak did, he had to be right. He didn't mean it in a boastful way. He was genuinely sincere.

"So, what amount of the credit goes to Harvey?" I queried.

"I don't know if I could assign a percentage to it, but I do know this. One could make a case that if he had never shown me the night sky and provided the accompanying narrative, I might never have been set on the path that got me where I am today.

By now it was getting dark, and we were getting hungry. Rather than make a big production, we threw together some sandwiches, and grabbed some beers. Eventually we made our way to the observatory out back, which was much nicer inside than the outside would suggest. Solid walnut floors held big captain's chairs on wheels - it was clean and comfortable. There was a telescope of impressive capability that he had connected to a thirty-two inch flat screen monitor which allowed for shared viewing, while Pasternak manned a remote switch for the telescope. He had several coordinate positions preset for aiming the telescope, so he didn't have to manually search for each star field or planet he wanted to discuss.

He spoke, and I listened much the way I imagined a young Evan Pasternak did years ago when Harvey was the teacher. It was like watching a live version of a hi-def astronomy documentary. Pasternak waxed on about star groupings and how various cultures treated them differently. This lasted for several hours, although it seemed like much less.

Our celestial journey complete, we retreated back to the house from the observatory. Pasternak pointed me to a guest room, and shortly thereafter, I was in deep slumber.

Fifteen

◆ ◆

"I will never look at the stars again the same way," I thought, lying in bed the next morning. I also contemplated the impact of Harvey's simple act of selflessness to introduce an impressionable boy to the subject of astronomy and the cultural narrative joined to it. On the other hand, to say "selfless" makes the assumption that there was some sort of sacrifice involved. It is quite possible that Harvey found it rather enjoyable to be cast as mentor. Something tells me he did.

Regardless, judging by the house in which I was a guest and the exquisite furnishings, Evan Pasternak had cultivated the seed Harvey planted, blossoming it into a burgeoning career. Granted, Pasternak had a lot to do with it himself, but given our discussion the day before, Harvey's influence was important to his present course.

I showered, gathered my things, and headed down the stairs to thank Pasternak and then bid him farewell. My departure flight time was well into the afternoon, but I was keen not to wear out my welcome and wanted to take the spare hours to explore the Seattle area. I left my bag by the door, and wandered into the kitchen. Pasternak was making coffee.

"Off so soon, Mr. Preston?"

"Yes, I'm sure you're very busy. I wanted to thank you for your hospitality and sharing your information about Harvey."

"Not at all, Dennis, I enjoyed reminiscing. I hope I didn't ramble on too much about my work."

"Absolutely not. It was really quite fascinating."

"Black?"

"Pardon?"

"Do you take your coffee black, Dennis?"

"That's good for me."

Pasternak poured cup for each of us.

"Join me on the deck, Dennis."

I followed him onto a spacious and elegant platform overlooking Puget Sound in the foreground with snow capped peaks behind in the distance. The air was crisp. A gas firepit provided a glow of warmth to the wicker lounge chairs facing the view. We each took a seat and sipped from our steaming cups of coffee, taking a moment to drink in the beauty as well. Pasternak broke the silence.

"You know when you called the other day, I couldn't believe it was you."

I returned a puzzled look.

"You know, Dennis Preston...the writer...I couldn't believe you called me up, out of the blue."

I was getting a strange sense about where this was heading.

"I can't tell you how many times I have looked CEO's in the eye and cautioned them of the tale of Thatcher Crowne."

"OH, GOD!" I thought. "Here it comes." I took a quick gander and considered the damage if I bolted from my chair and hopped the deck railing. The drop was in the neighborhood of fifteen feet. I would at least break an ankle. I could have sworn I also heard the rumblings of Mt. Rainier ready to follow in the footsteps of Mt. St. Helens.

I was stunned speechless.

"Do you know how much is spent by corporations each year on defensive strategies to guard against rogue journalism?"

I shook my head.

"Nearly eleven billion dollars."

I returned an incredulous look.

"Seriously, I've crunched the numbers. Granted, they're open to interpretation, but it's a LOT of money, money that could be used for expansion, hiring employees, improving benefits, R&D...."

"Are you trying to argue that there was nothing unscrupulous going on at TC?" I defended.

"Not at all, but..and I know you know this..the whole company did not need to be put through the mill."

Again I was speechless. I took another sip of coffee. It tasted bitter.

There was a pause.

"So what's your point?" I asked.

"None really, and my intention is not to lecture you, I'm just telling you my side of the story, what I see....again."

"Again?" I queried.

"You don't remember, do you?"

Again speechless, a new record for Denny Preston.

"1996. You and Carson Rodgers interviewed me as a material source concerning the health and viability of Thatcher Crowne."

I tried to un-age him 15 years, to remember the interview. Then I asked,

"Was it over the phone?"

"No, it was in Virginia. I was based out of there then. You came to my office."

I fidgeted in my chair, wracking my memory for any spark to remember that day.

"I'm sorry, Evan, I don't remember."

"I'm not surprised. I don't recall you taking many notes. I wasn't telling you what you wanted to hear."

"Look, I don't know what to say. I'm just going to have to fall back on a mea culpa here. I am not proud of a lot of what I did back during that TC episode. I know I can't go back and control-z the whole thing. I'm not trying to brush you off. I realize it was a serious thing that is...."

"I know, it's been a long time. I just wanted to see where your head is on the matter."

"It's not so much my head as my heart."

I proceeded to tell him all about my day with Dorothy Trombley in Kansas City. He listened intently, then spoke.

"This is all good. You asked my intent. I wanted to see if you were worthy of my recollections of my experiences with Harvey. I wasn't going to give my blessing for you to use it if I sensed you were the same arrogant prick that walked into my office 15 years ago."

"Thanks," I said.

"You're welcome...and, yes, you are no longer arrogant."

There was a pause...

"And the prick part?" I asked.

"Well....," he said, shrugging his shoulders, then he laughed. I joined him with my own laugh. Then he continued.

"You know the whole business with TC was bound to happen sooner or later. Corporations were going to have to guard against predatory press eventually. It's not like you invented it, but you were decidedly one of the pioneers of the modern era."

"Thanks?...I guess?"

Pasternak retreated to the kitchen and returned with a coffee pot, topping off each mug. We sipped some more, and then Pasternak charitably changed the subject.

"You know Harvey, he was a bit of a ladies' man from time to time."

"No," I said. This was the first I had heard of anything like that.

"He never married, though. We kept in touch a little. He always wanted to know about my love life, who I was dating through college, that sort of thing. He would reciprocate. Not in a prurient way, mind you. I think he just wanted to guide a naïve boy from rural Kansas through the slings and arrows of outrageous relationships. I did marry once. It lasted four years, and that was twenty three years ago."

"And nothing since?" I pried.

"I date. I have close friendships with women, even almost proposed a couple of times, but I look at my life and the pace I keep, and it just isn't conducive to a healthy serious relationship. In the end, it would inevitably result in two angry, broken hearted, bitter people with regrets. I know that sounds cynical, but it's just a fact."

"So, define 'Ladies' Man'," back to Harvey.

"Oh, he just liked to *discover* women, what made them tick. He liked to make them feel good about themselves, and in a genuine way. It wasn't just to get some play."

"I'm flabbergasted really. All this time I've followed him, and I have yet to come across a former romance of his. Frankly, I was considering he might have been gay. Do you have any names or contacts that could tell me more about...?"

"Hmmm...not really..."

We polished off the rest of the coffee, and soon after, I was settled in my car. I felt unsettled inside though. It's always unnerving to get incomplete leads on a story. Somewhere out there was a whole side of Harvey's life that was a treasure trove of information, but once again, I had no starting point. I should have been used to that by now, and I should have been accepting of the fact that so far, no matter how slight the leads were that I followed, I had been rewarded in some way. I told myself to trust that I would be again.

In a matter of hours, I was back in St. Paul sitting on the comfy couch, with no apparent inkling as to where the next door would open let alone where the doors actually were.

Sixteen

◆ ◆

It was an unusually warm day in St. Paul. I was sunbathing on my balcony when an e-mail arrived from Evan Pasternak on my handheld. It had only been six days since we met, but it seemed like two months. I read the message.

"Greetings, Dennis,

Our meeting prompted me to review some old photos and I found these..."

I didn't wait to read the rest, I just opened the attachment. There were three photos - two portrait style looking into the camera and one candid shot. They were decidedly from three different times on the same day, as the subjects had on the same clothes. The subjects were two people - Harvey, and a young woman. I looked the photos over for a few minutes and then finished reading the message text.

"After you left, I remembered something. Harvey met me in Hawaii for my junior year Christmas break from college. He met Leeann there, and they hit it off. I think they were an item for a while. Her last name is (was?) Gabriel, "like the angel", he used to say. Sorry, that's all I got.

Take Care,

Evan"

I responded, profusely thanking him. It took some searching and a subscription to a people search website, but I had narrowed the field to three "Leeann Gabriels". One was in Hawaii, with a married name of "Branders". I struck out on finding a phone number, but I found a family reunion page on a social networking site that yielded some pictures. A couple of the picture posts contained a woman who closely resembled the woman in the photos with Harvey (plus forty years, that is). I crafted a generic e-mail to the sitemaster with my information requesting a forward to Leeann Gabriel. I waited, and waited some more. Four days later, a door finally opened in the form of a phone call from Leeann herself. We chatted a bit, and once again, I decided these things are only best face-to-face. In-person brings so much more to an information gathering session. Besides, I'd get an extra day or two to hit the beach. We arranged a meet on Oahu. I cringed at the airfare cost but bit the bullet.

As photographs the pictures were nothing spectacular - spur of the moment snapshots. The first was a straight-on shot of Harvey and Leeann seated at a restaurant or bar table. The background indicated it was some sort of beachside tavern or tiki bar. They both had ear to ear smiles and, judging by the bloodshot eyes, appeared to have partaken in some of the establishment's libations.

The second shot was in some sort of botanical setting. They were standing side-by-side under a natural canopy of tropical floral bushes or trees. It appeared this was meant to be a portrait of sorts. They were more posed, and the smiles were more subtle.

Finally, the third was a candid shot on a beach at night. The amber glow of firelight was the sole source of illumination. The shot was in profile of the two looking into the distance, presumably staring out at the ocean. They were relaxed and content, both sitting, Leeann leaning back against Harvey's chest, Harvey's arms wrapped around her.

Leeann was clearly younger than Harvey. Judging by Pasternak's recollection of this being his junior year in college and the clothing and hairstyles in the photos, the timeline would settle in around 1972 or 1973, setting Harvey's age right around fifty. I would estimate that Leeann was likely around thirty. Despite the age difference, they looked to be a natural fit. It's hard to gauge the dynamics at play from three snapshots though.

My assumption was that Leeann was a native Hawaiian. She was Polynesian-Asian, with perfect mocha skin, rich mahogany eyes, and flowing silky black hair which fell to the center of her hourglass figure. She was, in a word, beautiful. This was a new side to Harvey, and I couldn't wait to find out the details.

◆ ◆

I arrived at McCray's about 5:30 P.M.. The meeting was set for 6:00, but I wanted to get settled in. McCray's was Leeann's suggestion, which was of all things a rib joint situated just off the beach. It featured island decor, but the hickory smell wafting through the air seemed more appropriate for Kansas City than Hawaii.

At 6:00 on the nose, Leeann entered. I spotted her and waved her over to my table. She seemed to float as she moved across the dining area. As she approached, I reached to shake hands, but she went straight for a hug.

I calculated she had to be close to seventy years old, but her face and the way she carried herself spoke to nothing more than mid-fifties. She wore her age magnificently. What she did show of age was on the outside only. Her eyes were full of life, and she projected the energy of an ageless spirit.

"I am so glad to meet you, Mr. Preston. Hearing from you about Harvey was such a surprise. He has been on my mind since I spoke to you. Those are such good memories."

"Please call me 'Denny', and do go on."

"Well, I'm not sure where to start."

"How did you meet Harvey?"

"I was a cocktail waitress in a hotel bar. Harvey was waiting for a friend whom he had just flown out to meet, and he decided to order a drink. Well, we hit it off right away. I don't know, maybe I was having a bad day or something, but he came along at the right time and picked me up."

"Define *picked you up*," I asked.

"Well,...oh..yes...! I guess that could be interpreted another way," she laughed and then continued. "I mean he made me feel better. I can't recall what prior to that made the day so bad. Perhaps it was the patrons. I am a pretty patient person, but sometimes the parade of mashers and gropers that made their way into the bar was too much to handle. Harvey was just the opposite - sweet and respectful."

"What happened next?"

"His friend arrived, a younger fella (Pasternak, no doubt), and they left, but the next evening Harvey was at the bar, and then

191

again the next evening. Then he asked me out, and asked again, and then again. I had a strict rule against dating patrons, but he was so persistent, and persuasive, and kind of cute about it, so I eventually said 'Yes'. He took me to a barbecue restaurant." She motioned to our surroundings which served as explanation for her location of choice for our meeting.

"You came here?"

She nodded. I took a moment to reexamine McCray's, given the new information. "How long did you date?"

"Oh, I don't know. It was a normal amount of time, three or four hours."

"No, I meant..."

"Oh, how long were we dat-*ing*?" She laughed.

"Correct."

"I guess it was about nine months or so, but we lived about five years worth of good times in those few short months."

"Describe *good times*."

"Oh, fine dining, travel, theatre, long talks, discovering our hidden talents....it was like a nine month honeymoon without the marriage."

"Were you in love?"

Surprisingly she paused to think about my question.

"Hmmm....I think so...."

192

"I would think that would be an easy yes-or-no answer," I suggested.

"You'd think that, but love is a complicated word. I would definitely say we loved each other, no question about that, but I wouldn't say we were actually *in love*...at least not for long periods of time."

"I don't know why, but that makes me a little sad," I told her.

"Really? Why?"

I thought about it for a moment.

"Well, I guess I'm looking for a happy ending that never came to be," I said, a bit surprised at my own sentimentality.

"It *was* a happy ending, Denny, for both of us. We both knew going in that our togetherness was not destined to be a permanent thing. We kept in touch throughout our lives and shared everything. 'Happily ever after' doesn't always mean 'together ever after'."

"Were you both on board with that?"

"Sure, I think so. Does that make any sense?"

I thought about it.

"Sure, I get it, but it still seems sad somehow."

"Well, it isn't. I'll try to express that better as we talk more."

We ordered and talked our way through dinner. A couple of hours or so later, we were set to leave, when Leeann invited me to lunch at her house the next day to show me some pictures and tell me more. She said she was certain once we started going through some of her memorabilia of her times with Harvey that more detailed memories would start to drift back. I accepted her invitation wholeheartedly.

Since the invitation was for lunch, I took some time to drive around and leisurely take in some sights the next morning. I wanted to keep things on a light note, but I was somehow drawn to the USS Arizona Memorial. The attack on Pearl Harbor was nearly seventy years past but there is still so much meaning and powerful emotion still present there. I was glad I chose to spend my morning there.

Leeann lived in a moderately sized ranch home overlooking the harbor itself. It was clear the home's cachet was the view. The Arizona memorial was even visible from the front porch. Leeann reached the door before I could ring the doorbell. She had set up shop in a screened porch area to one side of the house. We walked through the living room to get to the porch. There was an ample collection of framed family photos, none featuring Harvey, which caught my attention. Leeann carefully explained each of the photos, the subjects, and locations.

She married some time after she and Harvey went their separate ways. She was now a mother of three and grandmother to eight. Her husband, Nicholas, was a naval officer, now retired (and spending this particular day on the golf course).

Leeann and I eventually made it to the porch. There were mostly photo albums, but a few trinket type items of sentimental value were also strewn about on a larger-sized card table. Leeann decided to celebrate a little, so we sipped mimosas while sorting through the tokens of her brief time with Harvey.

There were photos of everything they did and the places they went - Venice, New York, the Florida Keys, Grand Canyon, Australia, Tahoe, Vegas, you name it. There were letters, even Leeann's own personal copy of Harvey's Christmas letter that prompted my trip to Mendocino. A thought was nagging at me about how Harvey was able to afford this jet-setter lifestyle, though, so I had to ask.

"Oh, Harvey had some savings from a business sale or something. I urged him to hold on to it, but he decided he wanted to spend it. It's what made it possible for him to come to Hawaii in the first place. We met within an hour of his arrival here in that bar where I was working. He decided it was fate and that he wanted to spend it, and spend it on doing things with me," Leeann answered.

"Wow, talk about your impulse buying," I added.

"I was against it really, but he kept coming up with things, and we kept having a good time, so I gave in and went along with it."

Judging by the Cheshire grin occupying Harvey's face in every single photograph, it was clearly a superb investment. Putting myself in Harvey's shoes, I imagined what I would do given the same opportunity, a large sum of money, a beautiful lady on my arm to share the wealth - it didn't seem so crazy really.

I glanced at Leeann. Her energy was high, she was aglow reliving the moments in her memory as she reacquainted herself with each snapshot, and narrating the specifics of each. Eventually, it seemed she had stopped directing her comments to me and was instead telling the story of each picture to herself again. I became less interested in the details of her commentary and more so in the effect the recollections had on her. It appeared Harvey's positive influence had no expiration date.

Then she stopped cold. She was staring at a photo of Harvey in silence. I don't think it was anything particular about that exact photo, it just happened to be the one she was looking at when she flashed on a powerful memory. I waited a few more moments.

"Who was she?" She said softly...not to me...but to Harvey's picture.

Her slender index finger caressed Harvey's image, as she again returned to silence.

"Why would you never speak of her, dear Harvey?"

I suddenly felt like an intruder. The moment was a deeply personal one for her. Leeann was in some sort of communion with Harvey, asking forty year old questions that had never been answered. Leeann's bearing eventually relaxed a bit. I saw it as a chance to inquire. Unwittingly, my words took on the tone of a counselor, not a reporter.

"Is everything OK, Leeann?"

She gathered herself. She had apparently forgotten I was in the room.

"I'm just fine, Dennis."

She looked up from the photo and turned her head to look directly at me. She smiled, causing a suspended tear to roll down her cheek.

"I lied, Dennis."

"I'm sorry?"

"I told you we never looked at our relationship as permanent, but I lied."

She sniffled and wiped another tear from her eye, then continued.

"Only Harvey felt that way. I wanted to spend my life with him."

I was taken aback. Harvey passing on this spectacular lady was beyond comprehension.

"He was everything to me, my friend, my lover, my guide, my purpose, my savior…. my passion."

My heart ached at Leeann's pain. I felt a tear of my own beginning to form. This was a first, some measure of pain inflicted by Harvey. I was trying to sort it out. Leeann continued.

"He was right, though. The time had come to move on."

Now I was confused.

"From time to time over the last forty years, I have imagined the course of our life had we stayed together, and I truly believe things would have faded and maybe died. There was no way to sustain the level of emotion and excitement that we found in those nine months. We really were different people at the core, not to mention the age difference. Harvey saw that, anticipated the inevitable, and ended it while we were still at our peak. It took me a couple of years to recover, and then I met Nicholas, and he became that person for me. Harvey was still a dear friend, and the few times

197

we saw each other after we parted were so fantastic. We stayed close, he knew my kids, even helped me sort out some parenting issues with them, but it still hurts that I lost the closeness we had."

"So, you did love him."

"In every way possible, and even more after we parted. But I don't regret it so much now. If we hadn't ended it when we did, I wouldn't have all that I have now. And the same is true if I hadn't met him at all."

"How do you mean?"

"When I met Harvey, I was an incomplete person. I grew up without a dad. I had no male role models in my life. My dear mother was a strong, wonderful person, but she couldn't be that for me. Every child needs a man around. Harvey became that for me, belatedly."

"Do you mind if I ask about your father? Did he leave your mother?"

"Yes and no. I know exactly where he is, or was. He's still there even to this day. Every day of my childhood I knew exactly where he was, but I could never see him or touch him or talk to him."

This was bewildering, and it was difficult to understand Leeann through her sobs.

"Where was..is he?" I asked as delicately as possible. She merely pointed out to the harbor. I looked, and it dawned on me after a few seconds.

"Pearl Harbor," I whispered.

"He was on the Oklahoma. I never met him. My mother was pregnant with me at the time of the attack. She watched his ship go down, helpless to stop it."

She gathered herself a bit, then continued.

"She was a terrific mom.. After losing dad, she was afraid to lose me too, so she kept me close. I led a sheltered existence through much of my childhood. I was the shy bookworm. I considered working as a cocktail waitress a major step, you know, being out there among other people. Then Harvey came along and showed me the world, including all the parts of myself I had conveniently ignored. Every time I said I couldn't do something, he would say, "Why not?", and then I found out I could, and I just got that much stronger and confident."

"Anything specific?"

"One of the first things he had me do was try out for a modeling job, a swimsuit spread. I was scared to death, but he talked me through it. I know that sounds sort of shallow on the surface, but I never considered myself as that attractive. He wanted me to see myself as I was, to show me my full self. I was never self-conscious about my brains. I actually used to hide behind them. I hope that doesn't sound strange."

"No, I think I understand that, and in return, he could brag he was dating a swimsuit model."

"YES, he DID do that!!" she said as she broke out laughing. "It only got better from there. He found my flaws and fears and lovingly found creative, positive ways to challenge me into making myself a better person. Eventually, I developed that skill on my own. He knew I would soon outgrow our relationship, and that's when he moved on."

"Well, if it means anything, I don't know if that's an act of strength or utter foolishness on his part. You seem like an amazing woman, Leeann," I offered, once again surprising myself with my candor.

She thanked me. And we began to clean up the porch area a bit, since we had pretty much covered everything photo-wise. Then I remembered the "she" comment.

"Leeann, you said 'Who was she?' What did you mean by that?"

"Oh, I never knew for sure. Call it intuition. I became convinced there was someone else. Someone way before I came along that took Harvey's heart and never gave it back. It had long since passed when we were together, though, but I just always felt like some part of him was in the possession of someone else. I was jealous of that, but now it's just the one remaining enigma I have when it comes to Harvey."

The sound of the front door opening broke our conversation.

"Nicholas? Is that you?"

"Yes dear. Is the reporter fellow still here?"

"Yes, I want you to meet him."

Heavy footsteps approached the porch area, and a strapping, tanned, gray-haired Adonis entered. Leeann looked dreamily at Nicholas with a contented smile while Nicholas and I introduced ourselves. Any concerns I might have had that Leeann still held a flame for what might have been were rapidly extinguished by the clear depth of her strong devotion to the man who was at her side now. She loved Harvey, but to my eyes Nicholas was her soul mate. Yes, I said it... soul mate. I thought I didn't believe in those....

Seventeen

◆ ◆

I stayed in Hawaii for three more days doing some sightseeing and getting good beach time with an afternoon of snorkeling. It was all I needed to feel refreshed and renewed to once again board a 747 for the long trip back. One advantage to owning your own schedule and traveling solo is when the auctioning by the airline begins at the departure gate for managing an overbooked flight, one can bank some good booty, if one is willing to wait it out. For surrendering my seat and merely delaying my departure for just five hours, I was able to get a free domestic round trip for later use, and a first class upgrade for my entire trip back home.

I settled comfortably into my ultramodern, high-tech pod-seat but was more inclined to sample the old-school amenities of the elite seating arrangement, sipping a couple of single malts followed by beef stroganoff paired with a Willamette Valley Cabernet. I was enjoying some chocolate mousse with a cup of coffee when my attention was drawn to the coffee cup. It was real china, as was customary in first class, and featured a stylized version of the airline logo. Something about it triggered an unsettling feeling which nagged at me. I couldn't dial in on what exactly was bothering me. I tried to let it go by getting up and pacing the first class area. I was contemplating the fine amenities at my disposal, which led to the memory of the Lear flight to France, then pausing at a personal musing about Lillian Trentsworth, followed by spying even more coffee cups on tray tables. It clicked. I had figured it out.

What was nagging at me was my reporter's instinct trying to tell me something. It had put together a conspiracy at play, one so subtle it almost had me anesthetized into complacency. The coffee cup was the key because it reminded me of identical ones I had noticed in two unlikely places, cups not identical to the airline cup but identical to each other. The first time I saw the cup in question was on Evan Pasternak's deck. I held it in my hand, the vessel of the bitter black brew he served with a side of scorns. Its twin was to be found among the collection of Henderson keepsakes scattered about Leeann Branders' porch.

I struggled to recall the details of the logo and the words. It was a white cup with orange and black printing. It was for an event, some sort of conference or gathering. It had dates on it, fall dates. The location was Scottsdale, Arizona. Beyond that, I was blocked. I resolved the best plan was to call Leeann when I got back home to have her tell me the details on her cup. This freed my mind up to work on unraveling the conspiracy.

The path that led me to Leeann was started by an innocuous text message received on the golf course. I assumed it was from Grainger, and it very well may have been, but then again it didn't have to be. It could have been from anyone who had access to his phone, and what better tool to guard one's anonymity than a short text message on another's phone. Who sent the message really didn't matter. I certainly would have liked to know, but it wasn't that important really. It was the when and the why that were of interest.

I was a little perturbed at myself for being taken in by such a simple plan. The text message served as a bright shiny object to distract me from my decided-upon course at the time to pursue

Lillian Trentsworth. Instead, I allowed myself to be led down a path of pleasant distraction in the form of Leeann Branders. The beauty of it was that there was substantive, pertinent, valuable information to be had in the pursuit of the Harvey Henderson story. I marveled at Lillian Trentsworth's deft ability to disarm me so skillfully, at her keen talent to read my motivations so clearly and so deeply in the scant few minutes I was in her presence.

I presumed she ordered Grainger to send me the text - bait which led me to Evan Pasternak, which ultimately guided me to Leeann. She was banking that this version of changing the subject would keep me off her trail. It never occurred to me to question why I was being led to Pasternak. I was so taken in by his tale of stargazing, and subsequently, Leeann's love story, that the fire in my belly concerning Lillian Trentsworth was relegated to the intensity of a candle flame, or so it would have been had I not made the coffee cup connection.

I mentally tried to sneak up on the coffee cup logo again. Sometimes things refresh when you occupy your thoughts elsewhere and then dash back to what you were looking for. It was something like "Contact" or "Confluence", but a made-up word, a hybrid. I still came up blank. I returned to the conspiracy subject.

Where I faltered was assuming the text from Grainger was meant solely to be helpful and offered in goodwill. As I mentioned, it did lead to good things, but by letting down my guard I became unsuspecting of the true motivation. I should have clued in again when Pasternak grilled me about Thatcher Crowne. It should have tipped me to where his loyalties lay which was to those who put bread in his basket, and they would be corporations - more precisely, those who run them.

I began a mental inventory of Pasternak's home from my recent stay, recalling it was peppered with awards and swag from companies for which he had performed consulting duties. From my first class pod-seat Wi-Fi station I began to search them one-by-one over the Internet. Out of the dozen I remembered, eight of them were subsidiaries of the Trentsworth empire. It was obvious, Pasternak played his part in the deception, either instinctively as a loyal subject to the queen, or perhaps as a hired gun for that very purpose. It didn't matter.

I had no thought that Leeann was culpable. She seemed well above this sort of malicious mischief. She didn't need to be part of it for the plan to work anyway. Indeed, it worked even better without her knowing. Pasternak knew the Leeann-Harvey story and knew it would be a perfect diversion from any and all things Lillian Trentsworth.

"Connextion"! That was it!

"Con" for "Conference", and "Next" for "about the future". I searched that and found a reference to several conferences. It looked to be a once every two year event held in different resort retreats. It was indeed an invention of Trentsworth Industries. From what I could gather on the few still functioning web pages, it was some sort of brainstorming conference attended by representatives of all the Trentsworth Companies. One website dedicated to documenting the history of the event showed one in Scottsdale, Arizona - September 12th - 17th, 1996. Those dates seemed consistent with my recollection. I would no longer need to bother Leeann with a phone call, but there was one in the offing for Evan Pasternak.

My original thought was to call from home, but I looked around at my fellow travelers in first class, and the virtual variety show of high-tech gadgetry that was on display, and I figured, "When in Rome." I grabbed my handheld, found Pasternak's number, and began dialing. As the call connected and started ringing, I realized it was close to eleven P.M. in Seattle. I was expecting voice mail, but instead...

"Evan Pasternak," came a voice from the skyphone's earpiece. Similar to the first time I called him, I realized I was stuck for where to begin. I hadn't thought out my strategy. I didn't want to let on that I was hip to the conspiracy at hand, but I wanted to find out why Harvey Henderson had a "Connextion" coffee cup in his possession at one time. It was a miniscule, but concrete link between Harvey and Lillian Trentsworth. The most logical explanation was that it was merely a gift, perhaps even from Pasternak. I was prepared for that very response as the explanation, but I needed to ask the question right so as not to seem too eager to connect the dots. It had to seem like a throw-in question, a Columbo moment, the kind where, as the detective was walking away, he would turn around and, just as the culprit was thinking he had gotten away with it, would say, "Oh, one more thing..."

"Hello? This is Evan Pasternak. Can I help you?"

"Uh...Evan...This is Dennis Preston."

"Hello, Dennis. Nice to hear from you. What's up?"

"By the way thanks for the tip about Leeann Gabriel. She was immensely helpful and a sweet, sweet woman."

"No problem. I'm glad I could be of help. I only met her once, but you are most certainly correct. I always wondered why Harvey and she never lasted. He was nuts about her."

I was hoping through the introductory banter that I would be able to craft an elegant maze of questions to get what I needed from Pasternak without him knowing what I was actually after, but the more I tried the more any sort of clever inquiry escaped me. I decided, "What the hell?"

"Say, Evan, what can you tell me about something called the Connextion Conference?"

I was expecting a pause and the sound of a throat clearing, but he just blurted it out.

"You mean the biennial gathering of the Trentsworth Industries companies?"

I was stunned at his frankness, which caused me to hesitate, then clear *my* throat.

"Uh...yes that's it.... What is that about?"

There was a pause from his end. I had him.

"Oh, the coffee cup! You remembered that from the coffee that day? Man, that's some memory.... Well, if I recall, that was the 1996 conference in Scottsdale. You know what, talk about kismet, Harvey actually attended that conference. Talk about full circle."

OK, maybe I had him, or maybe I didn't. That was too easy. He just spewed it out, no Columbo moment needed.

"Why would Harvey attend a corporate conference for the Trentsworth empire?" I asked thinking, "Why not? Evan's in a talkative mood."

"I invited him."

"As a participant?"

"Sure. The spirit of Connextion is to foster innovative thought and forward thinking ideation. What Harvey lacked in entrenched corporate experience was more than made up for by his inquisitive, intuitive nature. He was a natural."

"How did he blend in with the suits and ties?"

"Actually, that's kind of the whole idea of Connextion. Each invited participant is charged with inviting another person they think would add an innovative perspective to the proceedings. It was encouraged to bring in non-corporate types. There were artists and poets, farmers and astronauts. It was really cutting edge."

Actually, it really was. I had to reluctantly admit to myself that this was quite brilliant. Pasternak continued.

"Ms. Trentsworth's vision was to have her captains of industry, CEO's, VP's et cetera, spend time intermingling with a wide spectrum of diverse personalities and skillsets, with the goal in mind to spark fresh, original solutions and a sort of holistic approach to corporate problem solving. She was way ahead of her time. The first conference was sometime back in the seventies. I was first invited in 1992 since I was doing some consulting for Trentsworth entities. I invited Harvey in 1996, because I thought he would be a good participant and for selfish reasons. It was my feeble gesture as a payback for the influence he had had on my life. I got to spend a few days with him again to catch up."

"So was he helpful?"

"At first, yes, but he actually didn't stay for the full conference. He had to leave early, and I never found out exactly why that was. I asked him later, but he just kind of changed the subject. He didn't want to talk about it. I can't be sure, but I think something happened at the conference."

"And you have no idea what that might have been?" I asked, knowing the answer was, "No".

"No," he said.

I tried to think if there was something else. There was good momentum, at least until the last question. Pasternak was a fountain of information, and while I had him on the line, I wanted to pump him for anything I could, but there was nothing I could think of. I thanked him, and we ended the call.

My head was full of thoughts. The first order of business was to run all this through my newly discovered conspiracy filter, but I didn't get a clearer picture of things. Instead of deflecting, Pasternak was forthcoming. He answered every question I asked and then some. I had no inclinations as to how this information could be an elaborate ruse. I decided I would pay attention to my reporter's gut instinct to detect any irregularities. That aside, I acquiesced that I had to go with what I had, just more questions, one especially big one. Why did Harvey leave Connextion 1996?

I still had a good four hours of flight time left. It was almost 2:00 A.M., so I decided to try to sleep. It seemed like a big waste to sleep away half my free first class upgrade, but I was tired.

I was awakened three hours later by the bump of slight turbulence. It was an hour before the flight landed in Los Angeles - From there, a slight layover, a change of planes, and on to St. Paul. I remembered I could check my e-mail from my ultra-modern pod-seat, so I did so to stave off some boredom.

To my surprise there was an e-mail from Evan. The subject line was "Harvey: Connextions follow-up". The body of the e-mail said,

"Dennis, I recalled someone who may have witnessed first-hand Harvey's departure from the conference in 1996. His name is Ian Aronson. He worked for Trentsworth's mining interests."

There was some contact information, including an e-mail. As an introduction to the subject matter, and as a reference, I simply forwarded Pasternak's e-mail, introduced myself and inquired as to what he might recall from the day Harvey departed from Connextion 1996. I expected a two day turnaround, but before the plane touched down I had actually received a reply. As it turned out, quite serendipitously, he was sitting in the Los Angeles airport waiting for an early morning flight to the east coast. I checked some flight information and our gates were fairly close together. It looked as if we might have ten or fifteen minutes to meet. I agreed to meet him at his departure gate.

By the time I made it to gate 34 at LAX, Aronson was already in line to board his plane. Fortunately, it was a long line. I really just needed five minutes. Aronson looked to be in his late thirties, wavy

210

blond hair, spray tan, wearing jeans and a t-shirt. There were $400 sunglasses perched on his forehead. He also wore a gold Rolex which was absurdly obsolete as a timepiece given the arsenal of technology at his disposal, each of which could probably produce the time of day in a dozen spectacular ways. He had all the electronic trappings of a guy who spent half his life on a plane or in a red carpet lounge waiting for one.

He was the poster child for L.A. stealth-corporate style. Bluetooth in his ear, super-slim laptop with a satellite link, the aforementioned sunglasses and watch, and a Che Guevara T-shirt, as if to say, "I know I'm shamelessly materialistic, but this iconic, anti-capitalist, hemp-made T-shirt makes it all good."

It was pathetic really, but he made it work. I introduced myself. We shook hands. He spoke.

"Hola, Mr. Preston, Evan told me you were looking for information on one Harvey Henderson?"

"Yes, he thought you might recall an incident involving Harvey at the Connextion conference in 1996 where...."

"Yes I do... "

"What happened?"

"Yes, I do. But, it isn't going to happen without the involvement of Tejon properties, so they have to be written into this."

I soon realized he wasn't talking to me, and he probably didn't even hear my question. It seemed as if he were answering me because he was looking right at me, but, in reality, he was thousands of miles away.

"I'm sorry, Preston, I'm in a middle of a deal right here. Millions, I hope you understand."

That time he was talking to me.

"No problem," I said. The passenger line was edging closer to the jetway, which was making me slightly anxious.

"Tejon. T-E-J-O-N......in San Antonio......No, Texas.....Texas...T-E-X-A-S."

The line edged closer still.

"No, you need to tell them we can't move ahead with the sub-structural integrity analysis until the gradient pitch ratios have been established, and that can't happen without a nod from the geo-con team leads."

"So," I thought to myself, "Whoever this is on the other end, who can't even spell "Texas", won't have a problem grasping Aronson's last sentence?" I tempered my expectations of gaining any knowledge of Harvey at Connextion 1996 in this encounter.

"So, me and this Harvey guy are in this breakout session with about twenty other people at the Connextion show. I don't know, some topic like corporate cultural energy flow, positive versus negative integration cycles, or catalysts of change, something like that. And we're all just going about our business when..gradient...pitch...ratios...the soil gradient...S-O-I-L, not soy...jeez....where was I?"

"Going about your business in a breakout group when..."

"Oh, yeah, when in walks none other than...no geo-con's.... Geological Construction...they're engineers...you don't need to know that though...."

There were only eight people in line ahead of Aronson now, and I was still at square one.

"I couldn't believe it. She never used to even come to those things anyway, but there she was in *our room*."

"Who?" I asked, pretty sure I knew who.

"LT."

"Lillian Trentsworth?"

"No, Lawrence Taylor, of course Lillian Trentsworth....No, you need to tell Zander, he will take it from there..."

Four people in line ahead now.

"Zander...from the party. Remember? The guy with the beard...no, dark hair...he had that...oh, you know.. you thought it was sooo cool....the..."

Two people in line ahead.

".....Yeah, nose ring thing...Zander...So she comes right in the room unannounced and calls out his name, then takes him out in the hallway, where they argued for..like..five minutes maybe. Believe me no one had the guts to try to eavesdrop, but everyone wanted to...no, with a "Z" like zebra....Zander."

One person ahead in line.

"…next thing I know he's….no, DO NOT tell him you think he's cute!! Remember, professionalism…right?…"

He covered the bluetooth with his hand.

"I know what you're thinking, and you're right, she's a bit dim in the smarts department, but she's got a righteous rack, dude."

He handed his boarding pass to the gate clerk and began walking into the jetway.

"What happened next?" I yelled.

"Oh, he was just uninvited. They ushered him out, and we never saw him again."

Aronson disappeared into the jetway. I was trying to process the bits of conversation, scattered as they were. I realized I had my own plane to catch. Frankly, I wasn't sure I could trust a thing I had just heard, given the scattershot nature of his recitation of a brief incident from nearly fifteen years ago. Was this guy a reliable witness?

A quick calculation on the timeline told me he must have been in his early twenties for Connextion 1996. Given the elite nature of the attendees from the Trentsworth side of the house, he must have been considered some sort of wunderkind. I pondered, the fact that because he projected an air of vacuous superficiality, doesn't necessarily mean he isn't highly intelligent. He's from L.A. after all. Vacuous superficiality might just be the persona du jour he has to affect in order to make an impression in the circles he's required to travel in. So his priority list of employee "skills" in his hiring practices might be a bit juvenile and inappropriate, but that doesn't necessarily suggest he's unreliable as a source.

Assuming what Ian Aronson said actually happened, it opened the door to a lot of questions, probably unanswerable questions, though. There were now two verifiable face-to-face encounters between Harvey Henderson and Lillian Trentsworth almost exactly fifty years apart - the first in Yellowstone park in the summer of 1946 and the second at Connextion in the fall of 1996. Somewhere in between, some level of animosity was reached between the two, perhaps some festering dispute, or maybe just something petty and innocuous that was isolated to those few days in Scottsdale, for example Harvey parking in her reserved space at the convention center. Who knows? It is a distinct possibility that during their spat in the hallway, neither was aware they had even met so long before. The task ahead of me now was to try to color in that fifty-year gap. Good luck! I thought.

Eighteen

◆ ◆

I arrived home, dragged myself to the comfy couch and spent a few hours recovering from the long flights back from the Aloha state. I'm always amazed how exhausting air travel can be even though all you really do is sit. Sure, you lug a bag around, but that's really not a big deal, especially how light I usually travel. Nevertheless, I found respite in some movies and a comedy special while enjoying some microbrews. The place still didn't feel like home though.

In the time that passed while I was on the couch, I had received a phone call on my handheld. I didn't hear it come in because I left my phone in a jacket pocket and hung it in the closet....oh, and I took a power nap. There was a message waiting in my voicemail.

"Mr. Preston, this is Dorothy Trombley...you know, from Kansas City..We owned the house that Harvey rented...Anyway, it turns out Harvey had a storage unit that he prepaid for ten years...We didn't know it even existed, but some mail was delivered to our house, and there was a renewal notice for the unit....Not sure why he used our address as the mailing address....Anyway.....There isn't anything of value in there really... dusty furniture.. a few clothes...there are some papers in file boxes...I thought you might get some value out of them for your book...Before I tossed it all, I wanted to see if you were interested in any of it...Give me a call either way...thank you..."

I called back immediately and told her as soon as I could, I'd be down there. I didn't bother to unpack my Hawaii bag. I did decide to wait until morning though. At first light, I was off for Kansas City.

216

The trip rounds off to about 450 miles and just under 7 hours straight down I-35 through Iowa. I arrived at Dorothy Trombley's right at dinner time. That was unplanned, but Dorothy must have anticipated my arrival time and had already set the table with an extra place setting for me. I refused at least six times, but Dorothy outbid me with seven "I insist" comebacks.

I also met Dorothy's husband, Frank. I took a moment to look at his hands. Last I heard, he was a diesel mechanic. His hands were not stained with any telltale grime of a mechanic, so I asked what he did for a living. He said he was now teaching cabinetry milling at a trade school. He was effusive about the rewarding aspects of his work.

That was good news given the fact that I crushed his entrepreneurial endeavor in that same field years ago with my Thatcher-Crowne investigation. Still, my guilt was grinding away at me, and I decided to come clean about who I was and what turmoil I had unleashed on their lives years ago.

Surprisingly, they were unfazed. They took it all in stride, offering their sincerest water-under-the-bridge response. They had clearly moved on. I decided I would try to as well. We feasted on Dorothy's homemade fried chicken, biscuits, and green beans. It was divine comfort food.

After dinner, we chatted some and played cards. As I picked up to leave, Dorothy handed me an old set of keys, apparently Harvey's last ever, which included one for the padlock on the storage unit containing Harvey's belongings. She jotted down some directions to the storage place, too. I thanked her and Frank and began motoring to the hotel which was just a couple of miles away.

About halfway there, I realized the storage facility was directly on the way to my hotel.

It was late, and I was tired, but I knew I would have trouble sleeping if I didn't at least take a peek at the stuff. I also knew I would have trouble sleeping, or not get to sleep at all, if I DID take a peek, but my curiosity won out, and in a matter of minutes I was standing outside the storage unit fumbling through the keys. I unlocked the unit and pushed up the door. I was excited. I didn't know what awaited me.

The door was now fully open, and the dim lighting provided by the common lighting outside the unit didn't offer much help. I found a light switch in the unit, but when I flipped the switch nothing happened. The bulb was burned out. I thought some of maneuvering the car to use the headlights as illumination but decided it wasn't worth it. I'd be back in a matter of hours in broad daylight to assess the situation.

At least I could tell what I was in for. The unit was about a third full, so I wasn't looking at spending the whole day there, probably three to four hours would get the job done. I locked the unit back up, found my hotel, and settled in for a surprisingly good night's sleep.

◆ ◆

On the way to the storage place the next morning, I stopped for some coffee at a convenience store. I spied some light bulbs on a shelf of household items and added them to my purchase. It was daylight, and daylight would be enough illumination for moving and lifting, but I thought I might need some better light if it came to reading some documents or looking at photos.

I opened the unit and spied exactly what Dorothy had described. There were a dozen or so old cardboard file boxes which were more to my interest than the furniture and lamps and such. Before attacking the first file box, I dragged a dusty armchair under the light socket in the middle of the unit. I could just barely reach it, but I managed to replace the bulb. While doing that, a truck began pulling up just behind the unit. I wondered if my car was in the way, so I peeked around to check. It was a generic medium-sized panel truck, a normal sight among a small city of storage units, I thought. I turned back and continued replacing the light bulb. I heard one of the truck doors open and close. The bulb replacement now complete, I carefully backed off the wobbly chair, and a voice directly behind me said,

"Still standing would be good thing now, mister."

The broken English was uttered by a gravelly male voice of Eastern European origin. Instinctively, I turned my head which met with a fist moving in the opposite direction. Dazed, I felt a pin prick in my neck, and within the count of three I was out cold....

...Cold....the sensation of cold on my cheek.... Cold on my painful swollen cheek.... A cold pain in my horizontally oriented cheek....connected to my horizontally oriented body...lying on hard concrete....A cold, wet cheek....the taste of dirt...and dust...and drool...A rude, cold blast of air coming from where the light was....Light unbroken due to the absence of objects between the outside and my blurred vision....Brain signals to limbs....no response....try again....no response....headache.....Oh God, what a headache!....the sound of footsteps....I can't move....I hope it's not Broken English coming back to finish the job....

"Hey is anyone in there?" came a voice in unbroken English. I saw a shadowy figure enter the light.

"Hey!", quicker footsteps towards me. "Are you all right, sir?"

Brain signals to mouth.....no sound.....

Shadowy figure reaches for a gun from a holster. Panic..but can't move....Shadowy figure puts gun to his own mouth...the sound of a trigger......the sound of static....

"Jimmy...yeah it's me...call 9-1-1 there's a guy in trouble in unit 481."

Voice from the gun..."Ten four."

Shadowy figure puts gun back in holster....thinking not a gun, but a walkie talkie....

"Stay still, mister. Some help is coming."

"Stay still?" I thought. "No problem." Passed out again.....

Eyes open...Four people hovering over me, sky moving above...White shirts...stethoscope...doctors...I'm moving....floating....no, on a gurney....Paramedics...try to move....Body begins to rise....

"Stay still, Mr. Preston...You're going to be all right. We just need to get you to the truck to get you stabilized."

I nod, "OK."

"We think you were drugged, Mr. Preston, nothing serious though."

"You should try it from my perspective, pal," I thought. "Seems pretty serious from here."

I began regaining coherence gradually. Eventually, I was sitting upright in the ambulance, still on the gurney with an IV in my arm and a blood pressure cuff on my other arm, which was pumped by a technician every few minutes or so. The storage unit manager came to check on me.

"Sir, are you OK?"

"Yeah, I think so."

"I thought those guys were with you, hired movers or something. I was checking the security cams from time to time, didn't see anything fishy. They left, but it was almost an hour later and your car was still here, figured you were cleaning up or something, but something said I'd better check."

"Thanks," I muttered through the remaining fog. "Did you get a good look at them?"

"No, they parked the truck so the camera was blocked. They wore baseball caps that covered their faces. Some cops are back in the office looking at the video now. Maybe they can see something I didn't."

As if on cue, a policeman walked up to the ambulance.

"Hello, Mr. Preston. You're looking better. That's good to see. Can I ask you some questions?"

I nodded.

"It doesn't look like the security video is going to yield much. We're running the plates from the truck, but I will all but guarantee they will come up stolen or fake. Do you have any idea what these guys were after?"

"Not at all. Actually...."

I paused realizing it might sound a little strange if I simply blurted out that I was here to go through some dead guy's stuff, and really had no legal right to do so, despite the fact that several years had passed since his death.

"No, nothing but old furniture and papers. You're welcome to go through it if you want to."

"Would if we could, Mr. Preston. They took everything."

"Everything?"

"Everything," The cop parroted.

The drugs were finally wearing off, and my thoughts were clearing. "Everything" I thought again. No offense to Harvey, but most of it was mangy, old crap. Think about it, Harvey spent his last days living in sparse surroundings. The stuff in the storage unit didn't make the cut for the collection of "sparse". What in God's name could have been in this storage unit to be worthy of a possible jail sentence to the two Cossacks who rolled me?

"Is there anyone you know of that might want to harm you, Mr. Preston?"

The usual suspects ran through my head, one especially, but I wasn't about to let that cat out of the bag just yet. I had no proof, and there was too much of a story at stake.

"Not really, officer. Not for a pile of junk."

The rest of the day was spent at the hospital doing some tests and recovering from my morning of excitement. Since I spent a good deal of time sitting and waiting, I couldn't help trying to connect the dots. The person behind this was undoubtedly none other than Lillian Trentsworth, directly or indirectly. I couldn't say if she gave the actual orders. She seemed smart enough to maintain enough plausible deniability from such distasteful matters by having some "project manager" in charge of petty crimes. That seemed more likely. "She isn't stupid," I thought.

One thing it did resolve, once and for all, was that somewhere along the way, Harvey got some dirt on LT - Something so damning, it still had juice seven years after his passing. It could be some evidence of criminal wrongdoing on the part of some representative body of Trentsworth Industries or Lillian Trentsworth herself. It might not even be criminal wrongdoing, just something hugely embarrassing or socially deplorable. I concluded that either way it was something apparently worthy of going to great lengths to obtain and something to cause enough discomfort for her so as not to be content with the thought that it would just never be found.

Whatever it was, it had to be something so blatantly obvious, at first glance, as damning evidence to any random person who had access to it. In the world of corporate documents and legal-speak, it often takes a highly trained eye to recognize corruption for what it is. Context matters too. A given document may not mean anything until it is paired with another document. My instincts told me this is something that screams out bad things loud and clear.

Another indication that this was a highly volatile situation was that they took everything in the storage unit. This was a leave-no-stone-unturned command from on high. Send the goons, but don't trust them to make a decision on the importance of a given item, not even enough to leave the dusty old arm chair behind. Whatever it is could have been sewn into the upholstery, perhaps. Further evidence to that effect came from Dorothy Trombley, who took it upon herself to drive my car to the hospital from the storage unit. I gave her back the storage unit keys and advised her of the good news that she didn't have to worry about arranging to have the storage unit junk hauled off. She added that she and Frank finally sold the small house where Harvey lived out his remaining days. The purchaser was a private trust. No one ever moved in. Dorothy observed that there had been some apparent remodeling going on, but the work crew (two guys..hmmm) only showed up late at night, spent three days tearing up the interior of the house, and then left it as is. No one had returned in over six weeks giving weight to the argument that the activity was much more a ransacking than remodeling.

Why buy the house then? Why not just rip it up while it stood vacant? Simple. The purchaser needed time to go over every inch of the house without looking suspicious. The purchasing trust was anonymous, and, as I found out later, it had a Cayman Islands' bank address as the contact.

I patched together a likely scenario for the storage unit caper itself. I must have been followed, at the very least, from Dorothy

Trombley's house but possibly all the way from St. Paul. My own impatience did me in, I think. My visit to the storage unit the night before tipped the goons that there were goods involved. It gave them time to acquire the truck. They parked a safe distance from the storage place and waited for me to show up. They probably obtained the code to the storage facility gate by observing the keypad through some means of magnification from a strategic vantage point. They followed me in, and the rest is history.

I learned from the medical staff at the hospital that I had been drugged with sodium thiopental. In non-pharmaceutical parlance, it is known as "truth serum", the first of the three drug series used in lethal injection executions. It was a good choice because it acts fast and has a short half-life, so it doesn't hang around too long, just long enough for two guys to empty a storage unit and make a clean getaway. I was comforted by the thought that at least they didn't mean to kill me, at least not yet. Perhaps they were waiting to see if they got what they came for, and maybe my demise would follow confirmation. Who knows? That didn't matter really. My resolve was even stronger. The whole thing got my cackles up - it was time to unleash the A-game on Lillian Trentsworth. I would find what she was looking for, and she would go down for it.

Nineteen

◆ ◆

"No, dear, I wasn't being rude. I just asked her. I know her that well. You should know that." My mother defended herself against my accusation that asking Katie if she was still married, after running into her at the dry cleaners, was none of her business.

"Well, don't you want to know her answer?" Mom continued in an incredulous tone.

"It's none of my business, Mom, and none of yours."

"I consider her a friend, Dennis. She wasn't wearing her ring. I'm just concerned about her and her children."

I looked up from the magazine I was flipping through to give Mom a stern look of disapproval. There was a pause, but she was going to explode unless she said....

"Well, if you must know, she and Tom separated. She says they are working very hard to patch it up, but you know how those things go usually."

"No, Mom, how?"

"They don't."

"Mom, you are so NOT a gossip. Why are you being such a busybody about this?"

"I told you I'm..."

"Concerned," I said finishing her sentence. "Under what rubric of *concern* does telling me about it fall? And I hope I am the only one you are telling this to!"

She hemmed and hawed. With a fork, she began pushing a lone kalamata olive around the lunch plate that recently held her Nick's Deli Greek salad. She was about to burst, knowing her next sentence was *truly* none of her business. Then, the inevitable,

"This could be your big chance, Dennis. You might never get this opportunity again."

"I knew it! You just can't leave well enough alone!"

Mom was taken aback at my outburst. Then, there was an awkward pause.

"I'm sorry for raising my voice, Mom. I didn't mean to. I guess I saw that coming a mile away and anticipated....reacted...sorry."

"It's OK, Dennis, I just think...."

"Mom....pleeeease, leave it alone."

Instead of backing down, she doubled down.

"Why...Why should I leave it alone? I am concerned about you, too. I think she is just what you need in your life."

"You know what they say, Mom, 'Don't look back, you can never look back'." As soon as the words left my mouth, I was disarmed by my lame selection from all the options available from the source "they", that my weapon of choice was a Don Henley lyric.

Mom thought carefully about her next utterance, lowered her tone and with calm clarity delivered, "Dennis, you need someone. Think about it, you are over forty, and the only woman you ever confide in is your own mother. You are..well...whatever the male equivalent of a spinster is..."

"Geez, Mom."

"Well, think about it, honey."

I already had, and she was totally correct. I wouldn't admit that out loud though.

"Mom, I have lots of women friends."

"You mean platonic relationships with women married to other men is what you mean."

It was painfully obvious I shouldn't try to argue with the woman who knows me better than I do, so I buried my eyes in the magazine again. Mom waited a bit.

"So, that's it? No terse retort?"

"Mom, it's useless. I'm not ruling out a serious relationship with a woman in my life at some point, but whatever magic or specialness was there between me and Katie is dead and buried, not because of me, not because of her. It just faded. The window has closed....besides, technically she's still married."

"Fine, be that way, Dennis." Mom got up taking the dishes with her.

I buried my face in the magazine again, turning pages like I was actually reading something, but the only thing on my mind was

Katie. No, I wasn't even considering my mother's not-so-subtle suggestion to reacquaint myself with her. Frankly, I was experiencing a mixed bag of emotion. I had been removed from her life for so long I was surprised by the flood of thoughts I had for Katie, and even for Tom. Sure, at first there were some base, selfish thoughts playing out about how there was some incrementally greater marginal chance now for me and Katie to find each other. I even had a disturbing sense of vindication that I was somehow right so many years later, as if I had won something. Once I had weathered the unpleasantness of that ego-based reflex, I found myself wanting only good things for all of them and especially, their children. I knew what most likely would befall them. For some unreasonable amount of time ahead was a reordering of life and a slow, unfolding grieving process. I hoped theirs would be as painless as possible.

Mom had finished the dishes and was ready for a game of Gin Rummy or Scrabble. Before we got into that, something was on my mind, and now was a good time to ask.

"Mom."

"Yes, dear."

"In all the time you knew Harvey, did you ever get the sense there was ever anything going on at a deeper level?"

"Well, if you mean did he have a private side, of course. We all do."

"I'm looking for something out of the ordinary, something that may have given you some doubts or concerns. Did you ever get the sense he was in any danger at anytime?"

"Heavens, no!"

"Did he ever disappear for an unusual length of time or have any confrontations that seemed out of place?"

"Not really, he got along with everyone."

"… Maybe a break-in to his side of the duplex when we lived next door?"

"Now that you mention it, there was one. They just took some stereo equipment….some cash…It was just kids, I'm sure. The ironic thing is we were out of town. Our place was pitch black and vacant. Our place was the one they should have broken into."

It would have been easy to think this smelled suspicious, like a search that was made to look like a burglary. I did take note, however, and reserved my right to change my mind later if I decided to.

"Why do you ask? Have you found some intrigue in this Harvey project of yours?"

This would have been the right time to divulge the excitement I encountered in storage unit 481….for anyone OTHER than my mom. So, I just kept my mouth shut. She would have freaked if she heard all about Russians and hypodermic needles.

"Not really, just thought it was worth asking about," I responded dryly.

The post-lunch game choice was Scrabble. You would think someone who makes a living writing would be pretty good at that, but Mom is a word machine. She ultimately put the hammer down with QUIXOTIC on a triple word score. Oh, and a double letter score where the "X" landed. The resulting damage was 152 points. Shortly after playing that word, Mom added,

"Hmmm..I suppose that's my tribute to Harvey."

"Pardon me?"

"Quixotic, to be hopelessly naïve and idealistic....ridiculously romantic.... you know Don Quixote?"

"Are you saying Harvey was like that?"

"Yes, he was to a degree."

"OK, I'll bite mom. Give me an example."

She thought about it for a while.

"OK, I think this would qualify. He once told me he knew there was a beautiful lady out there that was 'the one'. They'd eventually marry and then the whole happily ever after business, you know..."

"What's so hopelessly naïve about that?" I questioned.

"He was seventy-six years old when he told me that."

"It was still possible, can't blame a guy for trying. At least he wasn't a brooding mess of sour grapes," I said, making Harvey's case.

"True. I think it was the way he said it. He had this love struck teen look on his face...at seventy-six! He just seemed innocently dreamy-eyed about it."

231

"So, did you then immediately try to hook him up with one of his not-quite-divorced-yet, long-lost former flames?" I quipped dryly.

Mom laid down her next word - TOUCHE.

I looked up, amazed at her timing, and she smiled.

We cleaned up, and I headed out. On my ride home, I thought about it some more - Don Quixote and his windmills. I had a windmill of my own to tackle, a windmill named Lillian Trentsworth. It was time to get down to business, and I hoped if there was any allusion to mom's scrabble word, it was as an homage to Harvey and not prophecy with regard to what I was after.

Twenty

◆ ◆

There was the question of whether the goons had already gotten what they were after in Harvey's storage unit in KC. That was answered fairly quickly. Within a week of the incident at unit 481 I noticed I was being followed and my condo was being watched. There was a red Mercedes Benz sedan circa 1980's, missing a hubcap on the passenger side front tire that made its presence known all too often. It wasn't as if they were trying to advertise their pursuit, but honestly how many cars are there like that around? They might as well have wrapped the car in flashing Christmas lights.

So, how does one go about finding something someone else wants when you absolutely have not the faintest hint about what you are looking for? You get them to tell you what it is, not an outright verbal confession, but indirectly. Their actions will tell you when you start to zero in on it. They will dial up the attention level when they think you are close and dial it back when the opposite is true. In my case, "they" were the Russians who were a direct extension of Lillian Trentsworth. They may not have known what it specifically was, but as they reported their observations to their superiors, they would receive instruction about when to intensify their efforts to obtain whatever it was.

Sure, there was some element of danger about teasing these two fellows to a level of frustration and the possibility of facing whatever consequences might arise from that. But I was now privy to some level of danger and would not be caught off guard again. I'd been here before, this kind of cat and mouse game, and I had always come out on top. The key to this kind of strategy is to project an air that you are hot on the trail of something and to continue to broadcast the impression that you are oblivious to the surveillance at hand. They have to believe they are the cat, when they are really the mouse.

So, how was I to execute this strategy given the situation? I had a general idea of what they were looking for, some sort of document, or documentation on disk, a photograph, or a videotape. It was information, not an item, software, not hardware as it were, something potentially small enough to be hidden in the tightest little space in a rental house necessitating ripping up floorboards and the tearing out of fixed cabinetry, or something capable of being sandwiched in between reams of personal cardboard file boxes hidden in a long forgotten storage unit.

I surmised my best approach would be to act as if I was hot on the trail of something major. My actions had to project an air of certitude and confidence highlighted by bold strokes and direct, decisive movements. I did some brainstorming, narrowing the field to five diverse but plausible venues to see what level of attention each would garner.

The venues had to be credible to the nature of the search, yet non-descript enough so my pursuers would be compelled to flesh out their own story of what I had found and how close I was to finding it, whatever "it" was, based on the clue-set I was presenting as bait. The five I decided on were: a public records office, some location where I had been earlier during my investigation, searching for something at a remote location, a high tech repair shop complete with technology prop, and eventually another storage unit. I decided the order of each mattered too. I had to create the illusion that there was logical method to my actions, so the chain of events had to come across as each being somehow connected to one another.

The public records office seemed the best place to start. It was the most generic of the five options and would lend itself to a broader spectrum of possibilities, but with a perceived credibility, when viewed through the eyes of my pursuers. After all, what can you get at a public records office? Anything, really, but whatever that might be carried the gravitas of officialdom.

To pull this type of charade off, one must have the conversation in the observer's head involving questions like, "Why go to a records office? What could be found at a records office that isn't already available on the internet? Something requiring a signature? Something more sensitive than a routine parcel search." Beyond that it doesn't really matter what conclusions they reach. What troubles them is that there is something out there they don't have, and, rather than take the time to research it themselves, their laziness prevails and leaves the leg work to the deceiver. In this case, I was certain I could count on that.

As it turned out, there is a regional National Archives center in Kansas City. It houses records for Missouri and Kansas as well as other nearby states. I realized I had just come from there, and that last trip was a rather stressful one, but it had to be done. I wasn't looking forward to yet another drive to KC, but it played right into the storyline that there was still something to be gathered in the last city where Harvey lived.

I waited another four days to leave. I felt it served my cause to force the Russians to suffer countless hours of droning, mind-numbing boredom waiting for anything at all to break the monotony. I was certain several days of tedium would only heighten a tendency to make something out of nothing, once things were set in motion. When I finally did leave, I made it look urgent. I packed the smallest bag I could that still looked like a travel bag. I made sure to look rushed, almost jogging to the car, and I even mocked a vital cell phone conversation throughout. They took the bait and followed me all the way to Kansas City. I did have to slow down a few times to be sure they didn't lose me, though. I concluded they could not have possibly followed me to Kansas City last time without me being aware of it, since they were so bad at it. It did make me wonder how they knew I was there in the first place.

After a night's rest in a hotel, I made my way to the Federal Archives making sure I had the Russians in tow. I had a long day ahead of me playing the role of someone doing serious research. I made sure to do something in all of the respective records departments to give the impression I was onto something. I even made a few photocopies and took some cell phone pictures of random documents. After eight hours, I headed back to the hotel, grabbed some dinner, went to bed and got up and did it again the next day. Halfway through, I pretended to find something. I abruptly packed up my stuff making sure one of the Cossacks saw me.

I drove back to the hotel and waited a few hours, then hastily left to find the nearest home improvement center. I had decided to incorporate two of my five planned options into one. I devised a plan too tempting to resist, or so I thought. I purchased a shovel, a pick axe and some large plastic garbage bags. The Russians followed the whole way. My next stop was the house Harvey lived in right behind the Trombley residence. I drove up the back way, since the drive up to the house was now cleared of the overgrowth that was there when I visited the very first time - no doubt the work of someone hired by the trust that owned the property. I parked the car out of sight of the Trombley's. I didn't want to attract their attention, because I knew it would involve them in something potentially dangerous. What I planned involved a slim chance that the Russians might be provoked into action, and who knew where that would lead?

I got out of the car and hid behind the house, so as not to be seen from the drive into Harvey's place. I listened intently for the sound of another vehicle, and, sure enough, I did hear one pull up further down the road. It was out of my sight though. I opened my trunk and grabbed my tools, then I ventured into the woods behind Harvey's house. I moved quickly but was careful to make an astute observation of my surroundings. I wanted to be capable of making a beeline out of there in case the Russians' curiosity got the best of them. I suspected they would probably get into position to get a visual on what I was up to. I wasn't expecting an encounter though.

I know I was giving them credit for more intelligence than they probably possessed, but it would be bad form to accost me a second time and come up empty-handed again. As long as they were under the impression I was doing the leg work for them, they would be wise to be absolutely sure I had what they were looking for and not make the mistake they made in storage unit 481. My finding whatever it was they were looking for, was their meal ticket. Otherwise, they'd be looking for a needle in a haystack, where the entire planet was the haystack. Chances were, under those circumstances, their employer would find another pair of pursuers.

After a reasonable amount of time, I stopped in the woods, grabbed the shovel and began digging, making sure I made a good amount of noise for the benefit of anyone who might be listening. After about ten minutes, with a few pauses to look over my shoulder a time or two, I decided I'd done enough digging. But instead of just stopping, I acted as though I had found something. I kneeled down and carefully filled one of the plastic bags with debris. When I decided I had enough debris in the bag to look like something, I tied it, grabbed the tools, and quickly hoofed it back to my car, taking special care to listen for footsteps not my own. I heard nothing.

I loaded my trunk with the tools and the bag, got in the car, and got moving. As I approached the end of the drive, I noticed no other car. However, there was some fresh road dust in the air. They had presumably made it back from the woods and exited before I crossed their path. I was impressed with that since, until now, they had seemed pretty hapless.

The trap was set. My plan was to set forth a scenario that I had discovered information of value from my records search that led me to some secret hiding place in the woods belonging to Harvey Henderson. I was counting on the Russians believing I had dug it up, put it in the bag, and made off with it. The next move was theirs. I would head back to St. Paul and see what reactions I had provoked. If the scenario was believable, I would expect it to elicit some sort of action from my pair of Russian shadows. I headed back to St. Paul straight from the scene and decided to handle my hotel check-out remotely. I had to give the impression that I was excited with what I had found, and wanted to get out of there as soon as possible. My performance would send the message that I had found what I was looking for and there was no further reason to remain in KC.

Surprisingly, I was not followed home. I took this as a positive sign they were convinced I had found something meaningful. I concluded they had taken the bait, that they knew I was headed home and, rather than risk me spotting them (at least they still believed that they were undetected), they would return at their own pace and deal with this at the St. Paul end. My drive got me in around 9:20 P.M.. Although I didn't see the Mercedes outside my building, I continued the charade, just in case I was being watched, by grabbing my bag of debris and bringing it in with me to my place.

I got settled, grabbing a beer and flipping on the TV, but I soon realized that I had inexorably cast myself as the mouse now. The most probable course of action I could expect coming from Russian goons was to break in and try to get at what I had presumably found in the woods behind Harvey's house. I could choose to be there, or not to, since there really wasn't anything to be had anyway, but it wouldn't fit the ruse scenario for me to leave the condo without my apparent prize, so it looked better to stay home.

I waited several days and nothing happened. The nights were the worst. I was lucky to get three or four hours of any sleep, given the adrenalized nature of the situation. Four days passed, and there was still no action. The Mercedes was yet to be seen. I thought they had possibly changed autos, but I didn't spy any around long enough to be considered a stake out. I began to speculate that perhaps Lillian Trentsworth, after hearing the chronology of events, saw through the masquerade and pulled the Russians off the job.

◆ ◆

It was early on a Friday night. Two weeks had passed since my last trip to KC. The hot pursuit I had sensed before had definitely turned cold. I decided it was time to plan the next phase of my ruse, incorporating the remainder of the five options I had set forth in my master plan. I was considering something that would appear as if I had found an old computer of Harvey's and decided to go to an expert to unlock some secrets that might be hidden among the ones and zeroes. I was uninspired though, given the apparent lack of interest from the Cossacks in the red Benz.

My handheld buzzed. It was Evan Pasternak.

"Denny Preston."

"Denny, greetings! I have a business rendezvous here in St. Paul and wanted to see if you could join us. Are you available?"

"Now?"

"Yes, we are at the Grizzly Parrot. We can catch up over some scotches."

"Well,...yeah, why not..I'll be there in a half an hour."

"We'll save you a seat."

The Grizzly Parrot, despite the name, is a high-end, bar-restaurant housed beneath a Hyatt in downtown St. Paul. I would need to class things up a bit, so I quickly washed up and threw on a sport coat. I would still be underdressed, but who isn't these days? I motored the seven miles, found a parking spot in level 3B of the Hyatt's underground parking, and took the elevator which opens directly into the Grizzly Parrot. Upon entering, I encountered a sleek dining room. It was throbbing with heavyweight conversations adroitly crafted with virtuoso precision in between bites sliced from thick slabs of red meat. The random snippets of conversation making their way to my ears covered subject matter indiscernible to the layman, given the vocabulary peppered with insider acronyms and sector-specific industry jargon. I felt as if I had stepped into the magneto of a finely tuned motor, the motor that made the world go around.

I spotted Pasternak at a corner booth and approached. Evan was accompanied by a dashing fellow who was introduced as Desmond Parrish. He stood about six-feet-two with rugged chiseled features and broad shoulders. His tanned face was set off by salon sculpted salt and pepper hair, brilliant perfect teeth, and the rare ability to sport a two-day growth of beard with debonair panache. When he spoke, it was with a British accent. He was a solid candidate to be cast as the next James Bond, but perhaps it was more accurate to assume that James Bond would rather be cast as the next Desmond Parrish. We concluded our greetings and settled into the booth.

"Mr. Preston, Evan here has told me all about you. He thought we'd hit it off, so I'm glad you could make it."

I picked up a pecking order dynamic that indicated Evan was acquiescent to the alpha-male Parrish. It wasn't hard to see why. Parrish was a specimen. He had a captivating aura. He oozed charisma as if he had stepped out of an imported vodka ad.

"So what brings you two to St. Paul?" I asked.

"Desmond has need of my unique abilities for a merger project involving a parent corporation in Minneapolis and a diversified agricultural enterprise in Paraguay."

"That sounds like a challenge. Talk about different cultures."

"Indeed, it is a bit of a spectral contrast, but Evan is perfect for this. There isn't any other chap I'd consider for the part," Parrish said glowingly of his new hire.

"So, you work for....?" I said looking at Parrish.

"Trentsworth."

"Industries?"

"Yes."

I don't know why I expected something other than that. I knew Pasternak was well connected there, so that was no surprise. I guess it was the breaking bread with the enemy aspect that had me ill-at-ease, bread being scotch in this case. Parrish was a Trentsworth operative and way more involved than Pasternak, who was just a contractor.

"Dennis has actually met Mrs. Trentsworth, Desmond," Evan spilled out.

"Really? Was it business?"

"Not really," I said, trying to diffuse the gravity of my sudden unexpected outing.

"He's been working on a project that appears to intersect with her life somewhere in the mix."

"A writing project? Like an unauthorized biography or something of that nature?" Parrish queried.

"Not at all, I had no idea she was even a player in the story. I probably still wouldn't if she hadn't brought it to my attention," I said trying to further downplay the seeming possibility that there was something potentially nefarious in the works.

"What did you uncover that got her attention?"

"That's the funny thing, I have no idea."

"Hmmm…that's strange," Parrish said, agreeably. "Well, good luck with your project," Parrish added, raising his glass as if to toast success.

The three of us spent the next two hours sipping scotch and noshing on Grizzly Parrot top-shelf tapas while trading stories of slaying dragons in our various chosen fields. Evan was right. Parrish and I did eventually hit it off. Underneath the sparkling veneer was a genuine guy.

Evan dismissed himself, citing an early morning meeting. I too decided to head back to my humble condo. Parrish decided to accompany me to the parking garage to retrieve some personal items from his rental car. Immersed in conversation, we exited the elevator and crossed to where my car was. Our conversation was rudely interrupted.

"Hands behind head and no business of being funny."

The voice was familiar, broken English. We both slowly raised our hands and placed them behind our heads.

"No move or shoot heads. Da?"

"Da," Parrish responded.

A car drove up behind us, the sound of a sliding door opening was soon followed by strong hands quickly applying handcuffs to both of us. Blindfolds followed soon after.

"Get in car and lie on faces."

The car was apparently a van of some sort. We were able to lie down fully. Soon after, the vehicle began moving, and we were on our way.

"Sorry about this, Desmond. I think this is my fault."

"I don't see how that could be."

"No talks," came a command from above.

The wheels were turning in my head. I couldn't understand what triggered my Russian pals to come back out of the woodwork. I could only guess they saw the meeting at the Grizzly Parrot as some sort of exchange negotiation for whatever they thought I had dug up at Harvey's place in KC. They must have constructed a storyline that had Parrish as the money guy in a blackmail scheme orchestrated by yours truly. Projecting ahead this would not end well since they were obviously after the money or the item to be purchased, or both, neither of which existed. They would never believe it no matter how much we protested. Unfortunately, Parrish was an innocent caught up in this. At the very least, I hoped I could convince our kidnappers that he was worthy of release.

Twenty minutes later, the car stopped. We were marched through a building of some sort. It was a large one given the reflected sounds from our collective footsteps and the cold air. Another door opened, this time to a smaller room. We were both seated, cuffed to our chairs, and then the blindfolds came off. That was unfortunate since we could no longer use as a bargaining chip the fact that we had not seen our abductors' faces.

I took the opportunity to look Parrish in the eye this time to apologize for the circumstances. He was surprisingly calm, perhaps coolly looking for a plan of attack to reverse fortune. Whatever he could fabricate would have to be amazing, both in strategy and execution. We were both handcuffed to steel chairs which were bolted to a concrete floor. Our captors each possessed firearms, and they put forth a posture as if this were just another day at the office. Our venue appeared, from what we could see, to be an abandoned factory - uber-cliché, but effective.

The Russians exchanged dialogue in Russian, presumably some sort of bad cop-bad cop scenario. For the most part they looked identical - shaved heads, grimy visages, even identical tattoos of some sort of eagle or stylized dragon on their outer left bicep. The only distinguishable difference was that Russian #1 had a scar on his left cheek, and Russian #2 had a tooth missing - his right incisor if my knowledge of dental anatomy was correct.

The room was unoccupied otherwise except for a steel table which held a duffle bag. Russian #2 opened the bag and produced a cattle prod.

"Oh goodie, pain!", I thought, engaging sarcastic levity as a denial mechanism to distract me from the severe predicament that was unfolding before me.

Parrish spoke.

"Preston, what's going on here? What are these guys after?" Apparently, he had exhausted plans for devising escape.

"I wish I knew, Desmond."

Russian #2 gave the prod a test run on the metal table, leaving a nasty looking scorch mark. Obviously, this was for our benefit.

"Give us what you dig from city of Kansas," Russian #1 demanded in gravelly voiced disdain.

"Guys, I don't know how to tell you this, but there wasn't anything there," I pleaded.

Russian #2 rested the business end of the prod on Parrish's left thigh and pulled the trigger. Parrish convulsed in his chair, trying not to let on to how much pain he felt. There were two holes burned through his finely creased slacks.

"Sorry, Desmond," I feebly sent Parrish's way.

"Stop apologizing," he replied. "It doesn't help, Dennis."

"You give us what you dig?" Russian #1 asked sternly in my direction.

"Guys....." I was at a loss. I could tell them a lie and say I had it hidden somewhere or make up some story. My thoughts were interrupted by intense pain, as the prod was applied to my sternum and triggered. My arms went into spasm, my shoulders were on fire. I think my heart may have skipped a beat.

"Come on, Dennis, tell them what they want to know. I have a feeling this is going to get worse, don't you?"

"Desmond, I'm telling you, there isn't anything."

"There's got to be. Why else would they be doing this?"

I hesitated to confess my charade in Kansas City, since it seemed so pathetic at the moment, but Parrish deserved to know.

"I may have given them the impression that I had something."

"Why would you do that?" he asked, followed by another convulsive reaction to the cattle prod, this time on his right thigh.

"I thought they knew what I was looking for, but it appears not to be the case."

"Brilliant!" Parrish mustered with a stiff upper lip, as he tried to sort through the pain.

We each received a total of three prod shots, the last of which for Parrish was administered *between* the legs. He passed out. I was dealing with my own pain, but it paled compared to my regrets that Parrish was involved in this and probably needed serious medical attention at this point. Russian #1 walked over to me and uncuffed me from the chair. He stood me up and turned me around. I could now see behind our chairs. There sat a large galvanized steel vat of some sort. It was about the size of a large bathtub and filled with water. I noticed Parrish was slowly beginning to regain consciousness.

247

"Get on knees," Russian #1 demanded of me. I obliged considering there was a pistol barrel resting on my temple. I was cuffed to the metal table leg which, like the chairs, was bolted to the floor.

"You watch," Russian #1 continued.

He uncuffed the barely conscious Parrish from the chair and recuffed his hands behind his back. He picked Desmond up by the hair and forced his head down into the vat causing water to splash onto the floor. Parrish's head was submerged down to the shoulders. His chest rested on the lip of the vat. The Russian held Parrish underwater for a good thirty seconds, while Parrish kicked and writhed for release. After what seemed like an eternity Parrish was let up for a brief two seconds, and then forced back into the tank. This continued at least a dozen times the last of which saw Parrish's struggle end. His body lay limp against the tank. Russian #1 grabbed the back of Parrish's belt and hoisted his lifeless body into the tank, Parrish's motionless legs stuck out of the tank like two straws in a drinking glass. Russian #1 took a moment to delight in his handiwork, then turned and fixed his steely eyes in my direction.

"Hope breath you can hold better," he said to me, laughing.

Russian #2 responded in kind. I was shaking to the core. I felt nauseous and proceeded to decorate the concrete floor with Grizzly Parrot tapas and 18 year-old scotch. I thought I might cry, but I was too scared. Adrenaline was coursing through my veins, clouding all rational thought. I tried to come up with some sort of tale to save me from the looming watery demise that was soon to be mine.

"My God! At least tell me what you think I have!" I shouted.

Both Russians moved in closer, kneeling to get right in my face.

"You have what we want. Not being truth is not good. You tell now!"

"I have nothing to tell. I wanted you to think I had something, but I don't. I have no idea what is so God-damned important that good people need to die over it!"

"This not good answer."

Russian #2 uncuffed me from the table, while Russian #1 grabbed me by the hair. The cuffs snapped back to trap my hands behind me. I was paralyzed as they led me to the tank and plunged my head down under. I was struck by the silence, and at least for the time my breath held out it was a strangely peaceful existence. But soon my body's need for oxygen forced me to take an involuntary breath, sucking in a good quantity of water. The pain was excruciating. My head was yanked out of the tank. Russian #1 yelled out.

"You tell now!"

All I could do was cough and convulse. Even if I had something to tell, I wouldn't have been able to speak coherently. I tried to breathe in, but my body was more occupied with expelling the water. Unfortunately, I got nothing in before my head was forced into the tank again. This time, the blurred, lifeless face of Parrish was directly in front of me. I closed my eyes. I lost count of how many times I was dunked, brought out, and dunked again, each dunking draining my ability that much more to hold my breath and gather air when the chance came.

Eventually, a warmth began to overtake me. My body continued to convulse and writhe, but my consciousness began to feel like it was rising out of me. I was now above the tank looking down at myself. I was at peace. Thoughts flowed freely, good thoughts, thoughts of my childhood, my mother and father, Katie, and eventually the utter joy as I relived, in vivid recollection, my first memory ever. Harvey, plain as day, was there handing me a wrapped gift. I quickly ripped the wrapping paper and there was Football Man, brand spanking new and all mine to love as my companion for life. Next, I had the indescribable sensation that it wasn't a recollection. It was as if I were living it for the first time.

Time had stopped. I was no age - child and adult all at the same time, the child wanting to know what lay ahead and the adult asking if this was all there was to my life. I didn't know the answer. How could I know the answer? How did I feel about it? What answer did I want to be the right one? The only outcome that would satisfy both was "live more, because there is much more to be lived."

Suddenly, I felt my consciousness suck back into my suffering shell. I had been pulled out from the tank again, but instead of being thrust back in, I was gently laid on the floor. I was on my side coughing up water and trying to make sense of things, when I saw a Russian fall right in front of me assuming the same horizontal plane I was on. My vision was blurred by water and oxygen deprivation, but I could see his eyes were glassy and distant, and his body twitched uncontrollably.

My ears detected a struggle between two people, then I saw another Russian crumple in the corner of the room. The sounds of struggle ceased. I rolled on my back to see what was going on. A figure kneeled over me.

"Dennis? Can you hear me? Are you all right?"

The voice registered. I searched for a match in my scrambled brain. It finally came to me.

"Danger," I replied groggily.

He responded with a sigh of relief, then....

"Can you stand? Are you hurt?"

"I think I'm OK..." I coughed up some more water.

"What the hell took so long, Danger?" I managed to wise-crack through my coughing fits. "Just so you know, I didn't tell them a thing."

"About what?"

"Wouldn't you like to know?" I continued joking.

Grainger helped me up. I noticed that Dirk was there too. The Russians were still alive. The one that landed in front of me was still out of service, as he was connected to the wires of a Taser. The other was barely coming to and appeared to have been rendered inoperative the traditional way with a good old-fashioned pummeling. Blood was pouring from his nose, and he was now minus another tooth. The violence that had just taken place began stealing my attention away from the out-of-place euphoria that was apparently a remnant of my out of body experience.

"Can you handle the cleanup here, Dirk? I'm going to get Preston out of here."

Grainger led me to the doorway out of the smaller room, into the larger abandoned factory floor, and motioned for me to wait there. He quietly walked back into the smaller room and carefully kneeled by the vat containing the body of Parrish. He reached under the vat and paused. Seconds later Parrish's body moved! He thrashed about and eventually got himself vertical on his knees in the tank. I was confounded. Resurrection powers for Grainger? That's a new one. Parrish was gasping for air. Grainger pulled a small oxygen tank from underneath the vat, said "Hi, Des," and then clocked him on the side of the head with the butt of the oxygen tank knocking him cold. Grainger looked up at Dirk and nonchalantly said.

"Take care of him, too."

Dirk calmly replied.

"NP, dude."

I had a thousand questions, and Grainger knew it. He let me know he'd fill me in on the way back.

Twenty-One

◆◆

Grainger's black Escalade was parked just outside the abandoned factory. Grainger got behind the wheel, and I dragged myself into the passenger side front. Grainger handed me the oxygen tank, and I filled my grateful lungs repeatedly with fresh, replenishing O^2 while Grainger drove. My recovery was thankfully a rapid one.

"You know we should be taking you to a hospital to have you checked out, Dennis."

"Look, I'm fine, a little dazed and sore, a few burn marks, no big deal. By the way, thanks for rescuing me."

"I suppose I should fill you in on what just happened there."

"It would be appreciated."

"What you just experienced is known in the business as the 'Innocent Minnow'."

"Minnow?"

"Yeah, so, one guy befriends the mark - that's Parrish befriending you - and if he does his job right, when it comes time to spill the beans, you gladly do so to avoid watching this innocent guy take the heat for your stubbornness. These guys knew you wouldn't cave easily if they just tortured you, but torture an innocent because of your actions, and they figured you'd roll over. If you didn't, they go on with the fake death and try to sell the you're-next-unless-you-talk angle."

"So, you don't think they were going to kill me?"

"They're not supposed to, but Constantin seemed like he was enjoying himself a bit too much there. He was getting close."

"He's the Russian?"

"Romanian actually, Constantin and Petran Dragos. They're brothers. Parrish has used them before in some unofficially sanctioned operations."

"And how does Parrish fit in?"

"He was telling the truth about working for Trentsworth Industries. We employ him, but certainly not for this operation. You see, in order for something the size of Trentsworth to function in today's complex global environment, there are any number of situations that may arise that require pushing the envelope a bit. Parrish is very skilled at that and in a way that doesn't attract attention."

"How long has he been in charge of that?"

"Twelve, thirteen years."

"And old Denny Preston comes along and asks a few questions to the random world, and all of a sudden, Parrish goes off the deep end?"

"Well, I know that sounds incredible, but that's what happened....not directly, but I don't think any of this would have occurred if the Denny Preston variable hadn't been introduced."

"Why?...That just sounds inconceivable to me."

"You see, Parrish has all sorts of security clearance and freedom to roam within Trentsworth Industries. You have to understand he has seen it all. This guy knows where the bodies are buried."

"Literally?"

"I don't know anything about any of that....It's just a figure of speech, Dennis... So, you come along and, for whatever reason, Mrs. Trentsworth takes this keen interest in whatever you are doing but doesn't let any of the inner circle types in on the secret. Again, Parrish knows ALL the dirt."

"So, let me take a stab at it, Grange. He figures this is something so big, because she is apparently hiding it from her most trusted lieutenants, that if he can get his hands on it, he can blackmail LT with whatever it is."

"Exactly, and he never had that opportunity before, because he was always hip deep in whatever muck was being handled. He was always more culpable than Mrs. Trentsworth, should any of it ever get out. He was the designated fall-on-the-sword guy. That was part of his job, really. But he thought he finally had something with leverage that didn't implicate him. He figured he could cash in if he could get his hands on it."

"So, Mrs. Trentsworth wasn't behind any of this?"

"No."

"So, how did you find out Parrish was up to no good?"

"There were suspicions for a while, just nothing we could pin to him because, well, he was good at his job. But then he got greedy and sloppy, so we put some eyes and ears on him, traced his actions. The real red flag was the purchase of the house in Kansas City."

"Harvey's old place? That was him?"

"Yes, he laundered it through several front corporations, but what he eventually tied it to internally made no sense. Once we figured that out, it all fell into place."

"So wait a minute, that was months ago. Are you telling me you knew he was orchestrating all this, and you let things get to the point where I was having a near-death experience in a dunk tank to finally pull the plug on Parrish?"

"There were no indications that he would go to the extremes he did. Mrs. Trentsworth wanted to track him to see what he might find in case you were unsuccessful."

"You mean she wanted to see if all the little ants on the anthill found a giant crumb, so she could swoop in and snatch it up."

"Look, Dennis, what can I say? After the Dragos brothers drugged you in the storage unit, she assigned me to keep a close eye on things to make sure you were protected."

"At least she put her best guy..well, guys on the case."

"If it means anything, I insisted on it, Dennis. We got here as soon as we could. We got word of Pasternak meeting Parrish and figured the con was in play."

"I suppose you have to report back something to LT, but I have to tell you, I honestly don't think there is anything out there, no giant crumb. I think everyone is chasing the most elaborate red herring ever conceived. It's all based on everyone else's assumption that the other parties are one step ahead of the rest. Look, I investigate things for a living, Grainger, and I'm just not getting the sense there is anything out there."

"Dennis, off the record, all I know is I have never seen Mrs. Trentsworth behave like this."

"Like what?"

"Oh...I don't know....obsessed?"

"About what?"

"All I can say is *she* believes there is something out there, and, if she knows what it is, she isn't telling anyone. I'd like to ask you to continue, if you can. I can even get some resources together for you."

"Thanks, but no thanks, Grange. I'm done. If there was ever a wake-up call, it's an out-of-body experience in an abandoned factory while a tattooed Romanian with a severe facial scar is trying to snuff your lights out. I have some sorting out to do before I do anything else. Besides, despite all your good words and openness here, I just don't trust LT. So, maybe I do find what she's looking for. I might never get a whiff of what it is. She'll grab it, and that's that. I have to tell you again, all my instincts say it's the wildest goose chase ever. I could spend the rest of my life looking for this...this...*whatever*. That doesn't appeal to me. I'm over it. I'm retiring from this business. I have a lot of good material, enough for a solid book. I don't need this added distraction and frustration."

"Sorry to hear that, Dennis."

"So, what happens to those guys, or do I dare ask?"

"The Romanians will be shipped back to Romania where they are sought after by the authorities for other crimes."

"I assume Parrish will be fired."

"Probably not."

"You're kidding."

"Oh, he will be dealt with. You'll find out someday, trust me on that."

"What about Pasternak, was he involved?"

"No, he was duped by Parrish too. That was all pretense for your benefit. He lured Evan with a lucrative job and used him as a prop to get to you. Pasternak's presence only served to lend credence to your meeting with Parrish as purely coincidental to erase any suspicion on your part. By the way, we'd like to keep Pasternak in the dark about this. We'll tell him the merger fell through and write him a big check anyway."

"No problem." I agreed.

Twenty-Two

◆◆

I wasn't just blowing smoke. I *was* retiring. I had a nice story about a nice man and his life-changing influence on the people he met, myself included. Granted, it didn't have the *big finish* I was hoping for, but there was a good message underneath it all. Most of all, I needed some personal time.

Whether you believe in near-death experiences or not, I do. I have to. I was there. Science says NDE is really just uninhibited chemical brain function brought on by lack of oxygen, and it's easy to dismiss it as that, until it's your brain. It took over a week to sort out the few seconds of thoughts and feelings I had while I was supernaturally separated from my physical being.

A lot of the images were merely memory replay, random moments from my childhood. I also experienced feelings, feelings unattached to any of the imagery. I felt the presence of my late father. There was no voice. There was no physical sensation, just a presence felt that language fails to describe in adequate terms.

There were other random bits, bits that seemed to be related to an unlived life, my life, but pieces of life I haven't been part of yet. These are even harder to understand since they have no relative point of reference. It was as if I were playing out pieces of life that needed to be fulfilled, reconciled before I moved on to the next life. I cannot express much more than that since these images often involved places and people with whom I was unfamiliar. Perhaps we all retain some store of life's unrealized moments, past and present, things that were sort of in queue, waiting to happen, but never were yet. Maybe these moments cling to us like static electricity, waiting for release, and, as the soul begins to unravel from the mortal coil, as death approaches, it sparks the stored energy to release and come alive in the way it was meant to be now that the physical world opportunity will apparently never happen. I know this all sounds rather trippy and cosmic, but all I have are the leftovers of something I experienced but can't explain how.

During my ordeal, after the rapid fire imagery and gamut of emotions, I was presented with a moment of slow-motion clarity. That was when I relived my first memory, Harvey giving me Football Man. My first impression was that I was simply presented with my first memory last of all, as if my grey matter hard drive had simply rewound itself to the beginning. But just as powerful was the sensation that this was not a memory, but instead a glimpse of the future. I was shown a memory, but it was not a memory. It was the future. Why present the future at the one instance in my life where there was apparently no future left to be had? Why show me a vivid image of my past as the representative vehicle of what is yet to come? This was unsettling. I could only try to dismiss it so as not to let it overtake me and rule my thoughts.

Overall, I felt changed, not transformed really, just expanded. The strange sensation I had that my condo didn't feel like home anymore was clear to me now. Simply put, I just didn't belong there anymore. My life was elsewhere, I needed a new domain. I needed to find somewhere else to live. I hadn't resolved where, but I was determined to begin looking. I took a few days to size up the local real estate market and residence options. I was quickly aware of how little attention I had paid over the years to new communities and the rebirthing of some of the older areas in the Twin Cities. Every time I returned home from residential reconnaissance, my feelings were confirmed again. It was all too obvious I had outgrown my current digs.

I was aware that not only did I need a new place to live, but I needed a new place to *live*. I needed a place to thrive with a new flow of energy more than I needed just a new floor plan. I looked at lofts. I looked at two story homes. I looked at luxury condos and townhomes. But instead of looking with an eye to functionality and affordability, my lead interest was *feel*. Sure, affordability and functionality matter, but I wanted to find the place where I belonged, not just the one that worked logistically. This was a new approach for me, so I had to practice at it. I looked at a lot of places, then one day my search ended.

The billboard said, "Discover Downtown St. Paul's Newest Neighborhood". "Discover" seemed to be the word that stuck. It drew me in. The community was a collection of three to five story warehouses that had been completely overhauled by one of the area's leading architectural firms. There were nearby shops and markets and restaurants. It was a vibrant urban center in the making. It felt right even before I walked into the building. I met a saleswoman who walked me through some finished show-units. I could see myself living there. I was ready to sign, and even though I was right at the top edge of my budget, I felt confident I belonged there and would make it work somehow. I just needed to get home, crunch some numbers and talk to a realtor friend and a mortgage lender I knew. That was until the door opened to the elevator, as I waited on the third floor. The elevator was occupied by two people, a man and a woman, a man and Katie - a man not Tom.

As the door opened, I noticed they were ending a kiss. I walked into the elevator even though leaping to the ground floor was preferable. It was a new level of awkwardness as I launched my best effort to feign an appearance that I was more pleased than ever to see her. Inside, I was devastated. I told myself I shouldn't be. "She has every right to do what she wants with whomever she chooses," I reminded myself. These were words of little comfort.

I was on such a high. I had found my new domain, but there was no way I could move in now. The place was stained indelibly, like omelets and Counting Crows. Katie tried to soften the blow by introducing everyone, as is her nature to try to turn bad into good. I don't even recall his name. I didn't want to know. All I wanted was to go back in time and tell the elevator designer to design this one elevator to go a lot faster so I could end this hell-ride sooner. I was certain I was going to burst into flames at any second and then hoped I would. After the elevator ride, we spent even more painfully long minutes discussing the location and the living facilities and how great it was to see each other. Finally, we went our separate ways. I don't remember my ride back to the condo where I didn't belong anymore. The last conversation with my mom was looping in my head, especially her words. "This could be your big chance, Dennis. You might never get this opportunity again." They echoed in my head over and over again.

I couldn't believe Katie had found someone else so fast. He was at least ten years younger than she was by my estimation. She had her arm wrapped in his. They kissed!! They drove off in his custom Audi turbo. I was fully aware now the depths of my soul that Katie had permeated so many years ago. It was fully apparent she would never be completely gone, permanently entwined in my being. I would have to live with her for the rest of my life - live with her, but without her. For the time being, my search for a new residence was on hold. Whatever confidence had inspired me before had come back to mock me.

I thought I would have to endure another couple of weeks of reorganizing my place, as I had to the last time I ran into Katie at the coffee house. Instead, mercifully, I received a call from my sister, one that changed everything, and I mean *everything*.

"Hey, sis, what's up?"

"So, I thought Jim was over this….this …disease he has."

"What disease?"

"We've talked about it. I've tried yelling at him, I've tried being the understanding wife, the non-judgemental counselor, but nothing works."

"What are you talking about, Karen?"

"Jim… He's still a kleptomaniac."

"This is the first I've heard of that."

"Are you kidding, Denny? I've told you about this at least a dozen times."

"When have you ever told me about Jim stealing things?"

"What do you mean stealing things?"

"You said he was a kleptomaniac."

"Is that what that means?"

263

"Yes, a kleptomaniac is a compulsive thief."

"Oh, then never mind."

A Pause…

"Are we done here then?" I asked.

"No, that's not it, at least it is about the klepto thing, forget I mentioned that."

"So what are you talking about?"

"What do they call it when someone can't throw anything away?"

"I don't know….*Dad*?"

"Well, he's got whatever Dad had."

"Honestly, can we end this call and try it again? I have no idea what you are trying to tell me."

"He had them hidden in the crawlspace. He never even looked at them after he put them there. He just puts 'em in there and expects some day he's going to use this shhh…."

"Whoa, Karen, chill. What in God's name are you talking about?"

"I think I have some boxes that belong to that guy."

"What guy?"

"Harold Haverson."

"Do you mean Harvey Henderson?"

"Yeah."

"Where did you get them?"

"From you."

"From me?"

"They were in the storage shed... Dad's shed.... You know last year, you brought over all the stuff..."

"You said it was all gone."

"I thought it was, but Jim went through it before I did, without me knowing about it, and found these two boxes that had some quote, *cool ashtrays,* so he stuffed the boxes in the crawlspace and totally forgot about them."

"Have you looked inside? What's in there?"

"I have to tell you, Denny, it doesn't look like much - junk, some random papers....oh..and some *cooool ashtrays."*

Her last two words were delivered in the all-world, sardonic tone that only Karen possesses. "Some random papers" is what caught my ears. I tempered my expectations and motored over to Karen's. The boxes were on her porch with a note that said "Had to run and get the kids. ...Enjoy". The last word was written normally, but I'm sure it was meant to be dripping with sarcasm. The ire fueling her sarcasm wasn't aimed at me. She has a chronic aversion to any sort of clutter, a by-product of living years under the master of all pack rats, our own father. Unfortunately for her she married one too, not unfortunate for me, I hoped.

265

I peeked inside the boxes. She was right, there wasn't much. In Jim's defense, the ashtrays were cool, hand-blown glass from some of the original Vegas strip casinos. I'd find a way to get them back to him and convince my sister they were works of art. They were probably worth several hundred dollars each, and there were a half dozen of them. Jim at least deserved that remuneration for risking his life to rescue these two boxes, even though he didn't know the importance of his actions at the time.

I decided to wait until I arrived back at my place to thoroughly examine the contents. I still had cautiously low expectations. When home, I set the unopened boxes on the coffee table and grabbed Football Man from the mantel to give him a better view. After all, he did have a hand in bringing this moment to bear. I tugged at the lid of the first box until it opened, a typical cardboard file holder. There were three ashtrays. I gingerly removed them one by one and set them by the kitchen sink. I'd wash the dust off them later then I removed everything else, which included some old matchbooks from restaurants, most probably long since extinct, some odd screws and nuts, a used paint brush, and a non-descript baseball cap, among other useless items.

So far, this wasn't promising. I moved on to the second box. There were three more ashtrays and the rest mostly papers, including an old road map of the Midwest and some odd scribbling, like phone messages. But then, at the bottom, I found three envelopes. They were business letter size and blank on the outside. They weren't sealed. I opened one. It contained several dozen uncashed checks for varying amounts dating from 1967 to 1999. There were two things in common - the Payee: Harvey Henderson, and the Payer: Trentsworth Industries. Each check had a different project number listed on the memo line, nothing more. The amounts varied from $5,000 to $47,897.00. There was one receipt as well.

Did this mean blackmail after all? If so, why not cash the checks? To make a point? That would be one hell of a point. The grand total was over $400,000! I decided to reserve judgment until the contents of the other two envelopes were known. The second envelope contained a single sheet of paper with an address and a key taped to the bottom of the sheet. The address was a storage unit. "Here we go again," I thought, "another storage unit." If the contents of the two envelopes were connected, one would have to assume the crucial item of the apparent blackmail was to be found behind the door of that storage unit.

After a pause, I slowly untucked the flap to envelope #3 and pulled out another single sheet of paper. The sheet was standard white paper, folded twice. Before I unfolded it I could see through the paper to notice it was hand written, and there was a lot of writing. I was looking forward to reading this. It was going to be some superb reading no matter what it was. I got myself comfortable, settling back into the cushions of the comfy couch for a good, long read. I read two words and stopped. I folded the page back up and returned it to the envelope. They were only two words, but they flipped the whole world on its axis.

It made no sense. What could be in the storage unit, then? I had to know and know now. I checked the address again. It seemed familiar. Of course! It was the same facility where this whole thing had started, the facility my father chose when he needed to house my parents' overflow. Harvey probably chose it for just that reason. It was convenient to the few times he came to stop in and see my parents, but how much could be in there? I got in my car and drove the few miles it took to get there. I wondered why someone would leave things in Minnesota while living in Kansas City.

I would find out soon enough. I stood outside Harvey's unit. Just three doors to the left was the unit where I spent a brisk fall day loading up my parent's stuff and eventually reuniting with Football Man. This unit was smaller than Dad's but still substantially sized. I unlocked the lock and pushed up the door to reveal boxes, more cardboard boxes. There were numbers on the side of each box. They were all taped shut. I used one of my keys to slice through the tape on one of the boxes. I opened it to find something rather ordinary, but, if what was in this one box was also in the others, it was almost unimaginable, incredible, monumental really. The tumblers fell into place. I looked at all the boxes again. The numbers made sense now. I said out loud to myself.

"He wrote it all down. The son of a bitch wrote it all down."

The contents of the storage unit were the clincher, they served to confirm what those first two words I read from the letter in the third envelope told me - that any notion of corporate espionage or blackmail was so much nonsense now. They were two words that summed up all the good things I ever learned about Harvey - words that eclipsed anything I encountered during this whole journey of discovery. Those words were

"Dearest Lillian."

It never dawned on me. It never crossed my mind. There was not one shred of anything to indicate the possibility ever existed. But, then again, it was right in front of me, the simplest explanation. Harvey and Lillian, two people from completely opposite worlds and temperament, somewhere along the way finding each other. No wonder she didn't tell her inner circle at Trentsworth Industries. It was none of their business. It wasn't business at all. This was huge, not in a story sense, but in a human sense.

I was tempted to open the third envelope again and read on, but the reason I stopped reading stopped me again. This wasn't meant for my eyes. It was meant for one person and to be delivered in person. I pulled out my handheld and texted Grainger.

"G, I found it, but I want to be the one to give it to her. Send the Lear."

He was surely back in France now. My calculations put the time at around 3:30 A.M. his time. So I would wait. I closed up the unit, and drove back to the condo still buzzing from the events of the last hour. I found my place on the comfy couch and sat in silence for nearly three hours absorbing the magnitude of what just took place, retracing my steps from the beginning of this journey. I contemplated what was about to unfold, what awaited me in France. Would it be revelatory or confrontational? I decided to go to bed and check for Grainger's reply when I woke up.

Twenty-Three

◆◆

Thump! Thump! Thump!

Someone was at my door. I threw on some jeans and stumbled downstairs. It was déjà vu. Looking through the peephole, I saw Grainger standing outside the door. He had received my text and wasted no time ushering the Lear out to fetch me. I took about ten minutes to pack a few things including a large padded envelope I put together containing the three envelopes and one of the items from the cardboard box, I opened as a sample of sorts, proof of what I had found.

The whole flight Grainger didn't ask, and I didn't bring it up. He projected an air that he understood the gravity of the situation and a respect for my side of things and my needing to be the one to deliver this to Lillian Trentsworth personally. We arrived late at night in France. The ceremonial handoff would take place in the morning. I was shown my accommodations and advised I would be awakened at 7:00 A.M., with a target time of 8:00 A.M. for breakfast. I was to bring whatever I had brought with me.

My jet-lag influenced sleep was intermittent. I had some hours to kill in my room, and the temptation to violate my own self-imposed oath not to snoop at the third letter was difficult. Grainger tapped on my door at 7:45 A.M.. I grabbed everything and followed him to a very pleasant three-season room that overlooked the French countryside. There was a roaring fire which kept the morning chill at bay. There were coffee and some of those incredible croissants, shirred eggs, and juice. I was seated at one

270

side of an eight foot dining table. Grainger left for a minute or two and returned with Lillian Trentsworth in a wheelchair. I stood and greeted her.

"Forgive me for not standing, Mr. Preston. My arthritis is at its worst in the mornings."

Some moments passed as she was assisted from the wheelchair into one of the dining chairs at the end of the table to my right. Grainger remained standing to her right.

"So, without any further ado, Grainger says you have something of interest for me."

"Yes. First, you should read this."

I extended the third envelope in her direction. Grainger stepped forward, took it, and handed it to her. She slowly opened the letter. In order to give her some measure of privacy, I chose a croissant and quietly started taking a few bites of breakfast. She began reading and gasped slightly. As she continued her hand began to shake. Grainger steadied the letter for her. Then something extraordinary began taking place. I watched in disbelief as the hardened dragon lady, the most powerful business magnate in the world, slowly let the armor plating fall away to reveal an ordinary, vulnerable human being. It was apparent that whatever words Harvey had written in his letter held powerful meaning, undiluted from the years separating the writing of them and the reading of them. She was a bit of a wreck, but it seemed to me a good wreck. Her tears looked more the kind of relief than of grief. She finished reading, wiped her eyes, and looked sternly at me.

"Mr. Preston, I thought I gave you plain instructions to leave this matter alone, that Harvard was off limits."

I couldn't believe it. This couldn't be good.

"Ww...well...yes, you did, but...."

"Thank you for not listening to me."

Her countenance softened to one of gratitude.

"Grainger, I am fatigued. I wish to go to the garden room to collect myself."

She excused herself, and Grainger lifted her from her breakfast chair back into the wheel chair and began to push. I interrupted.

"Mrs. Trentsworth, there is something else."

I extended the padded envelope. Grainger took it, and handed it to Mrs. Trentsworth who took a moment to examine it, before setting it on her lap.

"Thank you, Mr. Preston. I am eternally grateful."

"By the way, by my estimation, there are about two hundred more just like it waiting back in St. Paul."

Grainger left with Mrs. Trentsworth. I took the opportunity to enjoy some of the fine foods and the superb setting. I decided I had done something good. I wasn't entirely sure what that was, but the air of tension that seemed omnipresent at the Trentsworth estate in the brief time I had previously spent on the premises seemed to have lifted.

Grainger returned after a while.

"Mrs. Trentsworth has requested you stay the day and then fly back with me tomorrow to gather the remaining items. She would also like to request you join her for dinner this evening."

"Works for me, G."

The day involved some puttering around the Trentsworth estate. I ran into Danielle, my rescuer from the cow pasture during my first visit to France. She was attending to some landscaping on the estate. We had a good chat. I even had time to take in a wine tour of a boutique winery that caters exclusively to Trentsworth tastes. The vines are over two centuries old, and they make only a few hundred bottles each year.

As evening approached, I received word on when I was to join Mrs. Trentsworth for dinner. I cleaned up and put on some "casual" attire provided for me. There was a suit, including a tie, something I hadn't worn in as long as I could recall. Everything fit perfectly, and, judging by the quality of the complete array, the ensemble was probably worth more than my car. Normally this kind of opulence would make me uncomfortable, but strangely I was not. I had decided it was appropriate and respectful given the occasion. My normal rebellious nature would take a night off.

I was led to the dining room, which at first glance was intimidating. The table itself had to be twenty-five feet in length. It was solid cherry with gold leaf inlay and surrounded by majestic hand carved chairs with finely woven seat cushions. There was a chandelier that was definitely worth more than my car, and at least as big. The table, which would have easily seated over thirty guests, was set for only three with silver, fine crystal and, Wedgwood china. Mrs. Trentsworth was already seated. Grainger was there and looked a little uncomfortable. He was dressed for dinner. Tonight, he was not her assistant but her guest.

"I hope you enjoyed your day, Mr. Preston," she voiced in the same, post-tears softened tone from our breakfast meeting.

"I did. Most agreeable. Many thanks for your hospitality, and please call me Dennis."

"I hope you don't mind if Grainger joins us. I feel it important for him to be here, and to hear our conversation. It's high time he was aware of the reasons for all this intrigue, and because he knows me better than anyone else, I thought he should be in attendance."

While saying this, she reached out and tapped his hand looking at him more like a son than her assistant. Grainger acknowledged with a nod of tacit appreciation.

"The letter, did you read it before giving it to me, Dennis?"

"No ma'am…. Well, the first two words, but that was it."

"I'm sure that was enough to give you a sense of the subject matter. It is true Harvey and I were in love. It was a long time ago."

"What happened?"

"We enjoyed one year together, 1945. He came over and was stationed in France as part of a stabilizing force after the Normandy invasion. I was here with my family. My father was a liaison to assist in reestablishing the local provisional French governments to insure a smooth transition from the German occupation and to revive industry and culture. Father was born German and fled to America to escape the growing Nazi regime in the late 30's. Harvey and I spotted each other at a dance, talked and were immediately enchanted with each other. We saw as much as we could of each other. We were so much in love."

"How did you come to be apart then?"

"I protested vehemently. I wanted to stay with Harvey, but my father's work was done, so my family moved back to the U.S. Shortly thereafter, my life took off in a different direction. The nature of my father's work brought him into contact with a great many persons of significance. Through a sort of cultural attaché, I was noticed by a talent scout, given a screen test, and, as it turned out, I was a natural actress. Harvey stayed in France with his unit, promising to find me as soon as he returned to the states again. By the time he made it back, my film career was off and running. I was suddenly spending time and travel with elites and celebrities. Eventually, that led me to Gordon."

"I found a picture of you and Harvey in Yellowstone with some other actors. When did that take place?"

"Yes, that was Harvey's doing. He thought up the idea and suggested it. He decided to take the park ranger job right out of the military, because my film schedule would bring me to Wyoming during that summer. It was a brilliant way for him to arrange for us to meet again and spend time together. Gordon was not part of my life yet. Harvey and I enjoyed a few weeks together, promising to find a way to return to each other's lives more permanently. Harvey was going to finish out the summer in Yellowstone and then move to Los Angeles."

"But before that happened, you met Gordon and fell in love with him."

"We met, but at first, he was just a mentor of sorts. He was captivating and larger than life, at least as large as I could imagine life being through the wide-eyes of a young woman. Gordon was slowly sweeping me off my feet, but Harvey still owned my heart."

"So, what happened then?"

"As Gordon became more a part of my life, we eventually did fall in love."

It was my turn to speak, but instead I paused. I felt an unsettling feeling come over me. It must have made its way to my facial expression.

"Dennis, I can see confusion welling up in you."

I *was* confused. Within the last couple of minutes, I had heard about two people being "so much in love", and then in a flash a decision to throw all that away for a life lived elsewhere with another. Throughout this adventure, I had come to know Lillian Trentsworth as a calculating, self-absorbed, shrew, and then, just hours before, I had witnessed a pure glimpse of her humanity. I really needed an explanation. Which version of LT was the real one? She continued.

"From where you sit, based on what I have told you, I imagine my actions so long ago might come across as coldly cavalier and thoughtlessly selfish, as if the decision was an easy one, but I assure you it was quite the opposite. My decision was torturous and heart-wrenching." She paused, shook her head a bit, then said, "It must

276

sound ludicrous to hear my choice described in terms of anguish and doubts, knowing the gilded path my life eventually took."

"Well, yeah...From here, it seems you just dismissed Harvey rather unceremoniously for an existence of status and prestige."

"It was nothing of the sort. The mere appearance of it is a fanciful pretense in comparison to the actual living of it. I spent each day back then torn between two loves, two lives. There was Gordon's universe of majestic grandeur, luxury, and status, contrasted by the care-free, unassuming purity that was Harvey's. Each one spoke to a different part of me equally. I was divided, and the thought of having to make a choice was increasingly dreadful. I loved everything Harvey and Gordon were, one as much as the other.

"But, you did choose. You stayed with Gordon," I blurted.

My statement was met with silence. A troubled expression grew on her face, which told me she was still struggling with her decision. More than sixty years had come and gone, yet whatever distress had tormented her as a young woman was still operating on her to this day. Both Harvey and Gordon had died years ago, but she was still trying to sort it all out, still trying to make a decision that confronted her a lifetime ago.

"It could just as easily have been Harvey. It didn't matter, either choice was both the right one and the wrong one, and either choice was a life with someone I loved and sure to be a good life. But it also meant I was discarding another different life with someone else I loved. I prayed for some event or some other person to make the decision for me, and it never happened. What I didn't expect was to be so often haunted by the life I left behind,

277

not because of regret at making the wrong choice, but because of love that defiantly refused to be summarily dismissed."

"So why did you choose Gordon?"

"He asked me. He proposed, and I said, 'Yes'."

"So if Harvey had asked first then?..."

"Yes....maybe...I don't know...he didn't..."

It was so matter of fact, so simple and plain in its frankness. Harvey missed out on a lifetime with Lillian simply because he waited too long? I had to ask.

"Surely, you must have said something to him...to let him know?"

"I tried to reach him. Harvey had no direct telephone access at Yellowstone. I wrote some letters, but he never replied. I think he must have learned through the press. They found out shortly after our engagement and ran with it. I even traveled to Yellowstone to try to find him, but he was gone. I assumed he was heartbroken and decided he had been humiliated enough."

I looked at Lillian, her defeated expression betraying the fact that she still loved Harvey deeply. I began to see her differently, to look at her and the entirety of her life. I saw the woman she had become, the controlling, forceful being that defined the titan-like persona that rules a domain of global scale and wondered. Could the force behind it all have been the cauldron of churning grief she carried for the half of herself she had to leave behind when she forsook Harvey for Gordon Trentsworth? It was possible. I began to wonder: if she had not been faced with her impossible choice, would she have even approached being the woman she became? From the moment she chose Gordon, she was choosing to never be with Harvey again, yet he still possessed her, even to this day. Harvey's hold on her was inescapable. She spoke again, holding back tears.

"Dennis, I hope I am not giving the impression that I was not in love with Gordon. We were fabulously in love, but Harvey never left me or my heart. I expected that sooner or later my feelings would resolve, but they never did. Early on, I felt guilt over that, but eventually I found a way to see it as a blessing to love both of them."

"That's a lot to carry around for a lifetime."

"Yes, and initially it was. I struggled with it for some time. In order to survive, I realized I had to come to an understanding with myself that the circumstance of it all was how it was going to be, and that fighting it was more of a burden than appreciating it. Once I did that, there was a certain lightness to it all. My life and purpose seemed to unfold before me. Gordon and I grew even closer. He saw my potential and encouraged me to undertake the pursuits that resulted in....Well, I'm sure you know where that all ended up."

Indeed, I did. She was downplaying it greatly. A complete accounting of it could fill a large book by itself. Naming the charitable foundations and aid based corporations established by Lillian Trentsworth under the encouragement of her husband who captained the profit-based entities would comprise an all-star cast of world renowned assistance organizations. They are the bedrock to virtually the entire structure of humanitarian assistance currently throughout the world. For all intents and purposes the Trentsworth model, even decades later, is THE modern-day template for global scale medical and hunger aid. There is no telling the millions of lives fed and saved and the communities, even countries, stabilized by the pioneering foresight and good work, all at the behest of Lillian Trentsworth. For the most part, this side of Lillian Trentsworth is overshadowed by the ruthless bitch persona more favored by the agenda-driven information dispensers the world over. Unfortunately, "bad" sells more ink than "good", as a rule.

I contemplated the ramifications of her choice and the perspective now provided me by Lillian's words. I was overcome by a sense of extreme clarity and insight. I was presented with a possibility, the possibility that maybe her choice was not her choice. Choice is a relative term. We all make choices. There are those of the unspectacular variety such as, "Should I have a ham sandwich or a turkey sandwich for lunch?" Then there are those choices where the outcome might be too important to be left solely to the imperfect knowledge and the naïve unawareness of human beings alone. In these cases, where the difference between a right choice and a wrong one carries with it a greater level of risk to the whole, an unacceptable margin of negative circumstance, then one might presume "choice" could be trumped by some assistance from a guiding hand, a force beyond our direct awareness, call it "the Universe", "God", whatever you like.

I asked myself, "What if Lillian Trentsworth's gifts, at that time unrealized, were of such value to so many that instead of her choosing her life it chose her?" Perhaps her imminent role in changing the landscape of industry and technology and pioneering the advancement of humanitarian progress on a planetary scale was too important to be squandered. After all, her eventual influence could not only be described as revolutionary, but *evolutionary*. Had she chosen Harvey over Gordon, one could assume that without Gordon Trentsworth's vast resources and global-sized reach at her disposal, she would probably never have reached the rarified air she occupied. One could postulate that it might be hard to find a single person on the planet whose life was not affected in some way by Lillian Trentsworth. It would be difficult to imagine the world today without her wide-ranging contribution, and whether the average observer deem her worthy of such attention or disagrees with her methods and general disposition is irrelevant. Good or bad, she has had impact of immense proportion.

Could it be hers was a life constructed from an architecture of greater design, one that required the loss of Harvey as the furious fuel to drive the engine that yielded her many accomplishments? Was she meant to know of two destinies and suffer the loss of one, both destinies real, both alive, but presented in a physical realm that only allows one per person? There was the one she would have chosen with Harvey and the one chosen for her with Gordon - destiny number one spontaneously born of the desire of two hearts randomly encountering each other at a dance in post-war France and the second crafted by extra-natural forces carrying out some structured outcome, because there was too much at stake to be lost to another. A cosmically arranged marriage, if you will, one still carrying with it no less love than the other, but one too important to be left to the uncertainties of random chance.

It was extraordinary to fathom, a chain of thought not common to the mind of Denny Preston, one that entertained influences not readily observable in the physical realm, one that assumes interventionist behavior, one that involves…well….a god. Normally, this might bring me some level of discomfort to carry on a chain of thinking such as this, but looking again across the table at the conflicted state of Lillian Trentsworth and the clear physical manifestation of her bittersweet grief so long after the fact compelled me to consider it. She was still trying to work through it all, and this was a woman who, one could imagine, faced all manner of difficult choices throughout her illustrious life. I not only held it as a possibility, I considered it a strong probability, yet I had no arguable reason as to why I believed it except that I had a feeling about it. "So," I thought, "If her choice was not her choice, then perhaps all the events now unfolding mean to serve as some form of recompense for the choice made for her, the one she was never truly free to make for herself. The powers that be were making good on the destiny she had to leave behind, the one she missed out on with Harvey."

It was then that I arrived where I always did in my search for Harvey. Like so many others in his life whom Harvey had unwittingly changed for the better, he had done the same for Lillian. Yet, in her case the impetus for the betterment lay in his absence, not his presence. Without him, she became a world changer. I wondered if Harvey figured that out, if he had some depth of understanding of Lillian's destiny on the arm of Gordon. There was no evidence to that fact, only the knowledge that Harvey made himself no longer available to Lillian once the news had been leaked. He surrendered his pursuit of Lillian, for Lillian. Sure, his exit might have been spurred by simple heartbreak but, what if? What if he had experienced the same moment of clarity and insight that had overcome me regarding Lillian's life and destiny, but before the fact? What if?

On a personal level, I was reminded of the choice I made in my version of the same story. I lost the girl, lost myself, and made a mess along the way. Was there a destiny in my existence, a "guiding hand" that tried, but ultimately was pushed away due to my failings and inattention? I feared that ship had sailed long ago. I resumed my dinner conversation with another question.

"Why didn't you and Harvey find each other after Gordon died?"

"It was too late. We were different people. It was fifty years later. Whatever dreams and fantasies we had fashioned at such a young age about how our life would be together could never be met through the limitations of reality. We were both old and living in completely different worlds. My responsibilities would have made any time we spent together a punctuated life."

"But that was your decision. Is that actually how Harvey felt about it?"

Her composure began to crumble, to one of growing dread. Grainger noticed.

"Is something wrong, Mrs. Trentsworth?"

She began sobbing again.

"Oh, and I made sure that, if there were any chance of us spending some final years together it was dashed."

"How's that?" Grainger asked with concern.

"The last time I saw him, I blew up at him..."

The wheels began turning in my head, I exclaimed.

"Connextion,...right?"

She was a bit taken aback that I knew of that.

"Why, yes...I found out he was there and, for some reason, took it as an intrusion into my territory, not as a chance for reunion. I marched in and pulled him out of his meeting. Then, I suppose, I took fifty years of longing and frustration out on him in a matter of five minutes. He tried to tell me something, and I was so consumed with emotion that I didn't listen to what he was saying. I don't know why I was in such a state. It surprised even me. I finally had him right there in front of me, and all I could think about was that we lost out on the best years of our lives together, how self-conscious I was that I wasn't the beautiful girl he fell in love with anymore. I was all wrapped up in utter confusion at the flood of emotions that the moment presented. I asked him why he never tried to reach me. I told him I never wanted to see him again and then walked away. He was stunned and seemed to be broken."

"Why didn't you try to find him again to tell him you made a mistake."

"I was too afraid. I was mortified at my own behavior. I had destroyed what we shared together. I was afraid I'd do it again or worse. I was so confused. All those years I held a love for Harvey in my heart, and there he was right in front of me, and I became someone else. Maybe I had become someone else. I didn't want him to see what I had changed into. I wanted him to remember me as I was when we were together....I know, it makes no sense."

She began sobbing again. She was in pain. We were all in pain. After a minute or two, she had composed herself enough to say,

"After some period of time, I recalled what he was trying to tell me in that hallway through my ranting. He said something like, "I want to give you my life," or "My life is yours if you want it." I assumed he was simply wanting to rekindle something, but something about the way he said it was unusual. By the time I figured it out, he was gone forever. Whatever he was referring to was lost to me."

"Until I came along, right?"

"Correct. I discovered you were following Harvey's life, and I believed it to be my only chance. I knew you would find whatever it was he was talking about."

"Because of my skills as an investigative journalist?"

"No, because I know you, Denny Preston, you never give up."

"Not if you followed my career lately. I gave up on serious investigations some time ago. I gave up on a lot of things."

"But that's not your nature, young man. You are as stubborn as a mule."

"I am that, but…", and then I thought about it. It was time to ask a serious question.

"By the way, how did you find out I was working on a project about Harvey? That's not a common knowledge thing…that's a…"

"Beverly told me," She said interrupting me. The name was familiar. I knew a Beverly but it took a moment to put it together because I don't call Beverly by her first name. I call her, "Mom!!"

"That's right, Dennis, your own mother told me," she said with a playfully sly laugh.

"How? Torture? Threats? Snickerdoodles?" Then it all came together. "Lil…, you're Lil?!"

Mom had talked about "Lil" from time to time, but never put a last name to it. I was speechless.

"Yes, I met her through Harvey…well, because of Harvey. On a crazy whim, I stopped in once to see him when he lived next to you. It was unannounced. I was in town and mustered up the courage to try to see him. He wasn't home, but I met your mother that day, instead and we were like sisters right off the bat. You were a small child. We even talked, you and I. She was my indirect connection to Harvey's life for a time, but soon your mother and I became good friends."

"I….I…so I don't get it…When you had me kidnapped you acted like I was your mortal enemy, threatening me with abandon. Why didn't you just come clean and tell me you were looking for something of his?"

"That would not have interested you in the least, and even though I knew you were Beverly's boy, I still didn't know what you would do with that information once you obtained it. I knew you would redouble your efforts if you thought there were some sort of clandestine goings-on afoot and if you were instructed not to pursue it. If I had just asked you to find it, you might never have done so."

She was right. If she would have told me what she was after, even though she really had no idea what it was, I would have been

286

accepting a demotion from investigative journalist to private investigator. Sure, it would have been for the richest person in the world, and probably would have netted me some solid income, but I would have been less motivated to follow through to the end, especially with the passion I exhibited.

"But I talked to my mom several times about this. She knew I was working on it and never once mentioned she knew you, or…"

"When she first mentioned to me that you were pursuing Harvey's life story, I simply told her I could be of no help since I hadn't earnestly spoken to him in decades. She knew that was true, agreed, and that was that. She was under the impression the story was about what Harvey meant to you, not me. There was no reason for her to tell you."

Lillian spoke the truth. I looked back and realized that when it came to Mom, I had kept the details of what I was after regarding Harvey pretty much to myself. Mom only knew the basics, not that there was some intention to that, it just worked out that way.

"Lil…I can't believe I didn't put that together," I sighed falling back into my chair.

She smiled and paused, then she spoke.

"So it appears as though I may still get to have some measure of sharing Harvey's life with him after all. Isn't that correct, Dennis?"

"The book…books…They are diaries aren't they?… He wrote his whole life down for you, *to you,* actually."

"Yes, Dennis. I believe that to be the case. I finally have a chance to share his life now, and I would be eternally grateful if you would assist Grainger in making sure I have that chance. Would you go with him and gather the remaining diaries for me?"

"I would be honored to be part of that, Mrs. Trentsworth."

"Please, Dennis, call me Lillian."

The formal part of our meeting complete, we all took to some dining, small talk, and some exchange on what I had experienced and discovered during the journey that led me to Lillian Trentsworth's dining table.

I also asked about the stack of uncashed checks I found in envelope number one. She explained that, from time to time, she would send Harvey some money as a gesture to help him out. She meant not to try to buy him off, just to help him out in some small way. She said he only cashed one and that he simply signed that one over to a charity. Why he kept the others will remain a mystery. Placing them with the other two envelopes would imply he had clear intention to return them, to draw attention to them. It is unknowable if there was some sort of message in doing that. My suspicion is that these checks were his lone indication throughout his life that he was still present in Lillian Trentsworth's thoughts, that he still mattered to her. Maybe he kept them as a sort of touchstone to inspire him to keep writing. Perhaps, after he had put down his pen for good, he felt some measure of responsibility to return them as a reciprocal gesture of thanks or closure, so he put them in the box. But, it's impossible to know for sure.

After dinner, Mrs. Trentsworth retired for the evening. Grainger was given the night off, and we made our way to another wing in the estate that housed a billiards table once owned by Teddy Roosevelt. We sipped Armagnac brandy and shot billiards for hours, surrounded by a gallery of presidents, statesmen, and celebrities captured in portraits and candid photographs. Grainger, whom I now consider my good friend, let me in on some bawdy stories involving some common household names, but those conversations were off the record and won't be repeated here. At around 2:00 A.M. we retired to our rooms to get some sleep for our long journey home.

By 10:00 A.M. we were airborne and settled in for the long flight back. Grainger had some paperwork to manage, so I kicked back. Several hours into the flight Grainger handed me a familiar envelope and said.

"She wanted you to read this."

It was the third envelope.

Dearest Lillian,   *March 23, 1998*

My forever love. Our parting in France so many years ago is as if it was just yesterday. Despite the distance, I spend every day with you in my heart. I tell you my hopes and my dreams. I share my disappointments and frustrations. For some measure of time, I waited, hoping destiny would change its mind. But as the days mounted, I realized our life together would

289

never be more than what had already been, and perhaps that is the way it is meant to be.

I resolved that what couldn't be didn't mean that you would not have to lose the moments of a life that bless me each day. As days passed, I believed them to be wasted if not shared with you. So, I have written my life down for you, being with you the only way I am allowed to be. It fills me with pleasure to know that, possibly some day, you will be joining me, reading my life, one day at a time.

My first choice would be to simply deliver them to you, to give them from my hand to yours. But, instead, I am choosing to entrust them to the same fates that brought us together and then found favor in never again seeing us rejoice in the full richness of what we found for that brief time. I feel it only appropriate then to leave the delivery of such important goods to their discretion, so that whatever they decide may be a demonstration once and for all that our lives were joined not temporarily, not haphazardly, but with the intention that our love can traverse great distance and time, and that it was guided by forces beyond just you and me, and still is.

Therefore, I release these written thoughts and feelings that encompass the entirety of my life. I trust them to be brought to you by whomever and whenever fate sees fit. If you are reading this, then rejoice, as it is confirmation that we are bonded together forever and that wherever I remain, in this life or the next, I will wait for you. I will wait with a jubilant heart, reveling in the joy that we will once again be together, this time without the impediments and constraints of lives that must be lived apart.

Love Forever,

Harvard

So there it was, a lifetime declaration of love carried out on a daily basis as one lifelong act of monumental devotion. He wrote it all down, to and for the benefit of just one other person, someone he knew he would never see again, someone who might never even read the words. The years of writing alone was an achievement beyond most anyone else's consideration or desire, but it was an inspired triumph to then risk it all in an act of pure, unadulterated faith by hiding his writings so that they could only find the light of day through a series of improbable events. He did it as a means to demonstrate and underscore his deepest beliefs to the one he wrote it to. It was his way of witnessing that he knew some portion of their souls were undeniably connected by love and could not be restrained. He seemingly resolved that regardless of the events that left him unrequited, he would give of himself for her sake. He realized the agony of her choice, or perhaps not her choice, moved past his own grief, and chose an act of healing and forgiveness to be his monument.

I tried to think of just one thing in my life to which I committed even a fraction of Harvey's level of devotion, perseverance, and faith, and I couldn't even come close. I even threw in the towel on this very project. In the end, *it* had to come find *me*.

But, is it faith or foolhardy romanticism? A cynic would relegate the entire matter as an exercise in overarching corniness and futility. I wondered if in a weak moment I might be that cynic. But I lived it. I was there, and I am now a true believer. Corny or not, it had the impact to humble one of the planet's most callused individuals, Lillian Trentsworth. It was clear to me in the physical change I witnessed in her, once she was presented with the entirety of Harvey's handiwork all else was rendered pale in her life, it seemed undeniable to me that her soul was clearly transformed, perhaps even redeemed. She was gifted back the half of her life she left behind when she said "I do" to Gordon Trentsworth. I don't care how averse you are to sentimentalism one has to respect the power in that.

It was all too soon that we landed in Minneapolis. Grainger had arranged for a truck rental. We drove straight to the storage unit, and in a matter of fifteen minutes, we had loaded the boxes. Grainger took me home prior to heading back to the airport to deliver the precious cargo to his employer. I felt a tinge of emptiness knowing the journey had come to an end. I sat on the comfy couch in my now stale feeling condo. Football man was sitting in his place on the mantel. So much had transpired, especially in the last few days, but it occurred to me that my role was really one of spectator. Sure, I had been the point man for almost everything that had unfolded. I was at the center of it all but not the subject of it all.

Don't get me wrong. I was grateful to have been included in the events, to have seen and experienced the happenings as they played out. But I now detected an unexpected sense of envy for those now made whole. I wanted to be in that place, too. I suppose it might be akin to a play-by-play announcer and how he might feel witnessing the champagne soaked celebration of his team having just won a championship, the simultaneous experience of being part of it, but not part of it.

I was sure some of the emotion was just the result of a great deal of excitement followed by an abrupt ending. Maybe it was simply withdrawal. I had spent over a full year of my life chasing a story in the company of all manner of rich, vibrant characters, dangers, and new places, and then the merry-go-round abruptly stopped. I didn't feel changed or transformed, and this disturbed me to some degree. Sure, I had the story, a great one, and I would finish writing it. But my biggest concern, my immediate sense of unease, was why I wasn't a much different Denny Preston. I wanted to know I was noticeably changed for the better. For if the events of the last year of my life were not enough to spawn a metamorphosis, then I feared nothing could.

Twenty-Four

◆ ◆

Five months had passed since closing the final chapter on Harvey's life. I had resolved that a search for some sort of personal, defining assessment of what I was to take from all of it was the wrong approach. Sure, I had changed a little, engaging in some small but unusual acts of kindness, unusual for Denny Preston at least. I remembered to contact some industry insiders on behalf of Julie, the journalism major from Hays, Kansas. She landed a staff writing position at a small, but full-of-potential, blogging operation. I wrote a freelance piece on the Crazy Horse Café and made sure it found its way into a wide circulation travel magazine, hoping Wolf Schuster would benefit from that publicity. But, locating some tangible, before-and-after reckoning that would signal a purposeful seed-change in my life was not to be found. I wanted an epiphany, but it never came.

Epiphanies are events that cannot be conjured up on demand, though. I decided to stop searching for some seminal masterstroke and eventually came around full circle realizing Harvey was not about epiphanies. He was about being Harvey, and that was enough. That's where I drew the line on before and after. "Just be Denny," I told myself. "I am a storyteller, and a storyteller I shall be."

One crisp Tuesday morning, I received a phone call from Grainger. He delivered the sad news that Lillian Trentsworth had died. I felt fortunate to have known the genuine Lillian Trentsworth. I was honored to be considered someone worthy of notification prior to issuance of a general press release. The news itself would surely be global in scope, so I was grateful to be one of the few privileged insiders. I was in good company, as the next person on the list to be notified was my mom. Grainger, acting beyond the call of duty, had made arrangements for door-to-door transportation from our respective homes to the Trentsworth estate in France.

The funeral was grand, a stirring honor to the great Lillian Trentsworth, both through her accomplishments and her positive global impact across seven decades. The funeral was attended by an eclectic Who's-Who representing industry giants, diplomats, ex-presidents, prime ministers, and even a lowly freelance journalist and his mother. My mom and I stayed through the weekend, Mom taking the opportunity to show me around some of the haunts and personal sanctuaries she and Lillian shared in their few times together in their little corner of France. Unfortunately, the trip didn't include any time with Grainger. He was occupied with the considerable administrative duties that come with tying up the loose ends of a life that reached as far and wide as Lillian Trentsworth's did.

Mom and I traveled back to the states the way we came, as passengers together on our own Lear jet. We had long since had the "Why didn't you tell me you knew Lillian Trentsworth?" discussion, but we still mused about how even the most casual mention at any time during the Henderson journey could have changed the face of everything. For my part, I was satisfied with how it all played out. Had I known sooner than I did, I might have missed out on some meaningful experiences, although I could have gone through life just fine never meeting the Dragos Brothers.

In the meantime, I did receive one e-mail from Grainger that simply said, "This will interest you," accompanied by a link to a New

York Times online article. The article regarded an announcement by the government in Myanmar that a rebel resistance group had been quashed thanks to intelligence received from an anonymous source. The part I would be interested in was information uncovered in the investigation which led to a U.S.-based front organization headed by none other than Desmond Parrish.

The article said Parrish faced possible extradition to Myanmar where he would most likely face execution. The article also stated extradition in matters of this nature was rare, but that the investigation unveiled additional myriad illegal activities including arms dealing and money laundering for heroin cartels. Parrish was in deep sheep dip, but would probably not pay with his life, at least not completely, rather through spending some substantial number of years in U.S. Federal prison. I suspected the scales were balancing on his "cooperation" with the investigation, which probably included keeping Trentsworth Industries' name out of it. But that's just my speculation, I would have no other way of knowing that, of course....

◆ ◆

Six weeks post-funeral, my condo door rang out a familiar "Thump! Thump! Thump!" It didn't seem possible, but when I opened the door, I was greeted by my good friend, Grainger. He wasn't alone. This time, his sidekick was much more agreeable than the usual gorilla that accompanied him, a.k.a. Dirk. No, this time it was a more beautiful, but still familiar face. It was Danielle. Grainger and I shook hands, and Danielle passed up the same for a giant hug.

"Wow! What brings you two to St. Paul?"

"Actually, you do, Dennis," Grainger said matter-of-factly.

"Moi?" I responded.

I offered to make some coffee or break out something a little more celebratory, even though it was before noon, but there was no interest. We sat down in my slightly unkempt living room.

"We have some news for you," Danielle said, about to burst. Grainger tapped her knee as a tempering gesture.

"Dennis, although not the executor, I am a representative of the Trentsworth estate, and even though there hasn't been an official reading of the will yet, I am authorized to tell you that you have been given right of first refusal as the official Trentsworth biographer. She requested you be the one to tell her story, and Gordon's too, should you decide you want to do that. You will have full reign of the estate grounds. You will have unprecedented and exclusive access to any personal archives, unclassified business related material, and so on."

"I....I'm speechless, Grainger....How?....Why...?"

"You don't really need to be told why, do you?" Grainger said, incredulously.

"Well, ...I don't know... that's pretty huge, Grange."

Grainger looked at Danielle, and then looked back.

"That's right. You really don't know the rest of the story."

"Story?"

"Well, I took the Henderson diaries back, and Lillian tore into them. She abandoned all else, choosing instead to read every one of those diaries cover-to-cover in chronological order. It took her four months. In that time, she became a changed woman. I truly believe she lived a second life, dare I say a better, more personal life through those books. It was incredible to see her energy level increase, she almost seemed to get younger by the day. She even stopped using her cane."

"What do you think it was Grainger?" I asked.

While Grainger thought about it, Danielle jumped in.

"Even though he could never be with her, he shared his most treasured moments in her company, imagining she was there with him. He carried on a lifelong conversation with her in written form. He resurrected the life she never got to live, the one she thought she had lost forever."

I sat somewhat amazed at Danielle's words, but not surprised. Even without reading them myself, it confirmed what I had believed, that the words contained in those diaries, although not a substitute for the real thing, served as the way for Lillian to recapture the half of herself she left behind with Harvey so long ago. Apparently whatever he wrote had the desired effect given the changes observed in Lillian.

"After she finished the final diary she glowed for days. She was so happy. Within two weeks she just passed."

"Her heart stopped like it had just run out of beats." Danielle interjected.

"As if the last grain of sand in her hourglass had finally fallen." Grainger added.

The hourglass reference echoed back the exact words of Dorothy Trombley about Harvey's death. I wasn't surprised at hearing of the suddenness of her death upon the completion of Harvey's diaries. After living in his universe, there was nothing left to keep her on this Earth. Whatever import the responsibilities and weighty matters of her life as industrial titan possessed must have withered away when held against the renewing spirit found in Harvey's world. I'm sure she was ready to trade everything in for a leap of faith that what waited for her on the other side was the continuation of what she found in the diaries. Except, this time, it would not be read, but lived. I had a sense she made her peace with this life, realized it had nothing left to offer her, and bowed out with no regrets.

During my pause to ponder I noticed the body language of Danielle and Grainger. As if I wasn't curious enough that they showed up together, it was clear these two were an item. The ring on Danielle's left ring finger was the clincher.

"Congratulations are in order, it would seem," I proclaimed.

Danielle flashed her rock which had to be every bit of 3 karats.

"It was Grandmother's. She gave it to Grainger before she died with her blessing," Danielle confessed. (In truth, Danielle is LT's grandniece, but she called her Grandmother.) I processed her sentence, shook my head, and raised my index finger as if to scold both.

"Good cop, bad cop, huh?"

They looked at each other and smiled, then nodded affirmatively.

"That's just downright devious," I said admiringly.

The full deception unfolded before my eyes. I flashed back to the first trip to France when I was marched in front of Lillian Trentsworth, who drew on her acting talents from long ago to convince me of her ire and to create an atmosphere of animosity. Then, after being deposited in the cow pasture, I was "rescued" by Danielle. She was the real interrogator. She broke me down with hard labor, and then plied me with fine wine, succulent coq au vin, and pleasant female company to distract my attention from the true purpose, which was to pump me for information about what I was up to.

"Look, Dennis, Lillian had to find out what your intentions were and where all this might lead. She knew there was something out there and wanted to be sure you were sincere. There had to be some deception involved to put one past your keen investigative abilities," Grainger explained.

"I suppose, but it's still a little puzzling, since she knew my mom and could simply have asked her."

"Mrs. Trentsworth was a firm believer in looking into someone's eyes to find out the truth. She brought Danielle in for good measure."

We spent a little time catching up. Grainger and Danielle were enjoying a little leisure travel for a while, eventually planning to head to Northern California where Grainger's family lived. They would be married there, and then off for a month long honeymoon in several destination spots across the South Pacific. Beyond that, they had no plans. I was advised he would contact me when the LT biography project would be underway. I also learned there would be a sufficient trust set up to expense the project from which I would be compensated for my time and that all proceeds from the book would be mine to keep as well. I guess that meant I had a job lined up for some time now - a solid job - and one that would be meaningful.

There was one more thing, something completely unexpected. When we said our good-byes, Grainger reached into his blazer and pulled out an envelope. He handed it to me, looked me in the eye, and sternly said,

"Mrs. Trentsworth gave explicit instructions that I was to hand this to you in person."

He handed me the envelope and said,

"She said this would mean something to you and that you should act on this without hesitation."

I raised an eyebrow, curious as to what that might mean. Grainger and Danielle left, and I returned to the comfy couch with envelope in hand. I waited before opening it to ponder what her words might have meant. I drew a blank, and decided I would just open the envelope. Inside was a folded piece of paper with a lone receipt inside. It looked familiar, and after a second or two, I recalled it was the receipt that was tucked in with the stack of checks that Harvey had in the file box in the first envelope, the stack of checks sent over the years by Mrs. Trentsworth to Harvey.

The folded piece of paper was a handwritten note from Lillian Trentsworth. It said,

"Dennis, take a closer look. I'm sure this was meant for you."

I looked at the receipt. The amount was for $36,875.00. An amount attributed to "check 13458". The receipt was dated August 9, 1998. I remembered Lillian Trentsworth mentioning that Harvey never cashed any of the checks, save one, which he gave to "some charity". The next stop for my eyes was the actual name of the charity. The name recognition was instantaneous. I gasped. Adrenaline shot through me and up my spine. It was impossible what I was seeing.

I gently set the receipt on my coffee table and walked to a kitchen cabinet I refer to as my Private Reserve and found a bottle of whiskey. I took a big shot, and then another. I set the bottle down and slowly returned to the coffee table to reread the receipt, in case I had misread before. The charity name was the same.

I began deconstructing the event using logic as my means to prove coincidence, arranging thoughts to calculate the probabilities that there was a simple, rational explanation for what this lone receipt was trying to commit me to.

"So, Harvey gets one of these checks. At the same time, he has some contact with my mom who mentions this fledgling charity that collects unused, discarded materials from construction projects and then employs a network of charitable entities to redistribute the materials to non-profit, neighborhood renovation programs. He is so impressed, he signs the check over. As a matter of fact, he is right here visiting my parents, that's why he chooses to donate to a local charity. And then he takes the receipt and puts it in one of the boxes my parents saved for him. He puts it in the stack with the other checks as a token placeholder for the check that was signed over, an accounting thing, that's all. Then he leaves the boxes behind by accident, and they end up in my dad's storage unit. That's all it is, a massive coincidence. Whew!! No further action needed."

I moseyed back for another shot of whiskey as celebration that I was not now the object of some intentioned plan set in motion years ago. But then logic turned against me. Sure, there was a lot of junk in those file boxes, but one thing was for sure, the contents of those three envelopes was most assuredly intentional. The checks, the storage key, the letter to Lillian Trentsworth - all had purpose. The receipt had meaning too, and the only person it would have meaning for was me, and that was seconded by Lillian Trentsworth's insistence that Grainger hand-deliver the receipt. This was no accident.

Twenty-Five

◆ ◆

Harvard Wilson Henderson was born May 25, 1922 to Norman and Ernestine Henderson in Independence, Kansas. In 1932, the family moved to Hays, Kansas when Norman decided to try his hand at running a small dairy farm. It was a bold move given the state of the country's economy. It was just a few years into the Great Depression, and Kansas was also under siege from the effects of the Dust Bowl, but Norman was more inclined to stake his family's fortunes on his own enterprising spirit rather than pinning their hopes on someone else's in such uncertain times.

Harvey was an only child, an unusual circumstance in the days when larger families were the rule, especially in rural farming and agricultural communities. In the long run, it was an advantage to the family to be smaller than most. Larger families struggled to keep everyone fed and clothed, but since it was just the three Hendersons, they got by. It was a modest existence, but they never felt the extreme desperation experienced by so many others during such trying times.

After graduating from Hays High School in 1940, Harvey remained in Hays, helping his father with the dairy operations. He remained there until 1942, when he volunteered for the Army. His tour of duty included time stationed in Belgium, Italy and, of course, France, at different periods during the war effort. He never saw combat. His contribution was made behind the scenes performing logistical duties surrounding provisioning and supply management.

Perhaps his crowning achievement came in his contribution to the coordination of an operation for a convoy system of supply management called 'The Red Ball Express'. With all French railway systems destroyed, the Allied forces were faced with the gargantuan task of supplying the rapidly advancing D-Day forces as they progressed through Europe, primarily France. Harvey's contribution was to provide organizational strategies to a system of retrieval, refill, and redistribution of gasoline cans.

Patton's army alone consumed 380,000 gallons of gasoline per day, almost all of it supplied five-gallons at a time in standard issue "jerricans". In order for the troops to continue forward, there needed to be fuel. To complicate things further, there was a shortage of the cans themselves. It was imperative that the scattered, spent cans be collected, refilled, and sent forward to the front lines as quickly and as safely as possible. Once France was liberated from the Nazi's, Harvey remained there as part of a stabilizing military presence. In 1946, Harvey was honorably discharged.

He returned to the United States, landing a summer job as a park ranger in Yellowstone National Park. Later that year, Harvey returned to the dairy industry progressing through a variety of jobs in Wisconsin and Iowa. In 1953, Harvey was thirty-one years of age. The previous seven years provided him with a patchwork of management skills which he brought with him in an expanded role as a manager in charge of the transportation and distribution.

The rapidly developing U.S. interstate highway system provided a new frontier of regional transportation options heretofore relegated to reliable, but limited, destination rail transportation alternatives. Highways provided opportunities for more distant providers to reach closer to and more directly target smaller markets once thought impractical and economically unviable for perishable dairy products. Harvey's responsibilities revolved around establishing relationships with retailers in newer, developing areas west of the Mississippi, coordinating distribution routes and delivery schedules. He was essentially reliving his days in The Red Ball Express except instead of supplying Patton's army with gasoline, he was bringing gallons of milk and cartons of eggs to the households of the western United States.

After a highly successful four-year tenure in dairy distribution development, Harvey abruptly decided to walk away and instead pursue his nagging-itch fascination with an industry trying desperately to emerge from its embryonic stages, that of computer technology. Although lacking any formal education in computer sciences, Harvey began cutting his teeth in the practical application of computers for everyday use. Harvey found his niche freelancing as a beta-tester for some of the early stage prototypes of "small-use" computers.

In the summer of 1962, after successfully scratching the computer bug itch, Harvey again began dabbling in odd jobs. He opened an ice cream shop, which expanded into a combined hot dog stand and ice cream shop, which eventually grew to be a popular full-blown diner. The diner was located just off Interstate 70, which was a perfect location for attracting East-West travelers.

By 1973, his days in the diner business had grown stale, and he decided to sell and look for something with more normal hours. It had been over 15 years since Harvey left dairy, but before long, Harvey was back in the swing of things as a distribution manager. Barely six months in, Harvey had outgrown the distribution job and was asked to spearhead a project to investigate feasibilities for "stabilized dairy proteins" in the growing market of frozen and non-refrigerated foods. For the layman, that would mean developing uses for dairy derived food substances that can retain a consistency in flavor and molecular stability for long periods in frozen cuisine as well as in non-temperature reliant foods.

The results came in the emergence of flavored potato and tortilla chips, especially cheese based flavorings, cream sauces in frozen entrees, fitness based protein beverages, and powdered coffee creamers, to name a few. The project was a success, and although Harvey was never directly involved in the actual development of the products themselves, he was instrumental in coordinating the effort as the project manager. Harvey lasted six years in this second stint in the dairy industry, when he decided to bow out from the grind and take respite in something a bit more "colorful" - restoring grandeur and dignity to Victorian homes in the small California coastal town of Mendocino.

Harvey's days on the ladder were fulfilling enough that after four years, at sixty-one years old, he decided on something less physically demanding. He also needed to consider that a time might come soon when retirement was a necessity. He did still have a modest sum remaining from the sale of his diner, so he didn't need anything that would bring in a substantial salary. He was comfortable with a retirement of modest proportions. Harvey had never had a taste for a big ticket lifestyle anyway, so he was content to find a steady job and settle in somewhere.

Harvey determined Kansas City was the place to plant his roots. He took a position in a customer service call center for an insurance company. He was fast-tracked into a management position, remaining at the company for eight years, retiring at age sixty-nine. Harvey lived out his days as Harvey loved to live. He reconnected with some old friends, traveled a bit, worked part-time here and there, and then one night, his heart just stopped.

◆ ◆

When viewed in a nutshell, when seen from afar in abbreviated terms, Harvey's life brings words to mind like ordinary, typical, normal, and average. The vivid complexity of a person's life is lost in the rote recitation of dates and occupational accomplishments. Too often, lives are summed up in this "obit" style of people, places, and things. When presented as such, lives become freeze-dried and sterilized, but so often it is this shorthand version that becomes the inadequate two-dimensional representation of a greater human soul.

More and more, ours is a society of measured achievement, success that is defined solely in tangibly concrete ways. In order for the ever-shortening collective attention span to recognize meaningfulness, it has to be presented loudly in headline form. It has to be condensed and concentrated, or it will fall by the wayside surrendering to the next wave of concentrated info-data. It's the commentary of our age. Branding and single image recognition rule the day, and anything more intricate and subtle gets buried.

I say this merely as observation and not to pass judgment, nor to necessarily criticize a résumé version of a given life. There is a place for it, but it can't become our yardstick. It results in a world where, when we search for our heroes, we cast our gaze on the brightest stars. We turn our heads towards the loudest fanfare. To be fair, much good comes from works of greatness performed under the highly publicized spotlight. Often, along with the brazen attention grabs and look-at-me acts disguised as unselfish compassion yet designed mostly to bring highly visible, collective praise to the doer. We still find that diseases are cured, mouths are fed, and suffering eased. There is no need to fully discount works that result in lives saved, even if the primary motivation of the given life saver is to draw attention to themselves. Bottom line, a life is saved.

But overlooked go the multitude of great acts and selfless deeds that happen under the radar or that even the doers may not know of themselves. There is no measure or way to ever know of the impressions made or inspirations received every day from persons interacting with other persons. Words need not be exchanged, no emotional intercourse need take place for a moment to yield a life-altering observation or molecular level transformation in another's behavior. No epiphany need be experienced, no fund-raising goal or majestic metamorphosis need be reached to set another life on a better course.

I honestly don't know what Harvey Henderson's intentions were at any given time. It seems he was a good man. It seems he was a thoughtful person with a healthy curiosity for life, but it's impossible to know from where I sit, where his heart truly resided. We have to be resigned to that incompleteness. But, we do know this, something even Harvey might never have even known, he had an influence. He had an effect on others. He changed lives for the better. It's not really that important to know if he set out to do that, just that he did it. The net result was a positive one, and that's what really matters.

Unremarkable... Uneventful... was the life of Harvey Henderson, at least as defined by the spotlighted, sound-bite, headline-driven world we live in. But when considering the unquantifiable realm of unknown influence, the unnoticeable, indelible marks made on the spirits of others, we cannot say those two words. To be sure, we have to say the opposite. When we try to assign a specific value, we find no currency exists. When we try to posit a definitive equation, we find the variables flutter off like so many butterflies. We are relegated to a simple admission that there is a cause and effect, there is an increase in the wealth of the collective soul. There seems to be purity in that, and we must leave it there.

Twenty-Six

◆ ◆

I read it over and over again thinking it would change, a trick of the brain maybe. It never did. Harvey signed check 13458 over to The Grandheim Foundation. I could have rationalized that off as extreme coincidence, but the signature on the receipt made that a laughable proposition. The signature was that of a Katherine Langdon. Now, I know from personal experience that no one calls her Katherine. She goes by the name of Katie.

My mind was reeling. Seriously, how could he know? It had to be Mom. In fact, my earlier deconstruction was probably correct except for the complete purpose behind Harvey's donation. I'm sure he did find the foundation a worthy recipient based on the good work they do, but I have no doubt the catalyst to inspire the act itself was some conversation he had with my mother. I'm sure it was an innocent conversation. Mom was probably answering a typical small talk question of Harvey's, something like "How's Dennis doing?" Mom simply answered and took the conversation down the Katie path. The exact conversation is irrelevant. Something about it compelled Harvey to take a trip to The Grandheim Foundation, seek out Katie, sign over the check, and then plant his receipt among the rest of the items of import in his cardboard box time capsule.

Sure, it could be mere coincidence, but what if it wasn't? For me to ignore that this was an intentional act would be to disgrace all that had come before since that first day in my parent's storage unit. I had to follow through. There was no other option.

I thought to wait a day or two, but I knew it would just eat away at me and fester into some minor neurosis. Strangely, I recalled the tow truck driver from Story City, Iowa. The last comment he made to me was as vivid as if he were telling it to me at that very moment, "you will know exactly what you need to do to get back on the correct road," and "you'll know when to do what you need to do. Just pay attention!!" So I did. It had to be today. Just get it over with. If there was some element of fate involved, then whatever needed to happen, would happen. I cleaned myself up a bit, got in the car, and drove the fifteen minutes or so it takes to get to the downtown offices of The Grandheim Foundation.

My hands were clammy. My stomach was churning. My breathing became a bit choppy as I watched the floor numbers count off above me inside the elevator. I tried not to think of the gravity that was weighing on me. There was a lot of anxiety in knowing there was some architecture to the moments that soon awaited me once I stepped off the elevator to the front desk. Add to that the likelihood that what I would probably face at best was some sort of dressing down, or worse, a categorical rejection.

It was not as if Katie was going to ridicule me. That's not her nature. She would say something like the timing was bad, given her recent relationship with Audi Turbo Guy, or something like, "Dennis, that's so sweet, but that was years ago. Our time has passed, and we've both changed so much...you know."

Despite those distasteful scenarios, it became apparent that what scared me the most was falling into the bleak depths where absent is the belief that there can be magic in small, simple acts performed by good people - acts carried out with, or even without, intention that might forever change the course of a single wayward soul, or perhaps, in this case, two. I realized, if the moment that soon awaited me is merely a wrong turn, a misinterpretation, it meant that what I had clung to as unmistakable truth that the world is only made up of cold hard fact and concrete reality, it would only serve to solidify my subscription to that staunch mind-set, and I would operate from there for the rest of my life. But, if indeed there were forces at play managing providential outcomes, this would be the defining moment for that reality to reveal itself to me. There was a lot riding on this. It was more than just something about me and Katie.

The door to the elevator opened. Straight ahead was the front desk brandishing the familiar Grandheim Foundation logo featuring the signature "GF". I approached the receptionist and began to ask, "I'd like to see Katie…." Out of the corner of my eye, I could see her seated in a fish bowl conference room. A couple of seconds later, she looked up and spotted me. She rose from her chair and walked out toward me. She stopped at the fish bowl doorway and silently mouthed my name while carrying a look of concern on her face. I'm sure she had to think something was seriously wrong. For me to show up in person, she had to be thinking there was some bad news afoot.

She motioned for me to come over to her. I walked the ten or so steps.

"Dennis? Is everything OK?"

"Oh, I don't know," I said with a mild sigh, then mumbled to myself, "I guess we'll find out soon."

"Pardon?....Seriously, Dennis, if there is something wrong, *please* tell me now."

I looked at her and gave her a reassuring smile. She relaxed her posture and tilted her head a bit which was Katie's empathy tell.

"What's up, Dennis?" she said, returning a smile.

"Look, is there somewhere we can talk... in private?"

She opened the conference room door and addressed the gathering seated there. "Hey, everyone, let's finish this up later. I think we have enough figured out to keep us busy for a while. We will reconvene at two-thirty tomorrow."

When the room had emptied, Katie and I entered, and Katie closed the door. I looked out over the city skyline, which was framed in the conference room's thirty-third story picture window. A feeling of calm washed over me. I decided I would take some time getting to the point, or it all might sound a bit much.

"So, do you recall around 1998 a fellow coming into your office and signing over a thirty-six-plus thousand dollar check?"

"I do indeed. The largest walk-in donation we've ever had. Was it really that long ago?" Katie scraped her memory to garner verification that the date was in 1998. "Let's see, that was in the Halston street office so....yeah.. I guess it was that long ago....Geez...Why do you ask?"

"Do you remember his name?"

"Oh...no...I guess I should...I'm sorry I can't help you. I suppose we could look in the files if you really need the name. It's kind of bending the rules, but I think you can be trusted," she said, smiling again.

I thought about what she said, that I could be "trusted". I decided to bypass my usual internal conversation about how undeserving I was of that and move right ahead.

"Oh, I don't need his name. I know it."

"That sounds serious...are you investigating him?"

"In a manner of speaking. Do you recall the book I have been working on?"

"Sure...the one we talked about?"

"Yes, well, that was all brought about by a...well...it's hard to describe, but a personal moment that sparked a literary expedition that...well....It all centered around this guy. His name is...was....Harvey Henderson."

I pulled the receipt out of my pocket and handed it to Katie. She took a few moments to read it and let it soak in.

"Wow...... so you found this in your investigation. What are the odds?"

"Exactly...."

She paused to process the scope of the moment, the improbability and the incredulity of it all. She looked up from the receipt and looked at me.

"You know, I remember this now, he insisted on me helping him, asked for me by name."

So my theory about Harvey's action being prompted by a conversation with Mom seemed likely.

"This was purposeful.....from twelve years ago......this must be some kind of sign or something," Katie concluded.

She was always more dialed into the world of happy accidents and unexplained coincidence than I was, so it wasn't a leap for her to see the connections involved in mere seconds, when it takes me...well, more than a year. I could see her eyes begin to cloud with tears, but unfortunately not the joyful kind, they were the sad kind. I was puzzled and began to prepare myself for the worst, one of the "bad timing" scenarios I contemplated in my ride up in the elevator.

She turned to face the picture window, facing away from me. She began sobbing, I stifled the urge to approach and comfort her, something I had done so many times years ago. It was a reflex. She collected herself enough to say.

"It's karma... It's time to clear the air, Denny."

"Oh Boy," I thought, "Here it comes." But she was right. It was time to release the unspoken words from long ago, but she beat me to the punch.

"I....am... I am so sorry Dennis. I left you and never said a word to you. I was so selfish, and you were just trying to do your work...good work, but I talked myself out of thinking I loved you and ran away like a heartless...."

She began sobbing again. I tried to sort out what I had just heard. It sounded as if she were apologizing to *me*. That isn't how I remember things playing out years ago. I was the one that neglected her. I was the one who checked out. Who could blame her for doing what she did, given my level of self-absorption? Katie turned around, her swollen face still beautiful but wearing the pain of almost twenty years.

"Dennis, do you forgive me?"

"Forgive you?...There isn't...until about fifteen seconds ago I didn't know there was anything to forgive...I still don't think... Katie, dear, you didn't leave me, I *lost* you. I am the one to blame."

We both froze realizing that the crushing weight of guilt both of us endured for so long was lifting. The pain we had foisted upon ourselves was exactly that, self-inflicted. Involuntarily, we embraced each other. We lingered in the moment, then I spoke.

"Katie, I came here today to ask you something. Your whole life has been about recycling things. From the moment I met you to this day, you have worked so hard to bring new life to the discarded."

"What are you asking?" she said with a perplexed look on her face.

"I'm merely asking if you would consider recycling a slightly frumpy, high-mileage, occasionally high-maintenance, but very eager-to-please feature writer."

Katie briefly laughed, then fixed her eyes on mine. With the full depth of a heart expressing its glorious redemption, she said, "Of course, Dennis." We hugged again for a while. I looked into her eyes, still as windows to a soul greater than mine. We kissed, so easily, so effortlessly. It was as if fifteen years had been fifteen minutes, and yet fifteen minutes ago, this seemed fifteen million light years from a possibility.

The kiss ended, and from where I stood, I could see outside the fish bowl. All eyes were on the two of us. I whispered into Katie's ear.

"I think we are having a major impact on productivity."

Katie looked up at me, her eyes bulging a bit as she realized where we were again. She buried her face in my shoulder.

"Oh, my God!" She said.

"It's all right, they're all smiling. No biggie."

She laughed a bit, then said, "They're smiling because, just this morning, I held a mandatory training class on inappropriate workplace behavior."

We made our exit as gracefully as possible, both blushing, and with a hearty round of applause and whoops from the Grandheim Foundation's assembled staff. We grabbed a late lunch, which turned into a long talk, which turned into a walk, then dinner, more conversation, and a kiss goodnight. I did have to ask about the status of her husband Tom and Audi Turbo Guy. She and Tom had filed for divorce, which was official in three weeks. It turned out her time with Audi Turbo Guy was basically a long weekend, two dates total, ending when he abruptly proposed four days after first being introduced. Later, she found out he had been married four times previously, and he was only thirty-four.

Twenty-Seven

◆ ◆

It has been another six months since our fish bowl reconnection, and Katie and I are still going strong. We are taking it slowly, but contemplating a move together to the same community where we ran into each other on the auspicious Audi-Turbo-Guy-kiss-in-the-elevator day, a kiss she explained that was not as welcomed at the time by Katie as I had viewed it to be.

So much of our conversation, so much of who we are together now, is powered by two things - the fact that we both know all too well what life is like without each other, and more so by being the benefactors of the unlikely chain of events that brought us together again.

We marvel at the confluence of timing and circumstance, and we shudder at the thought that the delicate web which finally served to connect us again was woven with hundreds of delicate, essential moments one after another, perfectly placed by action and fate, any one of which not happening just right, would have resulted in the two of us not being together today. We are both convinced that, on our own, left to our own devices, Katie and I would have continued on with our separate lives blaming ourselves for the distance between us and seeing that as an impassable chasm. Our new foundation is built on the awareness that our being together again is so much more than just the two of us.

To think that my brother-in-law Jim not indulging his inner pack rat, looking through Harvey's boxes, seeing the ashtrays, and thinking them "cool", or Harvey, not putting the ashtrays in the boxes in the first place, could have dashed all chances for Katie and me is heady stuff. Had I not found Football Man to spark my initial curiosity or had Lillian Trentsworth not seen the importance of the receipt among the uncashed checks, where would we be? And to whom, or to what, do we owe our undying gratitude? Sure, we can fall back on the usual suspects of fate and destiny, but that would be somewhat disingenuous and incomplete.

No, much more than that, these markers were placed in destiny's way by one man and his staunch determination to just be himself, and to do so with no self-concerning intention, no self-aggrandizing awareness that he was ever being anything more than just Harvey - a stalwart, but unwitting instrument in the fervent desire of the spirit of life to see every soul filled to its capacity with meaningful purpose and having faith that doing this alone is purpose enough in life.

Katie and I have since noticed we have found our own versions of the Harvey instinct, an awareness of the meaningful moments hiding in the ordinariness of everyday existence. For us, it isn't a "What would Harvey do?" thing, or anything akin to the somewhat blithely naive and emotionally self-rewarding altruism of the notion to pay something forward. It is simply about being true to ourselves, doing what we do with purpose, having faith that our presence on this Earth matters, living our lives as if they mean something, and letting everything else take care of itself.

So, this search for one man found two. Finding the first led to finding the second by revealing that the one thing missing from my life was me. I realized life is about putting myself in motion, about being a willing participant. I have become be a walking opportunity and catalyst for the Universe… no let's call it what it is.. who it is…God… to work through me.

I seek no amount of recompense, adulation, or notoriety. I know that walking this path most often yields no emotional reimbursement, that I will most likely never learn of any measure of my influence on the lives of others. I am prepared for the obscurity and anonymity that living an unremarkable, uneventful life will bring. After all, Harvey died without knowing the full impact of his actions….. well, at least not in this life.

ABOUT THE AUTHOR

J.R. Baude is a freelance writer with credits as a sports newsletter columnist and editor, screenplay author, and songwriter/lyricist. Artistic curiosity has guided him to the joyful challenge of novel authorship, which he has passionately embraced in his debut work *The Unremarkable Uneventful Life of Harvey Henderson*.

Made in the USA
Monee, IL
25 January 2022

89831648R00189